About the Author

David Constantine is an award-winning poet and translator. His collections of poetry include *Madder*, *Watching for Dolphins*, *The Pelt of Wasps*, *Caspar Hauser* and *Something for the Ghosts* (all Bloodaxe) – the latter being shortlisted for the 2002 Whitbread Poetry Prize. His most recent volume is *Collected Poems* (2004). He is a translator of Hölderlin, Brecht, Goethe, Kleist, Michaux and Jaccottet. In 2003 his translation of Hans Magnus Enzensberger's *Lighter than Air* (Bloodaxe) won the Corneliu M Popescu Prize for European Poetry Translation. He is also author of one novel, *Davies* (Bloodaxe); a collection of short stories, *Back at the Spike* (Keele University Press); and *Fields of Fire: A Life of Sir William Hamilton* (Weidenfeld). He is an editor of the Oxford Poets imprint and, with his wife Helen, edits *Modern Poetry in Translation*. He lives in Oxford.

First published in Great Britain in 2005 by Comma Press
www.commapress.co.uk
Distributed by Carcanet Press
www.carcanet.co.uk

A CIP catalogue record of this book is available from the British Library.

ISBN 0-9548280-1-1

The publisher gratefully acknowledges assistance from the Arts Council
of England North West.

Set in Baskerville by XL Publishing Services, Tiverton
Printed and bound in England by SRP Ltd, Exeter

under the dam

David Constantine

Acknowledgements

'In Another Country' was first published in *The Reader*. 'Visiting' was originally broadcast on BBC Radio Manchester. 'The Red Balloon', 'All on Video', 'Under the Dam' and 'The Loss' previously appeared in Comma Press collections: *Manchester Stories 3*, *Comma*, *Hyphen*, *September Stories* (co-published with *Prospect* magazine).

Contents

The Loss

Nobody noticed. Apparently they never do. Or if they do, they misunderstand. It might be one of those sudden pauses – a silence, a gap – and somebody will say: An angel is passing. But it is no such thing. It is the soul leaving, flitting ahead to its place in the ninth circle.

Mr Silverman looked up, looked round. All the men were still there, the men and the one or two successful women, all still there. He resumed his speech. Perhaps he had never faltered in it. He continued, he reached the end. He invited questions, some needed answers almost as long as a speech. Then it was over, he saw that he had been successful. They were smiling, they wanted what he wanted. One after the other they came and shook him by the hand, called him by his first name, congratulated him, wished him a safe journey. Seeing them dwindle – soon fewer than half remained – Mr Silverman became fearful and, in some degree, also curious. Truly, had nobody noticed? He feared they had, and all the world henceforth would be gilded with pretence. Or he feared they had not, and he must go on now in the fact, enclosed in the fact, and nobody noticing. He took a big man by the sleeve and turned with him to the window in an old gesture of confidence. The big man – whose name was Raingold, who liked to be addressed as Ed – inclined to him, listening, frequently nodding, bespeaking friendliness with every fibre of his suit and with every pore of his naked skin where it showed in his hands and in his large and dappled face. But Mr Silverman, speaking quietly, aware that at his back there were others waiting to wish him on his way – Mr Silverman felt that it was too warm in the room and too cold outside in sunny Manhattan and that the plate glass between the warm and the terrible cold was surely quite impermeable. Mysterious then, the loss, the quitting. Would an adept be able to see his loss, like the dusty shape of a bird against the glass? It must be that the molecules of glass give way for the passage of a soul intent on reaching hell.

They were very high up, somewhere in the early hundreds. The surrounding towers of steel and glass seemed to be swaying slightly or rippling like a backcloth, but it was only an effect of light and shadows and clouds and reflections in the freezing wind. The towers were quite as stable as before. Yes, said Mr Silverman, tugging at the good cloth of Ed Raingold's sleeve, went very well, I should say. What would *you* say? Went *very* well, Ed Raingold said. And he added, beaming down, You can do it, Bob. In Mr Silverman's wonderment, in his honest puzzlement, there was a fine admixture of contempt. Had nobody noticed? Did it really not matter whether he had a soul or not?

At death, as is well known, the body lightens by a certain amount: twenty-one grams, in all cases. Aha, we say, that must be the weight of the human soul. The cadaver varies greatly. I saw a teenager the other day who must have weighed twenty stone. It was in the new mall at the old Pier 17. The food in there is on an upper floor and she stood at the foot of the escalator, wondering did she dare ascend or not. She wore a decoration in her hair, like antennae, such as elves and fairies are seen wearing in Victorian prints. On the other hand, one of those infants in, say, Ethiopia, can't weigh more than a pound or two. But the loss at death, apparently, will be the same.

But waking next morning Mr Silverman did not feel lighter. On the contrary, he felt heavier. Imagine a blob of lead implanted in you overnight; or that some organ, roughly kidney-sized, has been converted to lead during your sleep. So it was. Hard to say where exactly: at the back of the head, in the region of the heart, in the pit of the belly? It seemed to shift. Wherever he pressed his hand, there it was not. Perhaps it could dissolve and occupy him thoroughly, like a heavy flu. He dozed and dreamed.

Shaken awake again by his early-morning call – he had an aeroplane to catch to Singapore – Mr Silverman sat on the bed and tried to weep. He shook, he strained, he sobbed, but the tears that came were not much more than the wetness of a few snowflakes on his cheeks. No relief. He took a shower, he wandered naked around the overheated room. Again and again, touching, he received little shocks, from doorhandles, switches, a metal frame – quite sharp little shocks. They startled him, in little jolts they frightened him through his fingers to his heart. He collected them, each time giving forth a small yelp, until the room was dead. Then he looked out of the window. He was high, in the nineties, the sun was visiting the upper reaches of the towers. Down below – Mr Silverman looked down – all the silent hurry was deep in shade. Which was worse? The measurement of remoteness in no company but his own? Or proof of it when he clutched at Ed Raingold? Mr Silverman foresaw an icy interest in the ways and means and relative degrees of horror.

Car. Airport. Aeroplane. Singapore. Passing – so muffled, steady, multitudinous the tread – towards Baggage Reclaim, Mr Silverman saw an extraordinary thing. There was carpet, glass, more and more glass, and falling from everywhere like vaporized warm piss, there was the usual music: but the extraordinary thing was a bird, a common sparrow by the look of it, high up against a ceiling, perhaps only an inner ceiling, of sunny glass, beating and fluttering. Natural that the creature should seek the light and whatever sustaining air was still available outside, but incredible that it should ever have got where it was now. Nothing living ever came in there, blind-dogs or bomb-dogs perhaps in the service of humans, but nothing else that lived, except the humans in transit. Perhaps not even microbes got in there, only the humans, marching in their gross forms, but never a bird, certainly never a common sparrow, but there it was, fluttering, beating its life out against the sunny glass. That was the last pure astonishment in Mr Silverman's remaining years. A sparrow against the glass ceiling on the way to Baggage Reclaim! It was also, he acknowledged later, the last occasion on which he might have wept. Yes, he said, had I stepped aside and gone down on my knees on that thick carpet and bowed my head into my hands, knowing the bird against the ceiling high above me, then, God be my witness, I could have wept, the tears would have burst through my fingers, I might have cupped my hands and raised them up like a bowl, brimful with an offering of my final tears. Mysterious, the afterlife, lingering a while between New York and Singapore, between landing and Baggage Reclaim, an afterlife in which he might have wept.

But Mr Silverman was met at Arrivals by a smiling driver holding up a card which read: Mr Bob Silverman. Fidelity Investments; and soon, among smiling people, he was proceeding through his routine. Two days of meetings and presentations, all successful. He steered the company into wanting what he wanted. He had a clear mind, he set out the facts and figures clearly, he made shapely arguments, his conclusions were ungainsayable. No wonder he was so successful! He was a born persuader, persuading came as naturally to him as playing golf or the violin did to other mortals. And all the while it was like ventriloquy. He stood aside, listening to his own voice; he could even see it, his own embodied voice, and himself standing aside, observant.

In Singapore the rooms were, if anything, rather cool and the air outside (the little of it he had felt in passing to and from the car), if anything, rather warm. But the rooms were very high, in the hundreds, and the towers all around, very densely rising, looked – to Mr Silverman – liable to crumple at any moment. The men coming up to congratulate him and to wish him a safe onward journey were less tall than he was, they were slighter, but they were dressed like him and from behind their glasses they beamed on him with an almost ferocious admiration. When their numbers dwindled, again he clutched at a sleeve, stood at a window, speaking the words and the body-language of an old condescension. But he felt the leaden implant somewhere in his body, and suffered little starts of indignation that it mattered nothing to these successful gentlemen whether he stood and moved and had his being among them with a soul or without. Alone then, he had the distressing thought that perhaps it had never mattered; and a shadow fell like lead over all his past, all the life before his loss withered and died when he entertained the certainty that it had never mattered, he would have done just as well, he would have got just as high, even without a living soul in him. It had never been required of him that he have one.

He was met at Heathrow by his wife, Mrs Silverman. He looked her in the eyes, to see would she notice. She seemed not to. He kissed her with some force on the lips. Was it palpable there on the lips, as a shock of cold perhaps? Apparently not. She had brought the two children with her. It was easier than finding someone to look after them. She asked him had he had a successful trip. Yes, he said, very; watching, would she notice? Then he asked after her life in the interim. Busy, she said, and detailed the difficulties. Then husband and wife were silent, driving in dense traffic, and the children on the back seat were silent too. He sensed his wife returning to her own preoccupations and he saw beyond any doubt that what had happened to him would never happen to her. She was fretted to the limits of her strength, she had days, weeks, being almost overwhelmed; but below or beyond all that there was something continuing in her for which it was indeed required that she have a soul. Bleak, the few insights in Mr Silverman's remaining years. Before a man struggles to retain his living soul he must first be persuaded that he needs one.

Mr Silverman began to notice other men and women to whom the loss had happened. Angels wandering the world in human disguise are said always to recognize one another. Likewise the clan to which Mr Silverman now belonged. In one gathering or another, to his mild surprise, he knew and was known by his desolate kind. They were from all walks of life. At least, he met them in the few walks of life that he and Mrs Silverman had any knowledge of. Successful people. For example, at a Christmas party somewhere just outside the M25 he was introduced to a successful academic. They saw, each in the other, the fact of it. What to say? Nothing really. There was no warmth between them. They stood side by side, their backs to the company, looking down a garden at the fairylights in a dead tree. The academic, a Dr Blench, said: Most of what we know about the ninth circle comes from Dante, of course. And he had an axe to grind. But the ice must be true, wouldn't you say? Mr Silverman hadn't read Dante, didn't know about the ice, but at once acknowledged, after a few more words from Dr Blench, that what Dante reported on the ice must indeed be true. The thing I haven't quite worked out, Dr Blench continued, is why he says it is traitors that it happens to. I mean, are you a traitor? I don't think I am. So perhaps he got that wrong, even if the ice is right.

Driving home round the M25 Mr Silverman thought about treachery. Was he a traitor? Was he even a liar? Whom had he betrayed? Whom had he ever lied to? He glanced at his wife. She was concentrating on her driving among all the lights in a good deal of rain and spray. But he thought again: it will never happen to her. When she can relax a little she will revert to her own concerns, and for those a soul is necessary. Still he did not think that his worst enemy or the Recording Angel could assert with any truth that he had betrayed his wife. Two or three times on his business trips he had been with a prostitute. In Tokyo they sent one up to his room on the 141st floor, without his asking, as a courtesy. But always he told Mrs Silverman when he came home, said how sorry he was, how joyless it had been. He could not honestly say that she had forgiven him. He would have to say she had made him feel there was nothing to forgive. She appraised him, shrugged. She lingered over it briefly, as though it were a strange but characteristic thing. She seemed to be gauging whether it touched her or not, and to be deciding, with a shrug, that it did not. For a while he had even sustained a sort of affair, with a woman in Frankfurt, a secretary at several of his presentations. She told him he was a very persuasive man. They had sex together for a while whenever he flew in. But he confessed that also to Mrs Silverman, said it was nothing very much, and she contemplated him and the fact of it briefly and seemed to concur: it was nothing much. So he was not a traitor, he was not a liar, not to her at least, his wife, his closest companion on the upper earth. To whom else then?

Nothing much more to say about the remaining years – many years, interminable, as it sometimes seemed – of Mr Silverman's living death. Heeding the sort of information that must inevitably come, by accident or by grace and favour, to a man in his position, Mr Silverman shifted some money very advantageously, for the benefit of Mrs Silverman and her growing children. He told her so, with some wan satisfaction, quite without personal pride, and she appraised him as she had done when he told her about the prostitutes and about the secretary he had for a while had sex with in Frankfurt: thanked him, nodded, as though it were both very strange and very characteristic. And he watched her vanishing behind her eyes, to where she really belonged.

Mr Silverman thought a good deal about the ice. He connected it with his inability to weep – and rightly so. One evening in the lift, ascending very rapidly to the 151st floor in Manhattan or Tokyo or Frankfurt or Singapore, he found himself the sole companion of another of his kind, a bigger man than himself, in a suit of excellent cloth, wearing a confident loud tie and a very big signet ring on his left little finger. The man – Sam's my name, he said – told him at once about a particularly bad ending (if it was an ending) that had just come to his knowledge. The doors opened, Sam and Mr Silverman stood together on the hushed corridor. Sam continued. The man in question – he must surely be one of us – had taken an ice-axe to his own face, raised it in desperation against himself, in the firm belief, so the story went, that his face, indeed his entire head, was enclosed in a bulky helmet of ice, in the desperate illusion raising the ice-pick against himself, to make a way through to his eyes, to give exit to the tears that were, so he believed, welling up in there, hot melting tears welling up and not allowed to flow.

The Necessary Strength

'That horse makes me nervous,' Judith said. 'I don't like him being here.' 'He's all right,' said Max. 'We can do them a favour, I suppose.' Judith said nothing, but in silence took issue with both 'we' and 'them'. It was early evening, Max's time for being with his family – a pity, as he said himself, to spoil it by quarrelling. They were in the living-room, and against the large west window, full up against it in the teeming sun, the white horse pressed his face. The girls thought him funny; Max said that such a white long head with blinding sun behind it was a wonderful phenomenon; but it made Judith nervous, there was a quite deep gap between the house wall and where the horse stood lunging at the windowpane, and she feared he might fall in there and come through with a smash and a great deal of blood; and besides, his orange tongue and the slaver he made on the window disgusted her.

Megan asked could she ride the horse. Max said he didn't see why not, he would ask Ellie when he saw her next; but Judith said no she couldn't, the horse was too big and being on his own all the time made him peculiar and dangerous. Then the sunny room, with its western view of a bay of the silver sea, was crossed with strains and bitternesses, everyone fell silent and the horse stared in at them.

Judith stood up, with her book. She would go and read at the other side of the house, as far away from the horse as possible, though there was no sun in that room, it would be cold and to read she would need a light on. Max and the girls looked at her. She could wring their hearts merely by standing up, for then her smallness of stature was apparent and, if she took a step, her crippling at the hips. 'Stay,' said Max. 'It's nicer in here.' All three looked at her. The sun was merciless: it showed the cavernous darkness around her eyes. But her eyes were a sapphire blue, shockingly beautiful however familiar they might become to anybody. The alignment of her husband and her daughters, though one of pity, was still an alliance against her, she felt; and standing there she forgot her intention and felt merely apart and sad.

The horse turned, and chased away. Judith sat down again with the girls, and drew them in close, to look at their paintings. Esther's was of a house, any house, with flowers, a welcoming path, a curl of smoke; Megan's was of a loch, its blue surface almost snowed over with water lilies. 'What a sight!' said Max at the window. The horse was by the far fence, where the ground fell away to the rocky beach. 'A white horse, and the sun getting more and more red.' In him, like a reflex, whenever Judith had moved him to love and pity, came concern for himself. Soon then, rather sooner than usual, he said he must work and the girls went to kiss him goodnight. That done, he climbed the aluminium ladder out of the living-room into the loft above it, where he worked. He took very little time to settle, they heard his movements on the floor, their ceiling; then nothing. He was working.

Judith sat on, with the children. She loved that room and was glad not to have left it. It was where she taught the children in the mornings while their father slept. There were charts on the walls and posters and work the girls had done; vases of flowers and grasses on the windowsills; and in a corner, almost too small now even for Esther, stood an ancient cramped school desk. She took Esther against her and sang softly in Yiddish. The girls were hard to get to bed in summer. Even gone midnight it was never properly dark. Megan left off painting and went to the window. 'That horse is crazy,' she said. Esther was asleep. Had Judith been stronger she would have carried her away to bed. As it was, she sat there, dozing herself, and the ancient songs continued in her head. She wanted strength, she was dozing, soodling, and worrying at the question of the necessary strength when suddenly – a shock to her – she heard Max cross the floor above and saw his feet coming down out of the hole that was the entry into his own space. It was a shock, she could not remember when he had last broken off work and come back down into the living-room while his wife and children were still there. Megan at the window turned his way in amazement. 'What's the matter?' Judith asked. Esther woke up. 'The sunset is extraordinary,' said Max. 'We must go out and look at it.'

Judith was angry. All the sunsets at Acha were extraordinary. Why come down for this one? But because he had, the children were excited. If he came down, as he never had before, it was an occasion and they must all go out. Esther was wide awake. Megan felt curious, thrilled, apprehensive.

They all went out. The house stood in its own field that sloped away to the fence and a gate above the beach. The ground was rough, the children ran ahead, Max came after with Judith whose progress was slow. Half way down she halted. 'This will do,' she said, and contemplated the sky. There was a bar of luminous cloud across the whole view, but no sun visible, so that for a moment she thought Max must have been mistaken and the show was finished. 'No, wait,' said Max. 'It's just beginning.' And he laid an arm around her shoulders and so ushered her into a proper contemplation of the phenomenon. The sun drooped like something melting, all out of shape, down from the band of cloud. Slowly it eased itself into the gap between the cloud and the line of the sea, and there recovered its roundness and intensified its colour. The rays came over the water, over the fence, over the field almost horizontally, a queer orange light. The children were at the fence, on the low ferny cliff above the sea, and into the light, from nowhere as it seemed, approaching them, flushed by the sun, came the white horse. Judith started forward but Max held her back. 'He's all right. Only look at the sun on him.' There was a breeze off the sea and in thin clothes Judith was shivering. The sun seemed to have halted. The horse, leaving the children, walked towards her and Max in a very measured way. 'Phenomenal,' said Max. The creature was aureoled around by an orange golden light, but Judith said: 'I'm cold.' It would be twenty minutes before the sun, and all its extraordinary after-effects, finally vanished. 'See,' said Max, 'it goes down on a slope.' It would dip for only a couple of hours below the rim, and in its descent was dragged off the vertical by the pull of the north. 'So beautiful,' said Max.

'I'm going in,' said Judith. Night after night was beautiful. Why come down for this? Why bring everyone out? Why excite the children so late? 'Keep them away from the horse,' she said. 'And you put them to bed.' She limped in. Max turned to watch. She was too small for such large effects, and the tufted ground threw her from side to side. But her thin white blouse took colour like the horse's coat, and the house's windows blazed.

She lay in bed, angry, brooding on Max's descent into the living-room out of his upstairs lair. How he could do as he pleased, to trouble her; and all the old griefs revived. There had never been any discussion over whose the new room should be. The girls could have had a room each. It was wonderfully light, a skylight, a west and a south window. Now she never went up there, the ladder hurt her, it was too steep, as he must have known it would be. For months, her hips worsening, she had not been up there, not even climbed high enough to poke her head in and see what work he was doing in that place apart, that den all his to climb up to and climb down from above the living-room in the family house. She heard him come in and put the girls to bed – or heard him instruct Megan to put Esther to bed. Then heard him go downstairs again, not looking in on her; heard him in the kitchen making coffee; heard him go through to his aluminium ladder. Slowly the room darkened, but never completely. There was a cuckoo, all night; and worse, blundering in among her dreams, she heard the horse in the gap or trench behind the house, rubbing and banging against the outside wall. He had all the field under a vast summer sky, but chose instead to shove and snuffle around their dwelling where it was darkest and where he did not belong.

Max was working. In very fine pencil he was drawing bones. He might spend a whole night on a couple of sheep's vertebrae, or on the mechanics of its upper leg, the jointing. On a skull, on the wriggling script where the segments fitted, on the accommodation for the eyeballs, teeth and spinal cord, on the chambers, passages, apartments, all the housing, easily he could expend a month of silent nights. He learned the precise form and fit of these components, but also their texture on the surface and inside, healthy and in the pitting and delicate honeycombing and filigree of decay, clean as a whistle or stained in peat, bracken, weed. Nearly all his sorties from the house were in search of bones or bone-like things. On the beach he got dry claws and carapaces and the ridged and stippled casings of sea-urchins. In summer, more restless, at three or four in the morning, in the queer light with the sleepless crying birds he went out foraging, he crossed the thin pale road and entered the pathless wasteland of mauve rock, black peat, every shade of boggy green, and tumbling white water. Up there he found antlers, some still bloody at the base where they had left the living head, others cast years ago and shortened by corrosion. He found pebbles of quartz, like fossilized eyeballs, and lichens that are the dryest and least ample life there is. Up there the roots of the old Caledonian pines shone in the golden bogwater like giant starfish. Wood like that he approved of: hard and pale as bone. There was a particular river which, disregarding its Gaelic name, he called the Bone River. High up in it a carcase had lodged, and over months, by water with the help of a few crows, all the weight and stink and fleshly substantiality was got away and the animal disarticulated and passed downstream and Max collected it in pieces for his work.

Once he found the skull of a horse, came home with it under his arm, re-entered the sleeping house, climbed out of the living-room into his working space and there and then, until the children woke and it was time for him to go to bed, he began to draw the find that was as long, large, intricate and fascinating as many an animal entire.

In winter he made almost no excursions but kept to his upper room, and the dead but brilliant moon shone in at him through the skylight. He worked, on a high stool at a draughtsman's tilted desk, clamping the bones at the angle he wanted them, lighting them as he liked, and transferring them as exactly as his eye and hand and the fine tip of a pencil could do it, to paper. And when he had got them exactly, on scores of white sheets, then out of them in colours that were barely colours, using brushes sometimes as fine as a nerve end, he composed the pictures that were his speciality. He took bone, precisely observed, as his base and real material, and lifted out from it into beautiful chilly abstractions.

Now and then, while he was sleeping, the girls climbed into his space. Megan fingered and weighed the white objects – they were all around, on every shelf and surface – and looked through the folders thoughtfully. Esther made a cosy home in the corner, with her dolls. But Judith never came up, and he knew she did not. Her crippled hips would have made it very difficult; and besides, as he knew, she had grown to loathe his work.

Ellie came down to ride her horse. Judith watched her return, along the sea's edge at a canter. Yes, she was fit to be looked at. She was the image of freedom and wellbeing. On impulse, when she had stowed away her gear in the shed as Max had said she could, Judith invited her in. It was early evening. Max was still sitting with his family in the sunny living-room. 'Here's Ellie,' Judith said. Suddenly she took an interest in this girl and began to question her, gently but to the point. Why had she given up university? What did she think she would do in Acha, where there was no work, nobody her age, nothing to stimulate her intelligence? Ellie was not averse to trying to answer, but in the course of every attempt she glanced repeatedly towards Max, to see how she was doing. 'How beautiful she is,' said Judith to herself, 'and she is in love with him.' Ellie had found university harsh and cynical. There was no one you could talk to about things that really mattered, the boys only wanted sex and her teachers were always making fun. In the end it upset her, she stopped eating, she had come home, she was still not better from it. Sitting there in the beams of the sun, continually pushing back her heavy dark hair, she looked, Judith thought, too beautiful for her own good. Her face, flushed from riding when she came in, was pale as the moon now, luminously pale, her skin of an almost transparent purity. Still without vehemence Judith pressed her. Women needed their independence, they had to be competent, get qualifications, be always able to take their own lives in hand. Ellie shrugged, was lost for words, looked to Max. 'Ellie loves this place,' he said. 'Don't you have to work?' Judith asked him, and when he said no, not for a little while, she stood up and with a decisiveness that quite outweighed her lameness she left the room and came back with whisky and three glasses. She poured out, and said: 'If you're not working, I'll play. I don't like to when you work.' 'You could,' he said. 'It would help me.' 'Well I don't,' she said, but now sat down at the piano close to the foot of the aluminium ladder, and began to play.

Max saw how thin her hair had become, how dark with fatigue and pain her face, how slight her wrists. Ellie, when Judith turned, saw the shocking brilliance of her blue eyes and the bright chic clothes she had made herself, and when she began to sing that was the sense of her entirely: brightness, energy, a lively force, in her rapid fingers, in the lift of her head, in her more and more confident voice as it remembered the songs of her mother tongue and gave them out. 'Pour another, Max,' she said, 'and get your violin.' He did as he was bid, poured another three glasses, nimbly went up the ladder behind her and was down in a trice and tuning his instrument to her playing. Now Ellie, wholly of the audience with the two children, watched husband and wife revive their old unison. Judith led, but Max was quick on the uptake and adept at developing what she began. They filled the living-room with the peculiar gaiety that comes when a sociable skill is practised recklessly. Outside, another extraordinary sunset was under way, and against it the white horse came and stood at the window peering in. Judith raised her voice and sang at him. Max skipped across and serenaded him. They did not lessen his solemnity. He twitched at the shoulder, the flies teased his eyes, but he stared in steadily from under his fringe and his hot breath misted the pane. Judith sang and played, the children clapped and joined in, and under Judith's quick tuition Ellie was enabled also. They drank more. Ellie looked from Max to Judith in a rather breathless admiration. She was seeing them in a new light, but Judith especially: Judith seemed inexhaustible, and was indeed, as she sang, marvelling at how rich she and Max had been. Things she had composed herself, years ago, he remembered, and when she brought them back he worked up a new accompaniment. In build and appearance he was like her: slight, quick, with a girlish mouth, his good looks were as fine as a girl's. Over the violin, while he played, he watched her keenly, with a touch of fear. Her blue eyes disconcerted him, he felt mocked by them. At last, sensitive to what she wanted, he fell away into the audience, and, facing the wall, showing them her back, she sang something he did not know, something none of her audience knew, but he knew the tone and sense of it, and the three girls, in their different fashions, comprehended it too, it came up out of her in a dialect stranger and more ancient then hers at home, bitter, inconsolable, mocking its own beauty, harshly insisting that beauty is no redress, and yet still beautiful, but sadder, more stricken, more outraged than it was beautiful. Then briskly she said: 'You will be wanting to work, Max.' And to Ellie: 'You are a fool if you stick around in Acha.' And she limped to the children, took one by each hand, and swayed and stumbled like something smitten across the backbone, out of the living-room.

Max woke her. His hand, come in under her nightdress, rested on her left hip. Waking she struggled fearfully to recompose a world. It was their routine to meet in the kitchen, as his waking hours ended and hers began, and they might have a cup of tea together, before he went for his sleep in their bed. Why go against his habit now? Very gently, very tenderly he stroked her hip and a length of her thigh. The room was already light. Her eyes filled with tears of shame. 'Don't, Max,' she said. 'Please don't.' He desisted, and they lay side by side, looking up at the ceiling. 'Why aren't you working?' she asked. 'I thought ...' he began, 'I wanted ...' 'You were wrong,' she said. 'I'm leaving you. I'm taking the girls. I shall need some money. We must sell the house.' He wept. She let him. Then he said: 'You don't know how I love you.' She answered: 'When I thought it might be cancer and

I drove ninety miles to have my tests you wouldn't come with me, you said you'd be too upset, you said you wouldn't be able to work.' 'I couldn't work. All the time you were away I sat up there crying and couldn't do a thing.' 'You like that kind of pain. I don't like any kind. It hurt me to press the pedals in the car. The girls were sick – not once, half a dozen times – I had to keep stopping, getting out, cleaning them up.' 'There are different kinds of suffering,' said Max. 'You can't drive,' she said. 'You won't learn.' 'I hate the road,' he said. 'I wish they'd never built it.' Both saw only reiteration ahead, and were silent. Max had an apprehension of his future loneliness. He dwelled on it, his heart beat faster. He came back again, more tempted by it than ever, to the notion that in misery, guilt, icy loneliness, he might do better work. 'I have to suffer,' he said aloud. 'I have to. Then I'll do good work.' 'Your suffering stinks,' she said. 'All suffering stinks and is a waste of time.' 'No,' he said, becoming excited, 'we'll sell, I'll get a cottage on my own, I'll get one further up the coast where there is no road.' He saw, as something beautifully clean and purposeful, the reduction of his life to loneliness and work. His eyes shone. He sat up in the exhilaration of the idea.

Judith got out of bed and, turning away from him, dressed quickly. 'You are beautiful,' he said. 'The line of your back is beautiful. And now you won't let me touch me.' 'I'm lame,' she said, 'and it is getting worse.' Then when she was dressed she turned to him sitting up naked in their bed. He was thin and strong, fit, smooth-skinned. His face was alert and lit with the idea of loneliness and productive suffering. 'You'll get Ellie in,' said Judith. 'Ellie will keep house for you and sweeten the early mornings when you coincide in bed.' 'At least I can talk to her about my work,' said Max.

The girls were still sleeping, Judith went out. Cloudless early morning, paradisal. The little bay was brimful, quiet, shining. A couple of seals had come in close. Slowly, tried by every unevenness, Judith went down to the fence. The girls got to the sand in leaps and bounds, and through the bracken, on a rough path bearing left, Ellie could lead down her horse; but for Judith the fence was the limit. There had once been a way that she could manage, with everybody helping, but a storm, magnificent to watch through their southern and western windows, had rolled the boulders differently and spoiled it. She watched the seals. In the full water, their element, they rose together, necked, vanished, and reappeared apart. It seemed pure delight, in the water and the sunny air, that sinuous rolling together at the head and the neck, and diving vertically down and levelling again through the clear blue-green, like dancing. Max swam some mornings, she knew that. They met at the kitchen table, there was salt on his skin, his hair was wet, he drank a cup of tea with her and went to bed.

She turned away. The house in the one green field was sunlit. The first romantic adventure of the place, their work at it together, always with music and sharp thirsts and hungers, their love and mutual aid, woke in her now like temptation. The field had sprouted its pale and magenta orchids. The others, the common little flowers, Judith said them aloud as though teaching the children: eyebright, bedstraw, milkwort, tormentil. Visible south of the house was the road which Max detested. It was narrow, pale, insignificant, but seemed to Judith a brave idea, a brave undertaking, getting away south around a difficult coast. Behind the road, east, was the moor – moor and bog and mountain, that she could as easily have flown over as walked. But she knew: there were lichens in it with red and lively tips, there was cottongrass as soft as the children's hair when she cut it the first time and kept two curls of it among her jewellery; and in places where the shielings had once been, in spring the bracken unfurled more sweetly than she could bear to remember. At the back of everything were the high mountains, scraped raw, grey as ash in certain lights, pinkish, violet or red in others.

And so on and so on. Stars and the frozen waterfalls in winter, the sunsets all year round. Was she to live off beautiful phenomena, and bring the girls up addicted to them? Like nausea, always like nausea however often she felt it, there rose in her again the need for the necessary strength. She clenched her fists and set off up the rough slope back to the sleeping house. Then the white horse came.

In a wide arc, around the perimeter of the field, from hiding behind the house, he came down at full tilt, the rough ground never hindering him. Admiration, her instant first feeling, ran over rapidly into terror at his mastery and power, as he came down the slope and between her and the fence, through that small gap, passed with a streaming mane, and mounted again, and again went behind the house. She was left trembling at the rush, the din, the smell of the horse that had circled her, doing as it liked. Get home, was her only thought, get in and lock the door. If she was small against the mountains and the magnificent sunsets of Acha, that smallness was philosophical, an attitude of mind; but against the horse in common reality she was as fragile as a sparrow's skull. She made for the house, sobbing with fear, cursing her hips, and the horse came down again, set at her, as it seemed, full on, and swerved and passed and gathered himself up the slope, with all the lazy energy in creation to dispose of. A reasoning voice in Judith said: he is the image of strength, he is showing you what he can do, he can pass to right or left as he pleases, swish you with his tail for fun, without malice, he is young, he means nothing bad. But she tried to run, feeling she would break apart in terror if he came again, she tried and failed, she fell, her left hip came out.

Fainting on the pain, even as she went under she said: this has happened before, I know what to do; but when she came up again, out of a drowning sickness of pain, when she came up without any strength of voice to call for help from the sleeping house, the horse stood over her. He was the bodily apparition of every dread: the dread of utter weakness, of total disability, of the shame and helplessness of being lame, the dread of dependence, the dread of a cancer in a length of bone, and other terrors too, even deeper, in her blood, in the family, in the generations, in her race, the dread of them coming back; and on these she went under again, in more terror than pain, as the long white head of the horse, his swelling eyes, the black shafts in his nose, pushed down at her. One hoof raised gently on her chest would have crushed the life out of her, but it was the face, the orange tongue, the froth on the black lips, all her terror was concentrated there, on the steady face, she saw its strangeness as an utter difference, as a thing incomprehensible, a gap made in her apprehension of the world, and into that gap, as into a rent in nature, came nothing but blank terror that would never end. So she saw the horse, lying crippled under him.

Then not so. Then suddenly not so. On her back in a field as helpless as a flung sheep under the hooded crows, suddenly, and increasingly, it was not so. She saw that his liquid eyes were beset by insects, a vein in his left shoulder pulsed and twitched, and he dipped his long head down and with a clumsy gentleness knocked at her cheek, knocked and snorted softly, nuzzled and knocked, insisting. He trailed his fringe and sticky mane across her face, and raised his head in a long upward indication of how she might rise, and down again, nudging at her face and trailing the coarse hair until she understood and fastened a hand in it and gently, backing and lifting, he drew her up and she sat, tilting off her useless hip. So far so good. An inkling of triumph was in her now. She had a basis. She had done it before. Again the horse bowed his head. She twisted in both hands now, into the sticky, coarse, grey-white hair and hauled and he lifted and she rose and held against him in a queer *déhanchement*, all on the right. Last time it was the car, last time she had dragged herself ten yards up the rutted uncarriageable track, from among her spilled shopping back to the car, and heaved herself up bodily against its warm bonnet, and had then done there what she did now, pressing her face against the horse's throbbing flank, against her pain, did it again, shoved in the hip, ball into socket back where it belonged, and clung on to him patiently standing still, against the nausea and the pain.

Clinging to his mane, one step at a time, feeling the working of his near leg at the shoulder, its power held in to walk with her, she got home up the hill. At the door he left her, and resumed his lunatic courses down and around the field.

Judith opened the door. Megan was in the kitchen making tea. Her look was adult and officious. 'Dad's upset,' she said. 'I'm making him some tea.' 'Yes,' said Judith, 'do that.' And from the door to a chair, from chair to table, from table to a corner of the stove she got through to the sofa in the living-room, and lay down. She saw before her, stacked like mountains, great but not unprecedented trials of her strength.

In Another Country

When Mrs Mercer came in she found her husband looking poorly. What's the matter now? she asked, putting down her bags. It startled him. Can't leave you for a minute, she said. They've found her, he said. Found who? That girl. What girl? That girl I told you about. What girl's that? Katya. Katya? said Mrs Mercer beginning to side away the breakfast things. I don't remember any Katya. I don't remember you telling me about a Katya. I tell you everything, he said. I've always told you everything. Not Katya you haven't. She took his cup and saucer. Have you finished here? He had pushed them aside to make room for a dictionary. He was still in his dressing gown with a letter in his hand. *My* Katya, he said. I couldn't finish my tea when I read the letter. I see, said Mrs Mercer. It worried her. Already it frightened her. Quickly she cleared the table. Excuse me, she said, while I shake the cloth. He raised the dictionary. A name like that, she said, coming back the two steps from the kitchen door, I'd have remembered it. She's foreign, by the sound. I told you, he said. His face had an injured look. One thing he could not bear was her not believing him when he said he'd told her things. You forget, he said. No I do not, she said. When then? That made him think. A good while back, I grant you. It was a good while back. What worried Mrs Mercer suddenly took shape. Into the little room came a rush of ghosts. She sat down opposite him and both felt cold. That Katya, she said. Yes, he said. They've found her in the ice. I see, said Mrs Mercer.

After a while she said: I see you found your book. Yes, he
said. It was behind the pickles. You must have put it there. I
suppose I must, she said. It was an old Cassell's. There were
words in the letter, in the handwriting, he could not make out
and words in the dictionary he could hardly find, in the old
Gothic script; still, he had understood. Years since I read a
word of German, he said. Funny how it starts coming back
to you when you see it again. I daresay, said Mrs Mercer. The
folded cloth lay between them on the polished table. It's this
global warming, he said, that we keep hearing about. What
is? she asked. Why they've found her after all this time.
Though he was the one with the information his face seemed
to be asking her for help with it. The snow's gone off the ice,
he said. You can see right in. And she's still in there just the
way she was. I see, said Mrs Mercer. She would be, wouldn't
she, he added, when you come to think about it. Yes, said Mrs
Mercer, when you come to think about it I suppose she
would. Again, with his face and with a slight lifting of his
mottled hands he seemed to be asking her to help him
comprehend. Well, she said after a pause during which she
drew the cloth towards her and folded it again and then
again. Can't sit here all day. I've got my club. Yes, he said. It's
Tuesday. You've got your club. She rose and made to leave
the room but halted in the door and said: What are you going
to do about it? Do? he said. Oh nothing. What *can* I do?

All day in a trance. Katya in the ice, the chaste snow
drawn off her. He cut himself shaving, stared at his face, tried
to fetch out the twenty-year-old from under his present skin.
Trickle of blood, pink froth where it entered the soap. He
tried to see through his eyes into wherever the soul or spirit
or whatever you call it lives that doesn't age with the casing it
is in. The little house oppressed him. There were not enough
rooms to go from room to room in, nowhere to pace. He
looked into the flagstone garden but the neighbours either
side were out and looking over. It drove him only in his

indoor clothes out and along the road a little way to where the road went down suddenly steeply and the estate of all the same houses was redeemed by a view of the estuary, the mountains and the open sea. He stood there thinking of Katya in the ice. Stood there so long the lady whose house he was outside standing there came out and asked: Are you all right, Mr Mercer? Fine, he said, and saw his own face mirrored in hers, ghastly. I'm too old, he thought. I don't want it all coming up in me again. We're both of us too old. We don't want it all welling up in us again. But it had begun.

No tea ready, said Mrs Mercer, putting down her bag. He was sitting on the sofa queerly to one side as though somebody should be there next to him. No, he said. I didn't know what to get. The blood had dried black in a line down the middle of his chin. Besides, I'm not feeling too good. The one day in the week when you get the tea, said Mrs Mercer. I know, he said. I'm sorry. She went to see to it. He came in after her and hung in the doorway of the small room where they cooked and ate. His unease was palpable. Whether to stand or sit, whether to speak or not. Two or three times he shrugged. In the end he managed to say: Where was the trip then? Prestatyn, she answered brightly. We went to Prestatyn. You always enjoy your trips, he said. Yes, she said, I wouldn't miss a Tuesday trip if I could help it. He had lapsed away again. His face was desolate and absent. His fingers, under their own compulsion, picked at one another. Yes, she said. We went to Prestatyn market and I got myself a blouse. I'll have to see it, he said.

I've been wondering, Mrs Mercer said when they were face to face across the little table eating. Why did they write to you about that girl? So long ago it happened and didn't you tell me you were only passing through? I'm next of kin, he said. Mrs Mercer put down her cup. I beg your pardon. I mean they think I am. She'd have no mother and father, would she, if you think about it. Besides, they were Jews.

Dead anyway, of age. But very likely dead long before they died of age. And she was an only child, my Katya was. Yes but, Mrs Mercer said. Yes but so what? I don't see that makes you the next of kin. Oh I told them we were married, Mr Mercer said. I see, said Mrs Mercer. I had to where we stayed. Not like nowadays. You had to say you were Mr and Mrs in those days. And wear a curtain ring. We never did, said Mrs Mercer. We didn't have to, did we, Mr Mercer said. We didn't have to because we really were. And you two weren't? No, no, said Mr Mercer. I only said we were. You never told me you were another woman's next of kin. I did, he said. Besides, I'm not. And if I didn't it was so as not to upset you.

The meal went on and finished. They watched some television. They went to bed. In the dark it was immediately worse and worse. How old was she? Mrs Mercer asked. Same age as you, he answered. Nearly to the day. I told you, you're both Virgo. Same age as me, she said. Still is if you think about it. They thought about it.

So quiet that house was in the night, so quiet all the other little homes around it were that held the elderly in them and the old alone or still in couples sleeping early, waking, lying awake and thinking about the past. So much past every night in the silence settling over those houses that all looked much the same on a hillside creeping up against the rock and gorse and tipping down to the river where it widened, widened and ended in the sea. We went from village to village, said Mr Mercer in the dark. We had a map to start with but it soon gave out. We asked the way. Sometimes we had a guide from place to place. We had one when it happened funnily enough. To be honest, said Mr Mercer, I was a wee bit jealous of him. You mean she flirted? Mrs Mercer asked. I mean they had the language and I was only learning still couldn't always follow. They laughed a lot, they made some jokes I couldn't understand. Also they went ahead a bit more than they needed to perhaps. Or perhaps I let them, perhaps I lagged behind on purpose and let them go ahead, I don't know why. We were on a path around a slithery purple rock and the glacier on the right of us below. They were laughing. I must have let them go ahead. Then the path went round the rock face left and they were out of sight. Last sound but one I heard from her was laughter when she was already out of sight. And the very last, her scream. When I got there she'd gone and the guide was looking down. His face was dirty yellow, I remember. Was she a blonde? Mrs Mercer asked. No, said Mr Mercer, her hair was black. I thought she'd be blonde, said Mrs Mercer, being German. No, said Mr Mercer, I told you when I told you the whole story, her hair was like yours, black. Like mine, said Mrs Mercer.

Wednesday was library day. Same again? said Mr Mercer. His hands were trembling, he had a scared look. Same sort of thing, said Mrs Mercer. Mind how you go.

Whatever is in there behind the eyes or around the heart or wherever else it is, whatever it is that is not the husk of us will cease when the husk does but in the meantime never ages, does it? Explain him otherwise his agitation when he thinks of Katya in the ice: her bodily warmth and merriment night after night as Mrs Mercer in the wooden houses among flowers in the snow comes up in him, an old man near the end, inhabits him as thoroughly as does his renewing blood. Sweet first girl, sweet unimaginable shock of the simple sight of her the first time without her clothes. What am I going to do about it? he asks himself aloud. Nothing. What can I do?

At dinner time he said: This global warming... What about it? Mrs Mercer said. I read some more about it in the library in a magazine. I've read that book you brought me by the way, Mrs Mercer said. Sorry, he said. They're very worried in Switzerland especially. Where's all the water going? The glaciers are melting but the water's not come down yet. They think it's waiting, like a dam. I see, said Mrs Mercer. They fear it will all come down at once one day. Very likely, said Mrs Mercer. Then she said: When you tell me she's still there where she fell does that mean people can see her if they go and look? Yes, said Mr Mercer. That's what the letter said. Still there apparently, just the way she was. Twenty, in the dress of that day and age. She'll come down when the waters break with mud and rocks and anything human in the way of it will be wiped out. But we shall be dead by then and turning in our own clay in the earth.

In the night, in the utter silence of the nights among those little houses where old people live, she felt him leave the bed and in the pitch black reach his dressing gown and leave the room. She let him go. How it troubled her, all this. Not much to ask, peace of mind at nights and a bit of ordinary cheerfulness in the day, some conversation, something to laugh about and doing nobody any harm. And not all this. A slit of light came on under the bedroom door. She heard him fishing about above his head with the stick, tap tap, for the hook to fetch the trapdoor down and the ladder on it, to mount into the loft. He'll break his neck. But she heard the steps creak and the gasps of his exertion as he got up there. He'll freeze to death. How cold it was in the space under the roof above their little living space, bitter cold and draughty, where they stored the past, its bulk and minutiae, in boxes, parcels, bags, on sagging shelves, in hidey holes diminishing with the rafters. She heard him on the ceiling above the bed, rooting around. The slithering of cartons. Heard the efforts. Then silence. She slept. Woke in a sudden terror over his absence still. Stood in her nightie at the foot of the ladder, cold even there, calling up to him till finally he showed himself, wrapped up and shivering, without his teeth, leaning over the hole, his face a blue grey with the cold and grief, he leaned down over the hole above her upturned face, its halo of thin silver hair, and tried to say nothing to worry about but couldn't and made a gibbering noise, the photos clutched two-handed against his heart.

He slept late and shuffled in without a shave. His hand was shaking. She poured his tea. That's enough now, she said. Yes, he said. But asked could she remember where she had put the big atlas. I just want to look, he said. Under the sofa, since it was more wide than fat. And my boots, he said. I beg your pardon? My boots. But those aren't the ones. No, no, but I always bought the same. She thought they might be in the shed under the old fish tank. That stick I brought back might be in there as well, he said. I daresay, said Mrs Mercer. And will you make an appointment and get something to quieten you down?

He had found the photos and a book of hers he was carrying for her in his rucksack when she went ahead with the guide and out of sight fell down through the snow into a crack in the glacier. It was a book of poems in Gothic script with a Nazi eagle stamped on the inside cover. In the pages were some gentians, flat and nearly black. But blue if you looked long enough, an eternal blue. In the photographs she was just as she was: slim, in a long skirt, smiling, her black hair in a curve around her cheek. The white mountains were behind. The paths she stood on to be photographed often looked vertiginous but were safe enough in reality, until the last one. They were heading south, more or less, trying to find a way into Italy, as she said she had always wanted to. Her idea was there would be a last big climb, up very high where it would be hard to get your breath, and after that all the streams would run the other way and they would run down with them getting warmer and warmer through an unbelievable profusion of flowers and before long they would see the vines and that would be Italy. But some days they forgot where they were going and if a place was nice they stayed.

One thing I didn't tell you, Mr Mercer said next morning

after a quieter night though sleepless mostly, open-eyed and thinking. Oh? said Mrs Mercer. You made an appointment at the doctor's, I hope. Yes, he said. This afternoon. I was thinking in the night one thing I never told you. Never told anyone come to that. Not a living soul. Nobody ever knew. I'm the only one in the world who knows it even now, only one alive, I mean. Well? Mrs Mercer said. She was going to have a baby. My Katya was. More and more slowly Mrs Mercer went on with her toast and home-made damson jam. He sat, turning over his empty hands. His face, she knew, had she confronted it, was looking at her with its puzzled and pleading look, the eyes behind the glasses rather washed out. I suppose I thought it might upset you at the time. I see, she said after a while when her mouth had given up trying to eat. I suppose you would think that. Then she took her own things to the draining board and left him sitting there with his.

They parted company; ate together, slept together, but were in separate circles. Almost at once, as though it were beyond his failing strength, he gave up pitying his wife and fell back down the decades into the couple of months of a summer in the Alps. Between thinking and muttering he went to and fro, up and down, never knew which he was in, and in her company, face to face over another meal or side by side on a walk to the post office, addressed her or himself. I wonder where you put that big medical dictionary. It wasn't with the Cassell's behind the jars. In the loft perhaps. The ladder to the loft was permanently down, encumbering the way into the little living room. A breath of cold hung over the opening. Or the warmth of their living space, being drawn up there, was converted into cold just above their heads. He was often up there, rooting around. In the mechanism of her love and duty she called him down when his meal was on the table. But also at nights he went up there and she heard him moving and muttering over the bedroom ceiling. Then she wept to herself, for the unfairness. Surely to God it wasn't much to ask, that you get through to the end and looking back don't fill with horror and disappointment and hopeless wishful thinking? All she wanted was to be able to say it hasn't been nothing, it hasn't been a waste of time, the fifty years, that they amount to something, if not a child, a something made and grown between man and wife you could be proud of and nearly as substantial as a child. And now all this: him burrowing back though the layers, him rooting through all their accumulations, to get back where he wanted to be, in the time before she was. Once with a bitterness that twisted her mouth as if the question were vinegar she asked: How far gone was she? Six weeks, Mr Mercer answered. We worked it out it would be about six weeks.

The foetus at six weeks is a tiny thing hung in the mother like a creature in hibernation. The medical dictionary was in the loft in a very cramped place where the eaves came down behind a sort of false wall made of hardboard. But Mr Mercer found it finally and in it a picture of the foetus at six weeks and sat there under the bare bulb like an adolescent staring at it. What struck him most when he thought about him and Katya was their heedlessness. That was the word that came to him. We were heedless. Because really if it was bad where we were leaving, which was Bavaria, it was not much better where we were heading, which was Italy, and up there in the snow, the minute we set off what did we do but go and get a baby. Heedless. For obviously we should have to come down again sooner or later, out of the sharp air, the flowers and the snow, and face up to our responsibilities in a bad world getting worse. But then again when he thought about it it didn't seem heedless at all, because the thing he was most sure about, after all the years, was how sure they were all those years ago that what he wanted with her and she with him was to have a baby and go on living and living together for ever more. And you can't be called heedless when you know as well as that what your purpose is in life and you act accordingly. And though they weren't walking anywhere in particular, only to Italy and where in Italy it didn't much matter, every day seemed to have enough point to it getting from wherever they were to wherever they ended up and finding somewhere nice to stay as Mr and Mrs with her brassy wedding ring. And days when they didn't go anywhere but stayed in bed and took a little stroll in the vicinity when they felt like it seemed just as purposeful as days when they set off at four in the morning deadly serious. What did we do for food, I wonder, he asked himself up there in the roof space as though somebody else was asking him. What did we have for money between us to go on like that day after day, week after week? I can only suppose, he said to himself aloud or in his head, that God provided and kind people along the way. I have the feeling, he said, that somehow people liked us and somehow or other it gladdened them when we turned up. When Mr Mercer thought of himself and her he thought of certain flowers and not the gentians that were beyond having any ideas about but a bare and rather frail violet flower that came up *actually in the ice*, as soon as there was the least gap of grass or earth and the water unfreezing around it and running fast, there you would see one or more of these frail flowers sprung up. Then, and more so now, he wanted to call them, these flowers, brave: but a flower was a flower and neither brave nor cowardly nor anything else, yet the word brave came to mind when he thought of that quick seizing of a chance to spring up the minute the ice opened even only a little. And that was how he thought of Katya and himself after all that time with Hitler where they'd come from and Mussolini where they were going to, up there wandering around and making a baby the minute they turned their backs on civilization.

Tuesday again. Where's the trip today then? Mr Mercer asked. It seemed to Mrs Mercer he had aged ten years in a week if that were possible for a man his age already. The Horseshoe Pass, she said brightly, and the Swallow Falls, to see some scenery. You'll enjoy that, he said.

The minute the door closed after her he put his boots on that were not *the* boots but like them because he had always bought the same and packed a rucksack with the maps and some provisions for the journey. The maps were the very ones, in Gothic script with a pair of hikers on the cover in the costume of that time and place. He had found them in the loft with the photographs that he had against his heart now in a wallet with the letter to prove he had a right to see her in the ice if anyone in authority challenged him. When he was ready with a hat and stick and money from the place he hid his in under one of the joists, he wrote a message to leave on the table for Mrs Mercer when she came home from her trip. Dear Kate, he wrote, I am sorry about the tea again but trust you will understand that I have to go and see her as the next of kin and am sure it will all be back to normal here with you and me after that. PS I've made another appointment for a week on Monday. I think I'll ask him for something a bit stronger to quieten me down.

Where the road drops away from among the same houses Mr Mercer paused for a moment over the view, over the estuary, over the river widening and giving itself up into the endless sea. A sunny light was on that place where sweet and salt meet and the salt takes all the river in, all the streams of all the hills all along the way and feels not a bit of difference but continues vast and flat and through and through undrinkable. Kitted up to leave with money and some biscuits for the journey Mr Mercer brought his mind to bear on a six-week baby beginning in a girl of twenty in the ice now after sixty years uncovered because the glacier had lost its snow and discovered in there, fresh. The kindly woman whose house he was standing outside must have watched him for a good ten minutes from her front room window before she came out worried. And tried her best then, shaking him gently, speaking close up into his absent face, to get through to what was still alive in him in there behind his glasses and the glaze of tears.

All on Video

Straight after breakfast they watched the video. It seemed funny to leave the table just like that and funnier still, when it was only morning, to go through into the other room; but they did, as though for an adventure.

After breakfast, the flat day stretching ahead, was Leonard's bad time, or one of them; so Madge bustled, with an eye on him. Leave the curtains, said Betty. It will be more like the pictures. They switched the standard lamp on and the fire. Vic took his oblong out and went to the slot under the good-sized television. Never used it, said Leonard, a bit shame-faced. First time, eh? said Vic. Vic knew how. In it went, no problem. You never forget the first time, he said; but felt, as always, that he was wasted, with his fun, on Leonard. Still he found the right little button on the remote control and they settled down, Vic between the ladies on the sofa, Leonard in an easy chair, and though it was early morning they sat back in a dim light with the coals on low to watch the video of Sally's wedding.

Abruptly, and in silence, there were legs in a suit, two ankle socks, and a long flame-coloured dress; then the upper halves, at an angle. We're in the garden, Vic said. Behind the registry office. Redhot pokers, a weeping willow, and the couple and the little girl were posing, but as if on the deck of a ship in a tilting gale. Don't worry, said Vic. It settles down. Then the sound came on, like an abattoir. The women shut their ears. Vic bent over the other little buttons. I've got my wrong glasses on, he said. Don't worry, it quietens down. I expect we did make a din, said Betty. Happiness, so that's what happiness sounds like, or hope, the hope for it, the determined hope for happiness this time, after last time, everybody hoping for the best, very loud. Leonard saw himself, joining in. He was shaking hands with the young man and lifting up the child who knew she was the princess of it all in a white frock with her pigtails and bouquet. The next shots were disconsolate, the party trailing away down the common pavement. But Vic said he liked that, didn't they? The party trailing away smaller and smaller until they reached the off-licence where they turned left and vanished. Harder than it looks, said Vic. You have to hold it steady. He had also got the traffic in, and strangers, creatures, swam up very close and swam away.

Then the thing went haywire, like a kaleidoscope with migraine. Sorry about this, said Vic. Me running after you and tripping up. In fact by the time he had seen to himself and taken a drink and sent out for a part the hours of life had hurried on, the meal was ending, the speeches had begun, and there was Leonard trying to say, since it was only family and close friends, that anyone might make a mistake, in little things and in great things, and now by good fortune this was a new beginning. There he was, doing without his notes, trying to say it even better, and there was Madge beside him, willing him on, praying he wouldn't falter and lose his voice and turn her way with a look of dread and blankness, so that he felt ashamed, there in the almost dark behind closed curtains, that he should ever have been the cause of such a worry in another person's face. Sally replied. She had said all along she would answer back whatever the conventions were and so she did, standing between her child and her new husband. Men, she began. And so it went on: father, husband, father of little Gwen whom she hugged in a comradely fashion three or four times while she spoke. Here Vic had done very well. His magic eye dwelled on face after face and there wasn't one knew quite what to look like listening to Sally's speech. Two words – bitter springs – came up in Madge from the depths of long ago; then the rest, the whole line they belonged in: Mirth that hath no bitter springs; and the picture wobbled in her tears and not because Vic had not held steady. And Betty, who on the occasion – she was sure she had – had felt very sorry for her sister Madge and Leonard who after all had taken the girl back in and the baby too and were heartbroken now in the empty house, Betty watching it on video filled with bitterness and said again to herself: Where's the justice? And: Our Christine would have turned out nicer if she'd lived. On all the faces was a willingness to smile and laugh. All they all wanted was to be able to laugh and not feel bad. You never saw a gallery of faces showing so much willingness. Though in the end it was more like pleading: that the pretty young woman whose wedding day it was would say at least one thing they could feel all right about. Some nice shots, don't you think? said Vic. Ethel, for instance. Freddy with his medals. How much more is there? Leonard asked. He had got up suddenly and was over by the curtains making a chink between them and looking out. There's the party yet, said Vic. The party, said Leonard. What's the weather doing, Len? Madge asked. His voice had gone funny. It seemed trapped in his chest, as though his jaws and his teeth were barred against it. She knew he was struggling when she heard that sort of voice. The weather? he said. The weather's not so good. Madge reached out from the settee to bring him back into his easy chair. We can fastforward if you're getting bored, said Vic. It starts with the grounds and everyone arriving. Well I'm enjoying it, said Betty.

Fastforwarding crazed the screen and through a mithering interference the figures of humans came together, embraced and went apart at manic speed. Is that the dancing? Betty asked. Not yet, said Vic. Leastways he didn't think so. Hard to tell at that speed. Slow down then. He slowed and at once out of a confusion by which the eyes and the ears and even more so the mind were greatly tormented there came order, a wonderfully fluid, generous, shifting and various order, a delight. The jazz had begun. In a rush Leonard had back the happiness it had occasioned in him then. He was blind with tears. That's it, he said in himself. That's us at our best. He meant the ability, the sovereign gift and free bestowing of it on all who cared to listen and receive. And the interplay, the courteous, easygoing give and take. The way the pianist, a youngish man with a face like the moon (a moon with specs on) and his bit of hair in a ponytail, the way he nodded in the singer, her black hair how copious and beautiful! and the trumpeter, a gent, how he let her through, and the aloof bass went steady and she then to and fro against the pianist in a loving contest set her voice, smiling as she raised the blues, and he smiled back, the smiles of people who can do it, they know they can, they have gifts to spare, they knew each other and surprised each other, an edge in her voice suddenly, suddenly a sadder flattening under his hands, and then the horn came in, asking for space and at once allowed it, came in tilting his trilby, and reached up sobbing and howling to a sadness beyond the love duet, and the bass approached, more agitated, more in haste now, more on his mind, the blues, distress, and pianist and girl backed off for the necessary while, until it was over, the sadness, got over with, over and done with, and what was wanted was full measure again, voice and the instruments, all in concert, all in the triumphant joyfulness of their ability, and finished, laughing. Us at our best, that give and take, no bossing, everyone unique, in an order of our devising and our accepting. And when you looked around, as Vic's roving eye made possible, the room seemed a careless and coherent freedom too: dance if you like, or sit talking and drinking, move around as you like, the kids running in and out, the ages of man all mixed, a six-month baby here, and Freddy from the Somme. And the interdealings seemed – perhaps it was only the music – not chaotic or quarrelsome but intriguing, richly and bravely involved, a unity whose parts were quick and differentiated. The children, for example, with bright helium balloons ran in and out among the tables and the dancers like threads of living anarchy. A room of people would never set and die so long as it had its children running wild. The balloons were a good idea. We should always have balloons, ten thousand of them, brilliant and irrepressible, on strings, lightening even further the lightness of the children.

Then Madge said: Oh, that's Mr Williams. At a table full in the midst of all the goings-on, with a drink in front of him. And that's Stan and Mavis's girl sitting next to him. And people coming up to ask him how he is. We don't want any of that, said Vic abruptly. The picture leapt. Mr Williams and his wellwishers appeared to shatter, they hurtled forward in time and when the world was recomposed he had been lost in the mêlée of dancing, drinking, chatting. Didn't know he was on it, to be honest, said Vic. Fetch him back, said Leonard in a most peculiar voice. Fetch him back this minute, do you hear? Suit yourself, said Vic. Again the world shattered, music and conversation were driven backwards, the people unsaid every word, undid every gesture in one long spasm. Bit far, said Vic. But only a moment later, as Sally's child ran past almost lifting, as it seemed, on a string of red balloons, Mr Williams reappeared, with death as plain as daylight in his face. Nice to see you, Mr Williams, a voice said. How are you feeling? Pretty well, thank you, said Mr Williams. That's the ticket, said the voice. Then a hand on his shoulder, a squeeze, it was wonderfully clear, the affectionate pressure of a married man's left hand. Mr Williams continued sitting there, the smile lapsing off his lips and his look retracting fathomlessly into holes of bone. He dabbed at his lips with a bright handkerchief. Then a woman's voice:

Really lovely to see you, Mr Williams. How are you feeling? Fine, he said. A good bit better, thank you. That's the spirit, Mr Williams. And her hand came on to his, rested, departed, a beautiful hand, a bare arm, a fall of abundant blonde hair as she stooped. Should never have been there, said Betty. He wanted to, said Madge. He wrote and asked me would it be all right. He cared a lot for our Sally. Betty thought: Much good it did. Much good it did her if she got her ideas from him. Shall I freeze him? Vic asked. Vic froze Mr Williams between the efforts of his smiles, full on, in pain, lonely. Then let him go. How old was he? Betty asked. Younger than me, said Leonard. Now he was what I call ill, Vic remarked. Do you want the rest? Nobody said no. They saw it out.

Madge was upset by Vic's remark. She looked across to see how Len had taken it. Len was asking himself would it be possible to die of sadness, to be so sad that in the end, seeing no hope of any other condition, the little soul would dim to nothing and go out. Or of anxiety. To be so anxious that the head and the chest were paralysed by it and the nails clenched into the palms and stuck fast there and in that rigor mortis in the midst of life finally, imperceptibly, you passed over. Oh, you could fit the car up in the garage and end that way or find a rope and a hook or a fistful of pills, but that wasn't the thing itself, the sadness, the anxiety, actually itself doing it, the way a cancer did. And he wondered could you die of self-contempt, by being so persuaded you were unfit to live that in the end it worked, the persuasion was converted into its effect. He sat there wondering whether sadness and anxiety and self-contempt all in one, all at their worst in one, would ever without you lifting a finger be a *mortal* sickness. He thought they might, he could imagine it.

Off they go, said Vic. I like this bit. Pretty good for a first time, though I say it myself. They were leaving. See the moths in the lamplight, Vic said. Nice touch that. They were leaving, and Gwen, the day's princess, wanted all her balloons, she seemed to have gathered almost every other child's balloons, and had their leashes all together in her little fist, such a fullness and abundance of red and yellow and blue and green balloons, and there was no way they were going to get into the car with her, and hand them out or let them go, let them go up and up through the moths into the night and bump against the stars, that wasn't going to happen either. The boot, somebody said. So they lifted the lid and such fun was had by one and all getting umpteen bright balloons that only wanted to lift and be gone, getting them bundled in and held down long enough, like trying to drown something, before the lid was shut. Maybe they'll fly, maybe the car will lift off on the hill and they'll have all the lights of the towns and the motorways below.

Into the silence when they had driven off with cheers and bangings on the roof and on the boot full of balloons, into the sudden lapsing of the spirits then came the singer's voice and the piano and the trumpet and bass around her in a muted understanding. The jazz was coming through the windows of the upper room. I let it run a bit, said Vic. Ends it nicely, don't you think?

Madge was thinking of Gwen's bedroom. Just that. And the day's full routine under the rule of the chattering princess. Betty guessed as much, but thought: Count yourself lucky. I've had it all my life a room like that.

The thing ran out. Leonard opened the curtains. Not much better yet, he said. The others sat on a while. What's he do exactly, Betty asked, her new chap? He's in petrol, said Madge, not very sure. Safe at least, said Vic. We'll always need petrol. Safer than the first one anyway, said Betty. Leonard was standing facing the wall in a fashion the three on the sofa were bound to think peculiar. He had his hands in his pockets and was leaning his forehead against the wall. Madge wants a window here, he said. Don't you, Madge. His voice was hampered, stuck in his chest somewhere. Yes, said

Madge. We'd get a bit more sun. Evening sun at least. I'll do it myself, Leonard said, butting gently with his forehead against the wall. I used to do things like that, you know. Didn't I put a fireplace in the other house? And what will you do, Madge? Betty asked. Get a little job somewhere. Helping out somewhere. Leonard sat down at the piano. I used to play a lot, you know. I can't read music but I can play all right. Used to be able to anyway. We know, they thought. We know. Why are you telling us things we know? Haven't touched it for years, he said. I haven't touched it since ... I used to play jazz, you know. Like that chap. Funny face he had, said Betty. And his hair in a ribbon. Yes, said Leonard, like him. It used to be just like that, didn't it, Madge. Yes it did, said Madge. Leonard ran the tips of his fingers along the piano lid. Then opened it.

Estuary

The last half hour was the queerest. Frances wrote to Elizabeth about it: 'I had to get off in the middle of nowhere. There was just a platform and a little shelter. I said: "Is this right?" And the guard said: "Don't worry, lady. He'll be along in a minute."' Then the train, itself only a couple of coaches and almost empty, bore away south and Frances was left on the great space of the valley floor, the hills in a ring around her opening to the sea. She had no company but a few horses, and they were at a distance, grazing on the salt grass and mooching through the sedge. She wrote: 'There was one house near the railway track. And do you know what? They have no road to it. I suppose they use the track or come and go by boat. I saw a boat.' But the river where the branch line crossed it was fast and deep, its debris was everywhere, the land around was shaggy with grey dead trees and straw and other drifted things. Still, there were pools and channels and perhaps in a small boat a way could be found that would join them up, to reach a road. Otherwise whoever lived there must risk the river to where it widened and quietened in a vast lagoon, before the sea. It was late afternoon. Frances wrote: 'Then from nowhere came this one carriage. He must have been waiting in some siding back inland. And there was nobody on it, only the driver and the guard, and the guard got out and helped me in with my bags. I felt like royalty.' They bore away north, past the solitary house with its fuchsia hedge, across the river and over the littered and riddled flood plain in a curve to the firmer ground along an indent of the coast, and followed this, close to the water, as far as a village that faced the open sea. Frances concluded: 'My room is on the top floor in a quite tall blue and white house on the front. My landlady's name is Mrs W. She said: "What will you do with yourself?" And I said: "Look at the sea." And so I shall. The windows are very big. I'm glad you didn't tell me not to come. It can't do any harm. Nothing else has helped.'

Later Frances went out to post the letter and to phone home. She began telling Robert about the journey – the floods, the lambs, the snow, the primroses, and how the train had seemed to bring itself only gradually and reluctantly into its right direction. 'Oh, and before that, where I changed the first time, there was a poor man shouting his head off in the waiting room.' But thinking of this man she felt she could not tell the story properly, and asked instead: 'Have you looked me up on the map yet?' Robert hadn't, he had been busy all day. He added: 'And I've already decided what I'll do next.' She heard his little cough – really like a sob – of nervousness as he began to tell her what it had occurred to him to do as soon as his present work was finished. 'You always know what you'll do next,' she said. 'Best that way,' he replied. 'Then there aren't any gaps.' She saw, as though his face were close to hers, how the sweat stood out on his brow and how he dabbed at it with his clean white handkerchief. 'I do hope you will be able to sleep,' she said, but knew he wouldn't. Her spirits lapsed, the anxiety crept over her.

She lay awake, hearing the sea. It seemed to be beating at the very step of the house in which she lay, and between each stroke of the waves there was scarcely a gap. A slower tempo would have been easier on her mind. The waves insisted. Frances thought of the river, where it went under the branch line by the isolated house. Most of the journey was under the sign of water: the melt off the hills, tremendous sudden showers, trees knee-deep in the flooded fields, mist, a quickly dissolving rainbow; but it was only towards the end when the train, after much prevarication, settled at last on a straight line west, that quietly the river came alongside and they had run together as far as the little junction in one purpose and at some speed. Lying in the dark with her eyes open she saw the river as something darker still. It seemed to her a thousand times more full of purpose and concentration than she in all her youth and middle age had ever been. She saw herself as a little upright thing on the bare platform, in the fork of the track, waiting. What would she have done if the connecting train had never arrived? She tested her resolve. 'I'd have knocked at the door of the house behind the fuchsia hedge and they would have taken me on by boat.' Down the river? 'Down the river.'

Frances wrote to Elizabeth: 'Where I had to change trains the first time, in the waiting room, there was a man shouting and crying. He had created a big space around himself. We only wanted to read the paper and drink a cup of tea in peace, but he kept shouting out. He was quite a young man and had a frizzly great mop of hair. He was shouting: "It's no good!" Just that: "It's no good! It's no good!" Again and again, and rocking to and fro and sometimes covering his eyes. "It's no good!" Only that, but in different tones of voice, as if he were trying to find the one that would be the most persuasive. In the end two policemen came for him and led him away.'

Frances began to weep, there in a sunny room above the estuary, writing a letter. The man's feeble body came back to her, as he stood up between the two giant policemen, to be led away. Below the waist he seemed disproportionately small; or his head, with its vast aura of hair, looked too much for him to carry. His legs, in tight striped trousers, were spindly. He wore scuffed and pointed shoes that had once been red. And being led gently out of the waiting room he still cried: 'It's no good!' 'We get all sorts in here,' said the girl behind the bar. Frances put aside her letter.

It was full tide. The surf arrived quite placidly wave upon wave against the rivermouth. This mouth itself was a narrowish place pinced between banks of sand, but before it the silver water had filled out all of an available arena. Had the sea overwhelmed the river? No, there was the river still, water in water but distinct, as a current, a substantial ghost, still purposefully advancing through the leisure of its own great lake. Energies, different energies, from different directions, jostling and in combat. Frances went out, to witness them more closely.

Out on the sand, beyond the little harbour, on the north side of the river where it penetrated the sea, the wind was evident as it had not been behind the window glass; and with the wind, as its chief self-expression, came ceaseless changes of light. The wind was off the sea, but at an angle to the waves and sideways on to the river also, where the river came in. Light was flung about in these deflected collisions, and though the wind was no more than a sunny spring breeze it shifted the surface of the sand on the bank where Frances stood, so that the ground itself seemed more vaporous than solid. Hard to orientate yourself, since nothing stood still. Nothing held, except as an interplay. Everything shifted in its state as the elemental agents by their ceaseless give and take decided it. 'I'm breaking up,' she said aloud, but whether this was cause for anguish or relief she would not have been able to say. The process itself, when she viewed it over a period of time, seemed gradual and almost gentle. Only now and then there would be a jolt, a sense of fissure. A terra firma of ice as the sea warms and the icebergs calve and veer slowly away gives some idea. She could never determine the nature of the feeling at all conclusively. Sometimes it was terror, she was sure of that; but then at other times more like the excitement of a quickening.

In the evening, in the queer orange light of another sunset, she resumed her letter to Elizabeth. She wrote: 'I told you I was doing funny things before I came away, and that was why Robert said I should see you again, but I only told you one or two of them. Another was this: I went and sat in a catholic church and watched the people going up to make their confessions. I even went up myself, but ran away when the priest spoke to me through the grille. And another day I went and sat in that big council estate for a couple of hours. It was in the morning and I had nothing to do. All the same, I don't know why I did that. It was obvious I had no business being there, and the people looked at me when they went past. When I told Robert he didn't know what to say. It made him very nervous. Sometimes it's as though I frighten him. In the end he said: "Are you studying life, Frances?" And then he said I should go and see you again.'

Again she put aside the letter. Such a desolation came up in her she could not even weep. Where she had sat was nowhere in particular; not by a playground where she might have been thought to be in charge of one of the children; not at a bus stop; nowhere particular. Now she shuddered at it herself, that anywhere could be so unconnected. People came and went who knew one another and had some business in the place. They gave her a look. Her clothes were not like theirs, nor was her face. Her walk, when she stood up to leave, still had its peculiar grace, and the people looked at her as though she might be somebody famous. She had not thought the estate especially ugly; only the thought of herself in it, sitting without any business or connection, desolated her now.

The days ran into one another. They were good and bad, and the hours likewise good and bad, from one moment to the next, extremely. At her worst she lay under a flattening sadness, unable to move until – as beyond her control as the mass of the clouds – it thinned, let in the light, or by some benevolent hurricane was ripped away. And so anxious did she feel at times she believed her face must be ravaged by it, and then she hid. It was still pre-season, there were scarcely any visitors, she was soon known in the couple of shops and where she took her walks and where she sat looking at the sea or trying to paint or sketch the meeting of the sweet water and the salt. But in her anxious state she wanted nobody to see her face. She looked away, beyond the estuary if possible, or kept her eyes on the ground while people passed. She hid in her room, and shouted through the door to Mrs W. that she was fine. She felt unfit to be in any public place. But then the good in her rose again, or it was bestowed on her like light pouring out of an opening in the sky, a silver light, far off beyond the estuary, towards evening after a dull day, tipped down out of the heavens on to the flat receiving sea. In that state she was radiant, and knew it. The people looked at her as though they half-recognized her from television or from a film or a magazine, and she felt her tall and hopeful girlhood coming back to her out of a past when, as Robert had said, her beauty and her gifts shone in his nights. She wore boots and walked where she liked. She got into the zone of the river's floodwater and might have made her way through the maze of pools and channels across the flat salt marshes where the sedge-coloured horses stood, to the isolated house – whose little blue boat she often noticed now, moored by the bridge or pushing through the grass and reeds along invisible cuts. In the debris bulldozed outwards by the successive floods she found all manner of things: the tiny sodden corpse of a lamb from this year and the giant skeleton of a horse from last. And on all the wreck and on all phenomena when her spirits were high she bestowed an impartial passionate interest and hurried to telephone when she returned and beat against her husband's fearfulness with detail upon detail of a world she exulted in. Later, it is true, recalling his voice and the little sob of nervousness with which he prefaced his own accounts, she felt that between them there was a hated contest, which first she won by her vigour when her spirit was riding high and he won later by the mere echoing of his melancholy in her mind. 'If I face out to sea,' she thought, 'then everything is behind me. The light lights me up and I am beginning something new.' But it would be just as true to say that everything was at her back, forever coming and piling at her back, down all the hundreds of waters forever collecting in the river – in the river that dumped its cadavers on either side and went head down into oblivion in the sea.

Frances took to visiting the pub, a thing she had never done in her life before. The first time it was on a queer impulse, as when she had gone and sat in the confessional; but her nerve held. Knowing nothing, she went into the public bar and drifted to where there was some animation, as though that were the usual form. They were all local men. Their conversation, in some dialect or language she did not understand, ceased as she entered their smoky company. She stood then, like a gauche girl. One said: 'Are you looking for somebody?' Frances shook her head. 'Then what will you drink?' She answered: 'I'll drink what you are drinking.'

It was mid-afternoon, an odd time, but the men sat around in their idleness, out of the daylight. She was known to them already, in her singularity. Nobody ever forgot how she drifted in and stood there like a young girl who has, under all her fear of being wrong, some trust in her deep attractiveness. And it was easy. They faced her with a curiosity held in by a natural courtesy. If they asked it was because her openness invited it. They asked: 'How did you find out about us then?' 'You here?' she replied, 'you in this pub?' But they meant the place, the whole place such as it was – 'us out here at the ends of the earth'. Frances answered: 'I saw an advertisement in *The Lady*.' Nobody understood. She hurried to correct what she thought they might be thinking. 'I don't read *The Lady*, don't think I buy *The Lady*. I saw it when I was waiting at the doctor's.' But at once and for ever after they called her 'The Lady'. That was her name in the bar, and she was flattered. Their own names were all outlandish nicknames. She asked: 'Does one of you live in the house by the junction?' At this there was laughter, which they quickly checked in fear of having offended her, and Creel said: 'No, lady, none of us. It's Horse you want. He comes in now and then, or you'll see him by the harbour, hanging about.' 'I saw the horses,' Frances said. 'Are they his?' 'Sort of,' said Creel, who seemed to be the oldest.

Frances took a walk behind the village. The houses, the couple of shops, the pub, the chapels, made up very little depth. The road climbed steeply, and was soon only a track. The climb exhausted her, but she bore away from the sea and got a view over the valley floor, the junction and the fuchsia house, as they had told her in the bar she would. She could see the horses, and the blue dot of the boat moored where the railway crossed the river. It was late afternoon and cloudy. Watching, she saw the train arrive, its two carriages, and halt at the little platform; but nobody was left there when it moved away south. Still, after the due interval, coming as it seemed from nowhere, the connection, the single carriage crept over the watery floor; halted; waited; departed; and moving north towards her went out of sight under the hill she was walking on.

Frances felt the onset of her sadness again, and with it a terrible fatigue. She began to drift, hands in the pockets of her long coat, still away from the sea and climbing slightly until she faced the whole arc of the mountains. The house, which she had always in view, looked lost. A breeze came down the valley, cold. Where it came from there was still snow and her lifted face felt it. On a different day it would have been different. The sparks of gorse only wanted the sun on them. But the sky was a dark grey, inclining into an early darkness. Drift, disconnection, more and more heaviness. She wept quietly, still bearing around the curve of the hillside, climbing a little, and the boat and the dull dots of horses became too small to see and the house itself was dwindling to nothing. She was heading on to the bare mountain, against a stiffer and colder breeze, when a light came on in the house, and although it seemed fainter and further away than any star, she halted, and bethought herself.

There was a police car outside her lodgings when she got back. Mrs W. and a policeman were standing together in the hall. Frances said: 'Have you come to take me away?' Then she saw herself in the hall mirror and said nothing more. They were gentle with her. When it got so late Mrs W. had telephoned Robert, to ask what she should do. It was Robert who telephoned the police. No harm done, but shouldn't she phone and put his mind at rest? 'How tall I look!' Frances was thinking, 'and white. But not ugly, and really not old. That's what my face was like when I was a girl.' Mrs W. was handing her the phone. The officer watched, holding his cap on his chest. She heard Robert's fearful anxiety. 'I went for a walk,' she said, 'a bit far, that's all.' Then she began to tell him about the house by the junction, and how a light had come on and made her think, and how a man lived there all on his own, called Horse because he looked after horses but whom she had not met yet but in the pub they said she probably would before long. She heard Robert's sob of nervousness, and his bewilderment and his dread at what she might do and make him suffer next. Then he said: 'I'll come for you, Fran. I've looked you up at last. Or for the weekend. I'll come and see you for a weekend.' 'Don't,' she said. 'Please, please don't.'

The officer left. 'No harm done,' he said. Mrs W. was kind. Frances climbed to her room. The stairs were as hard as the hillside and often she had to pause.

Frances wrote to Elizabeth: 'I think I could stay here for ever. At nights I listen to the sea, so close, and so quick sometimes it sounds like oars beating, and to the birds that never seem to sleep but keep on crying all night long. And in the mornings this room is wonderfully light. I open the windows and study the way the river enters the sea. Full tide is beautiful, because of the huge bowl of silvery water, but low tide also, because of the white sand, more on the other side than there is on ours. I'll go over there one day. There looks to be no end to where you could walk on the other side when the sea pulls back for a while.'

Mrs W. brought her post up. There was one from Robert. Frances wrote: 'I frighten him, it's as easy as that. That's why he works so hard and can't sleep at nights. He doesn't want to think about me, and when he has to it upsets him.' Her writing got faster and was soon nearly illegible. But she had written: 'He shouldn't have married me. Or he should have left me years ago. He shouldn't have been so honourable. It has done no good. And now it is too late.'

On the street they were a good-looking couple. She was tall, graceful; he held his left arm stiffly across his chest, for her to link him. People had always glanced at them when they walked out. He wore a decent jacket and a collar and tie and with his grey moustache and neatly parted silvery grey hair he looked like an officer. The last time, when he accompanied her to the doctor's, the streets were frightening her again and she held him very tight. 'I'm sorry,' she said. Her tone was hopeless. She looked at him as though they were just married and she had already disappointed him and believed she always would. Often her face, under the years, looked girlish and helpless. And she saw his desperate pity, as though the time were running out in which he might have reassured her. Time and resources, time and his own will. She felt his pity for the two of them, the man and wife. He left her at the surgery. She stood on the step there and watched him leaving her to reach the library. His pace increased, when he went out of sight he was almost running.

Frances concluded: 'I often think of your room, as it was

the last time, more like your own room at home, I guess, than a doctor's room, you among your flowers and those pictures of houses and flowers that I suppose your children did when they were little. And the sun coming in, as it does here. And how you will always listen, and get behind with your appointments because you listen and talk, as any sweet-natured normal woman would. I admired you more than I can tell you in that pretty dress, when you were telling me about your latest book and how you want to help young people now by writing for them, and how well and happy your own children are. Mine aren't, I suppose it is well known. The girls have both come home, to look after Robert. They would rather be with him than where they ought to be. I haven't given them the will to manage as a woman should, and cannot get a man to go to sleep with me but he must be up half the night fretting and when he lies down next to me he cannot sleep. Life is so difficult. You need to concentrate, right from the start, and keep on concentrating and what you ever grasp you have to keep hold of, all the way through. It is much too hard. I haven't been able to do it, but you have and you always will. I'm glad you didn't stop me coming here. It has done no harm. Nothing else did any good.'

The day looked fine. She would take a picnic. She went downstairs. Mrs W. said she should wear her big coat nevertheless, so she did, and leather boots and a scarf and a woollen hat. She had her painting things in a little rucsack, also her letter to Elizabeth. In the hall mirror, setting her hat right and Mrs W. fussing over her, she might have been the younger woman's daughter.

She shopped quickly, to begin her walk; but then, on a contrary impulse, went into the pub. There they were, in the dark on a sunny day, swapping jokes and gossip in their barbarous vernacular. The mood was jovial. They called her into the fumes, and the one known as Hobgoblin, youngish but hunched, cried out: 'You missed him, lady. You just

missed him. We told him you keep asking after him.' The
laughter was more raucous than usual. 'Horse, you mean?'
said Frances. 'Horse!' they roared. She turned at once and
went out, so that afterwards everybody said she had come in
looking for him.

She got on to the white sands, just beyond the harbour.
The tide was still falling and in the sunshine the river,
slimmed to its essential self, hurried out after it; but off the
sea came the wind, as a counter energy, chopping up the
waters so that they danced with a quick sharp light. The sky
was blue, except far, far out, where a lid of cloud, horizon-
wide, was rising. The sand under Frances' feet flowed like
smoke. There, at the level of her feet, the breeze seemed
strongest. It seemed intently and surreptitiously to be
working at the removal of the sand in the time allowed before
the sea returned. She walked to where the river's bank
became the seashore, where the tiny nibbling waves, each
hustled by the next, beached with the wind incessantly,
against current and tide. Across the white-flecked dancing
water the sands on the south side extended like a desert.
Following the waterline, mesmerised by the constant
repetition of the little waves – it was an action that seemed to
be stimulating some state of body and soul to a climax, to be
whetting it to an unbearable edge – Frances was directed
back towards the harbour, and looking up from her boots and
from the silver insisting water she saw the blue boat close in
and rowing closer. Then the prow came through the ripples
and kissed into the white sand. 'Are you Horse?' she asked, as
the man at the oars turned his massive face her way. 'They
call me that,' he answered, 'because I look like one.' 'And the
horses are your only company out there?' 'At present they
are. Do you want to cross, lady?' He brought the stern round
for her to clamber in.

Crossing, he said: 'I saw you arrive. I always watch to see
if anyone gets out, and I saw you standing there that

afternoon.' Frances answered: 'I saw your light the other day, when I was walking where I shouldn't have been. It came on just in time.' 'And neither of us knew,' he said. 'And now we've met.'

The crossing was quick, and could have been quicker, but Horse took a diagonal line, to bring her further out and so that she got some feeling at least of what it was like at the very place where the river hit into the sea. He worked the oars swiftly, in short strokes. Then he beached, again with the gasp and kiss of a prow riding into banked sand, and looked her in the face. 'Shall I wait?' he asked. The question surprised her. 'I wanted a walk,' she answered, 'before the sea comes in.' 'Watch it,' he said, 'and watch the weather.' The lid of cloud had risen half an inch. Horse shipped the oars, stepped out in his seaboots and swung the little boat round, stern on. Then he reached for her hand, so she should disembark.

On that far side the wind was stronger, the flight of the sands faster, and since the wind came in at its characteristic angle they were not being driven inland but, obliquely, into the hurrying river. The movement over the floor was ghostly and, under the din of the wind, silent. Its shape was that of snakes, of countless snakes, progressing by writhing, as though down on its belly at its lowest and most secretive the wind took that bodily form and worked at diminishing the land, converting it into a harsh vapour that the water of the river and the infinite waters of the ocean could easily ingest. Under the vanishing surface was a ground firm enough to walk on, that showed through the layer of its own perpetual sublimation in pocks, ripples, frets actually palpable to feet on leather soles. 'It's goodbye to everything on a day like this,' said Frances aloud. Turning she saw the ground she trod on streaming away from her, she seemed to be standing ankle-deep in the smouldering of ash that might ignite or of ice that never would. It shocked her to see how far away, bobbing on the water, the little blue boat already was. She waved. He raised an arm. Was he waiting? She turned and headed away across the sand towards the line of surf. The wind rose. How ghostly everything had become. What lodged at all? Old whitened logs, rolled there by the flooding river and mauled by the tides. The sand crept over them. A black oil-drum, empty, rocked in an agony of imminent locomotion. There was a constant slide and skitter of dried wrack and other small detritus, and always the rustle, slither, low susurration of the fleeing sands. Now when Frances turned she could see nothing that looked attainable. The river, though it shone, was dwindling. Beyond, at a great remove, stood the sunny arc of the mountains – eroding, feeding their own substance day and night, year in, year out, into the streams. But it was the sea she had set her heart on reaching, the low white surf, whiter than the sand, milk- and snow-white, perpetual.

She bowed against the wind across a space too large for her strides and where everything was in motion except the heavy things fed there by the river to the very lips of the sea. One among these was very prominent and, heading always towards the surf, she came to it because it was in her path. It was a large and spectral thing, a branch, or more than a branch – most of a tree, an ash, ripped away from somewhere up the valley not long ago with all its buds. In another week or two they would have leafed, and there they were reared up on the sand at the mercy of the incoming sea, hundreds of them on clean silvery stems, black as coal and containing each in embryo a spray of living green. The wreck of this tree, the waste of so many buds, troubled Frances more than anything else she had discovered in the river's abundant debris. Its being wrenched from somewhere habitable and shipped out here to lodge in a shifting aridity, touched her as though its life were the life of lambs or fledglings or human helpless infants. She broke off a branch, a small bough, holding a dozen or more of the jet-black tips.

'They might flower,' she said, 'in a big vase in a warm room at home they might.'

She thought of her home, and of her family gathering in it without her, but could not keep hold on them, the line of the surf was more compelling, and towards that edge, clutching her bough of ash, she pushed on, against the wind, against the tide that had turned and was coming in to meet her now, closing the distance she would have to travel. She saw, but it did not trouble her, that the curtain of cloud had risen higher and was making for the sun just as she was for the incoming sea. Queer wish and excitement low down in her womb, to reach the edge, to say she had been out to the very edge, as for a dare, to wet a hand in the waves and turn and run, with a schoolgirl's vigour, safely back. The cloud was a yellowish black and on it the lightning was flickering like snakes' tongues. How fast it was travelling in fact. It would reach the sun before she reached the surf. She paused. It did. The sun went out. The temperature dropped as abruptly as a lift. Then came thunder. She stood, weeping in the wind without particular emotion. What did it matter? What did she matter? The waves were at a little distance still, but coming. They lifted, one behind the other, the white horses, an infinite number, from an inexhaustible source, steady as the wind. Frances stood. Her sense of herself, of herself as a distinct thing that lived and breathed and had a place in a web of connections, dwindled to nearly nothing. Everything streamed away, hurrying as fast as it could into extinction. That was the will, that was how things had set: triumphantly into extinction. And in that letting go she with her last iota of independent volition acquiesced. And she began again, the hard labour of setting one foot before the other, towards the sea. 'So be it,' she said.

Then came a shout. Not any distinguishable word, but a voice, two equal syllables of sound, only faint, but carrying so far, how great its strength must be, how colossal its determination, and it was that – the sense of a voice having travelled so far, across the flats, against the wind, against the tide, against the hurry of everything into dissolution, and that this voice arrived, it was that that halted her. And she turned: saw the river as a brilliant silver snake, still in the sun, sparkling and a little boat on it, far, far away, and between herself and that illuminated place she saw the shadow going towards the river in one terrific accelerating slide. She watched it hit the silvery water and pass over it and cross and pass over the sunny-fronted little houses of the village and pass on, for the mountains. But even as it hit and laid its cold over those things there came again that shout, the two equal drawn-out syllables that were not intelligible as a word, arriving where she stood with the surf at her back at the very limits of the power of a human voice. And again she thought: 'What strength! What faith!'

The voice decided her, and filled her now with the proper and necessary fear. She turned to the voice, she began to walk. But then came hail, horizontal, and the sand lifted higher and streamed away with the grains of hail. And such a wind now, and cold, a steady bodyline rush of cold whose shape and substance were the white hail. She knew the tide had turned and was at her back, coming. She knew that the flats were a pushover for an incoming tide. And she knew how weak she was, though tall and upright, and how unravelled in her thinking and her feeling, and how far away from anywhere, the only warm-blooded living thing, and that, having sought the edge, the edge was coming for her, in serrated waves, very fast. She said aloud: 'I've had it now', but answered that by an act of concentration, turned up the collar of her big coat and blessed her strong boots and her woollen hat and scarf. The ground sped from her feet, as smoke does, striving to ignite. Then came rain on the hail, and so level and dense was it that at once her clothing was as sodden as the dead lamb, and the chill of it came through into her bones. Everywhere around her was white and hastening, only the logs, the large remains, looked like people who had stumbled and could not get up. She reached the ash, it gave out a whining noise, she felt the fresh scar where she had torn off her bough as something she had suffered on herself. It lightened and thundered simultaneously overhead, which shook her like a tree. She thought: 'There'll be a police car waiting at Mrs W.'s.' Then she fell forward, on both knees. Like that she might have turned to salt in the blast of sand. But she got up again, saying in her head: 'Where this sand is going to is the river, I noticed that much, and on the river is the little blue boat with the man in it they call Horse, because he looks like one and only has horses for company at present out there in his house at the junction where he saw me standing waiting all that time ago.' Tide and wind and weather at her back she made her way, the one they called The Lady, towards the bank of the river, as she hoped, still holding her bough with its numerous black buds.

The Red Balloon

These long late summer evenings three or four times a week the balloon comes up over the gardens and the hospitals and drifts away. Comes up like a vast red sun from where the sun has set and drifts away into the quarter where it will rise again.

Tobias sits at his open window staring into the trees that conceal the nearest hospital. Then comes the balloon. He hears it first, he hears its fire. He hurries down into the garden with his binoculars.

Everything about the red balloon is pleasing to Tobias. Its colour for one thing. Such boldness astonishes him. And that it is not of this day and age but rises on hot air as it might have done two hundred years ago and goes with the breeze. Among the balloonists one seems to be captain. He wears a deerstalker hat and when he salutes a person on the ground he does it solemnly. The others are his passengers, never more than two or three. They change, they are never the same, but the captain is always there in his distinctive hat. Impossible not to think he is bearing them away. Their contentment is apparent, their friendliness extraordinary. High in the sky like gods with fire at their disposal they lean over Tobias's poor garden and salute him in the friendliest fashion as he stands viewing them. Their captain has mastery, they are in good hands. He has cognizance of the breezes. It must be the case that every evening a breeze starts up he knows that he can trust. How many people in the city's traffic have such knowledge? The captain and his passengers entrust themselves to a particular breeze and rise and drift over the modern city into the east, a little north of east, where daylight will first be palpable on Tobias's right eye, on his right frontal lobe, if he is sitting, as he often is, in the dark at his open window staring down the garden at the trees between him and the hospital. Who is that captain? Who are his chosen passengers? Three or four times a week the red balloon comes over and passes on. Tobias stands in the garden with his binoculars. The riders in the sky salute him courteously. His room, when they have passed, looks quite forlorn. By his empty house he is saddened to the core.

The first time Tobias saw Sam it was through a telescope upside down in winter when the trees were bare and not only the lights but also some of the nearer buildings of the hospital were visible. He had just bought the telescope to look at the stars and that afternoon was practising with it through the open window when he caught the flat roof of the Adolescent Unit and there was Sam, on the edge; but the image was inverted. Though people came every day across his vision and he looked at them, in the park or on the streets whenever he stood or sat, he had not bought the telescope for them but for the stars. He had thought that if he threw the sash open and dressed in more than his father's dressing gown he might use that little room as an observatory in the nights when he could not sleep, and learn about the stars; but by accident the first thing he ever focussed on was Sam there on the edge, in stockinged feet on a concrete edge, in jeans and a thin t-shirt leaning over and threatening to throw himself away. It was a powerful telescope and the image it offered to the eye was as sharp as ice. For a while Tobias could not understand what the drama was. Then, to right the image, he inverted his head and watched. The boy looked thin and cold and had you only seen his face you would never have said this is the look of a child about to throw himself away. That was the first sight Tobias had of Sam. Later he swore (to himself) that he had even seen the burn marks on the boy's bare arms. Sam held them crossed, almost as a very young woman might if she were naked there and trying to hide her breasts.

The hospital has extensive grounds. They are an old estate; the limes were left, the beeches and the chestnuts, also the orchards, gone to ruin, and hundreds of yards of damson hedge. The cricket pitch likewise pre-dates the hospital. Eastward there are open fields. The raggedness of the hospital's eastern boundary is peculiar. Tobias's garden, like the gardens of all the houses along his side of the road, finishes up against the hospital wall. Where he sits he faces north into the trees and from the air, if you include the public park, his part of the world must look mostly green, or black at nights. But the town is at his back, all its streets. The streets frighten him, by day when he walks them, by night when he sits in an empty house and they are at his back. He is on the perimeter, where the hospitals are gathered. He is out of harm's way if he keeps himself to himself. But the ambulances go in to deal with the city's accidents and savageries and come up again on long undulating screams. The house, devoid of any family, is only a poor insulation around his shoulders against the streets.

The hospital has a chapel whose bell for morning service on Sundays at eleven is very metallic and insistent. Tobias was there as usual after seeing Sam. He sat at the back and did not go up with the others for communion. How could he when for his uncommitted sins he was not at all repentant? Asked, he would have had to say he wanted to do them but was fearful. No members of the general public were among the congregation, though they might have been, as Tobias was, it was allowed. The worshippers were all inmates and staff. They knew him and said hello but he did not ask about Sam. He would have had to call him 'the boy on the roof' and admit to owning a powerful telescope. That night he opened the sash and viewed the moon. Her surface shone, he saw the dust, the disfigurements, the pocks. Effortlessly he extended his feelings into touch with the desolation and the cold. And the night was a quieter one. For an hour or more while he was viewing the brilliant loneliness of the moon he heard nothing that alarmed him behind his back.

Tobias sat in the park near the children's swings. To look at him, he might have been a youngish grandfather. Always when he walked in the park he feared somebody in a uniform might stop him and ask him what his thoughts were; but when he sat by the swings, smoking and watching, he dreaded being asked which child was his. By nods and smiles he tried to indicate his harmlessness; but it seemed to him he stank of shame and dread and every mother of a child must know.

Across his vision Sam came walking quickly in stockinged feet. Tobias stood up. To anybody watching, especially to an eye in heaven looking down, it will have seemed like an assignation. Their lines of travel joined and down the boy's, down the long green empty slope through the middle of the park, they continued shoulder to shoulder. I was drawn, Tobias said to himself, reflecting later. You might say I felt called.

'Why were you going to throw yourself off the roof?' he asked. Sam shrugged. He had bare arms again and was hugging them and rubbing them, for warmth. 'And why do you burn yourself like that?' Sam shrugged, but answered: 'Because I'm shit.' So the spots were the marks of the punishment he inflicted. I don't do that, Tobias thought. The burns were like the badges of an illness; or of an initiation, showing courage. 'Decoration' was a word that came to Tobias as he contemplated the cigarette burns on Sam's wrists and arms. 'Give us one, will you,' Sam said. His childish face was puffy, his eyes had a slyness Tobias did not like to see. 'You promise you won't hurt yourself?' He gave him a cigarette and lit it for him. The boy's mouth sucked on it. They were on the long slope of grass as far from any of the surrounding roads as it is possible to be. They halted. 'I said a stupid thing in there,' said Sam. 'I said I was so bad they should pour petrol on me and set light to me.' And now he feared they would, perhaps in the place where the gardener had his bonfires. This was so absurd that Tobias felt able to smile and to reassure the child with some show of affection. They turned, he laid an arm on his thin shoulders and step by step they climbed the hill again. 'When I was in there,' Tobias said, 'it was still called the asylum.' And: 'When I was in there I was always running away.'

Back home in the room where he was visible through the leafless trees Tobias marvelled at his carelessness. He had left the park and crossed the road and entered the hospital grounds all with his arm resting gently on Sam's shoulders. Soon they met a nurse. 'Tobias,' he said. 'Yes,' said Tobias, 'I've brought Sam back.' But now his boldness made him tremble.

Through the open window, high above the light pollution of the hospital, Tobias trained his powerful telescope on Jupiter. The planet lay in the viewing dish as a pulsing dot; three of the moons were piled to one side of it. There in the dish the specks of light looked like an experiment to engender life. Space must be very cold. An English winter, rising off an empty garden, entering at an open window, is not even the beginnings of the faintest intimation of the coldness of outer space. But Tobias felt something, a compound feeling made of cold, remoteness and loneliness, so that his soul, shuddering at its own temerity, edged out into an apprehension of the cold beyond the stratosphere. And out there, fetched hither into a dish close to his eye, was that cluster of dots that looked, though it was not, like a quickening.

Bad days, worse nights. He lay on his bed under the sloped close ceiling that was stained with years of nicotine. His fingers were black and calloused with it. How could he ever touch anyone? he wondered. Day came and night came and he sipped black coffee, scarcely fed himself, but lay fixed in a feeling heavier than any earthly substance, a compound of dread, revulsion, sadness, black as lead, heavier than Pluto. The sirens got closer, a car driven fast hit a wall somewhere very near, somebody rang the bell, somebody bawled obscenely through the letter box, he lay in the room furthest away from it, all encased in horror and melancholy, sucking in poison and exhaling it at the ceiling.

His appearance after these ordeals was much worsened. Anyone observing him must notice. He slumped in his bearing, dragged in his walk like an old man. The swags below his eyes were as black as nicotine, all his face seemed pendulous. He rose when he heard the chapel bell and went just as he was, unwashed, unshaved, to show God what a creature looks like after torment. He shuffled in and watched them take communion. He had the certain feeling that he was damned and that his eternity had begun already. More solemnly than ever he acknowledged the greetings of the inmates and the staff to whom he was well known.

The park was sunny, vast and cold. On the slope, at the midpoint, as far as it is possible to be from any roads and houses, a child was flying a red kite. Black and visible Tobias began the long crawl towards him. The kite dipped and soared. It and the child seemed to delight in one another. Fists full of silver, Tobias advanced. He would have liked to stand by the boy, as a relative might or an adult friend; stand and look up with him at that delta of red swooping on the empty blue. At most, when they were both enthralled, he would have laid an arm around his shoulders. But it was all so desolating and ridiculous. The day might be as breezy as it liked, he still fetched with him in his sweating skin the ineradicable smell of guilt and misery. A face like his, yellowish and black around the eyes, if he bowed that down to the child it would quicken less kinship, far less, than had he been a dog. Such a long way down the slope, and all so visible, especially from above, to make such a woeful overture. The boy had turned his way. He held his two hands steady as a gunner's. The kite, about as friendly in its shape and markings as a vampire, swooped at the head of Tobias.

That night he focussed on the Pleiades. He saw all seven and by a leap of the mind, a vast inversion, conceived all the fellowship in the universe to be out there in that little family cluster and all the cold and solitariness to be entering him, through the telescope, though his eyes, into his brain and heart. He viewed the Pleiades for a good long while, imbibing the full measure of his own remoteness. He heard owls and the squealing of a creature being killed; but at his back the streets were tranquil. The noise when it came was in the air and his viewing was obliterated by a colossal light pollution.

Police, their helicopter. It had come over and was searching. Into the gardens it put down a stilt of light. One after another they were stricken. They seemed to suffer death by sudden freezing, as though the cold of the stars had been harnessed by the authorities, to be a weapon. The light was silent, the racket above it was like the shattering of a mentality into the bits and pieces of an enormous panic. When he saw the sudden blanching of his few bare fruit trees Tobias felt a shock of pity for them and dread for his remaining life.

The patrol went from east to west and at the end of the row, where there is only a road between the houses and the vast empty park, it swung back over the grounds of the hospital. There it poked and probed, moving away east to where the grounds gave out into open fields.

The gardens were quiet again. Soon they resumed their own small light of frost and stars. But the policemen in their helicopter, not far off, still troubled Tobias on the right side of his forehead. If the night can unsheathe a weapon like that, out of the sky, he thought, what hope can a fugitive have nowadays? He will be seen, just as the owls see mice. There on the harsh lawn in his stockinged feet stood Sam. He was looking up at the open sash and at Tobias in the aperture smoking a cigarette and at Tobias's companion, the squat black telescope on its tripod. The man leaned on the sill, the boy looked up, his face gave off the queer pale luminance of fungus. He held a blanket round him, his fists showed, gripping it. The whole enclosure, extending to a shed and the hospital wall and the large bare chestnuts and beeches, was altogether pleasing. It had the aura, though the noise and the searchlight were not very far away, of somewhere safe and magical. 'Let me in,' said Sam in a voice as hoarse as frost. Tobias went down to him.

It was an ugly bare light in the kitchen. Tobias would have sat in the dark but did not wish to reveal this peculiarity. Sam sat at the table in his blanket. 'I came over the wall,' he said. Then: 'That light nearly got me.' 'Won't get you in here,' said Tobias. So far as he understood, the boy had been lying in the field on the blanket, on his back, looking at the stars, when the police helicopter came over and began probing. 'How close did they come?' Tobias asked. The beam illumined every frosty grass blade closer and closer to where he lay. 'You weren't still worried about the petrol, were you?' Tobias enquired. Sam smiled his sorry smile, his look was rueful and a mite ashamed. 'Yes,' he said. He thought the petrol would come down the beam, out of the belly of the helicopter in one vast drenching emission, and the light itself would set fire to him. Lying there, he was sure that was about to happen. But the light moved on, missing him, he said, by inches.

Tobias opened one of his tins of soup. Only when Sam put his bare arms out and began, like a little animal, to sip, could Tobias bring himself to ask who had done that to his eyelids. 'Me,' said Sam. 'With a fag.' 'I guessed it was a fag,' Tobias said. Sam smiled, Sam grinned and shrugged. The burns on his hands and arms had been renewed. 'Like I said,' he said, 'I'm shit.' 'When you did that to your eyes,' Tobias asked, his own eyes blackened colossally with fatigue, 'was no one there to stop you doing it?' 'I did it in the toilet,' Sam replied. Then came into the dayroom and showed himself. He was howling with the pain. 'Some cut a lot,' he added. 'But nobody else in there does burns like me.'

The noise was coming back. Tobias put the light out. They sat in the dark. Sam finished up his soup. They drank their black coffees. Again the garden was violated with a freezing light. The noise descended, it was lowered like a harrow as though with spikes to work a punishment into their stretched-out flesh. But lifted then, lifted, withdrew, the light itself retracted into the helicopter's belly. Frost, stars, another silence.

'When I ran away from there,' Tobias said, 'the farthest I ever got was Aberystwyth.' He saw that Sam did not know where Aberystwyth is. So he added: 'West. As far to the west as it is possible to go.' Sam nodded. Tobias said: 'I raised some money by doing something bad and took a train, with my shoes and socks on, like any ordinary person except that it was the middle of winter and hardly anybody else was travelling.' Sam's eyes were closing. Only the blackened lids looked at Tobias. But he went on a while longer. 'I changed at Wolverhampton, I remember. I had just enough money for a cup of tea and a piece of toast. Why did I head for Aberystwyth, you may ask. Most people head for London when they run away. The answer is I once had a holiday there when I was small. We stayed with my mother's Aunty Catherine. I must have thought if I got back there that lady would hide me. But of course nobody had heard of her in Aberystwyth. Very likely she was dead.'

Sam woke. It moved Tobias to pity when he saw what terror there was in hiding behind the child's burned eyelids. 'You're safe with me,' he said, and reached across the table to lay his stained hand for a second on Sam's wrist. 'Why do you like the stars?' he asked. 'Don't they frighten you?' 'They quieten me down,' Sam answered. Often, he said, he had run away no further than the eastern limits of the hospital grounds and lain down there, with or without a blanket, looking up at the stars. Only now it was spoiled because of what he had said to the nurses about setting fire to him. And he added: 'It's what they should do but I'm scared of it.'

'Come upstairs,' Tobias said. 'I've got a telescope. You might be interested.' They climbed to the little bedroom that also served Tobias as his observatory. 'Best leave the light off,' Tobias said. 'For safety reasons.' Sam sat on the bed. 'You on your own in here?' he asked. 'Yes I am,' Tobias answered. 'Since mother died I've been on my own in here.' He stood by the open window in his dressing gown. Suddenly he had no heart for trying to interest the boy in gazing at the stars. He had no conversation. He stood looking down his empty garden through the skeletal trees at the ugly orange lights of the hospital. North, well clear of the city's light pollution, the stars pulsed on infinity.

'Shall I suck you off?' Sam asked. 'For the soup and that.'

Tobias blushed. His cheeks, all his face that had been cold in the air at the open sash, now heated up with shame, he felt he was staining the whole chaste universe of stars and space and planets with his shame. Is it so obvious? he asked himself. Then, a while later, he said aloud: 'Funny you should say that.' 'What's funny?' Sam asked in the dark behind him. 'Well when I couldn't find my mother's Aunty Catherine in Aberystwyth and didn't know anyone else in the place I set off back again. What else could I do? It was nearly dark by then but I set off back walking along the road into the mountains without a coat. I expect if I thought about it I must have thought I might just as well go back to the hospital, not having anywhere else, but also I expect I was thinking I might as well be dead. Soon it started to snow and I would have died, it's certain I'd have died in a ditch before long, but a lorry driver stopped and picked me up. All I remember is he put a coat around me and I curled up in his cab, which was very warm, and went to sleep. The snow in the mountains was quite bad, so I believe. I believe he had a hard time getting through. I didn't wake up till we were in Wolverhampton and he stopped. I was a very pretty boy, like a choirboy or an angel, people used to say, and I thought he was looking at me when I woke up the way some men used to and women as well in those days. So I said what you just said to me – but for picking me up out of the snow, for saving my life in fact. I've never forgotten his face. He had the cab light on and I saw him blush. That big man blush. And there was a pause, him looking at me and me at him. Then he took a five pound note out of his overalls and gave it me. Five pounds was a lot of money in those days. And he pointed me towards the railway station that was only a couple of hundred yards away.'

Sam had fallen asleep. Under the hospital blanket but on Tobias's bed he was fast asleep. Tobias knelt by him. The frostlight and the starlight were enough to see. Sam had his hands together, in the praying position, and his head was resting on them, on Tobias's pillow. His lips moved now and then, as though he were moistening them and were about to speak. He made little whimpering noises, like a dog. His eyelids, where he had burned them, seemed like the empty sockets themselves of eyes put out. Tobias stood up, laid his outdoor coat over Sam, and turned away.

All night then he watched the stars, quarter by quarter, with deep satisfaction. He sipped his cold coffee, he exhaled a little warmth of cigarette smoke into the open air. And the boy slept. Once he began to mutter in an agitated way. Some words formed: 'Don't, please don't.' Then Tobias knelt by him and rested a hand on his shoulder through the coat and the blanket. Sam's eyelids did not open during his passage through the nightmare but again, because they were black, they appeared to be gaping. Tobias was able to soothe him. Kneeling there he hushed him. Then, back at the lens, viewing the light of worlds perhaps long since dead, he was content with himself.

The gasp of fire, the dragon's breath of the red balloon, startles Tobias out of his trance of loneliness. Then he goes down into his garden where the lawn is littered with unharvested plums. Some evenings the balloon is very close. The captain in the deerstalker hat salutes him gravely, him in particular, and the three or four young passengers wave. Another rush of fire. And they rise, they find the favourable stream of air. Tobias watches them pass over the treetops already turning red and gold, on a blue sky watches them diminish, flaring occasionally, into a quarter far beyond the city where tomorrow's sun will rise. He fears the winter. Then the trees are skeletal, they show the hospital, he has no company but the freezing stars.

A Paris Story

When Alice arrived at the usual place she found that her reservation had not been made. There was no bed for her. They were apologetic, named two or three other hotels nearby, offered to phone; but she said she would rather see for herself, took the addresses and left without ill feeling. It was September, a fine early afternoon, her bag was light. She walked for a while, following no recommendation, and close to the big cemetery, in the rue Fermat, a street she did not remember having been in before, she found a room to her liking.

She phoned home, as agreed. Rob asked, 'Everything OK?' 'Yes,' she said, and was about to tell him he would not reach her, should he wish to, at the old address; but hearing a particular tone in his satisfaction, she said instead, 'Is Lisa there?' 'Yes,' he answered. 'Yes she's here. You knew she would be, didn't you?' In the pause all thought of telling Rob where he might find her died. Then she asked, 'Any other news?' He answered, 'My proofs have come.' 'They'll wait till I get back, will they?' 'That's very kind of you,' he said. 'Rob,' she said, 'you'll be careful, won't you?' 'Trust me,' he replied. And he added, 'And *you* be careful too.' His joke dispirited her. She said, 'I hear they've started bombing.' 'Have they?' he answered. 'How awful. Must watch the news.'

Alice found a restaurant in the next street and ate alone. The *patron* was courteous, amusing; he told her he wanted to go back to Perpignan and marry again; then he let her be. She loved this city in which a woman could do as she pleased.

She had one of her authors with her, and read him now with the liveliest sympathy, sipping her wine. Her mind cleared of everything but the pleasure of being where she was. She savoured the reading with her food and wine. But in the hotel room, lying on the bed, she watched the news. Horror and pity came over her in a rush. She covered her face.

The plan was to follow her authors through the *quartiers* in which their stories were set. She would begin with Echenoz; his story, of a man loving his wife obsessively beyond her violent death; its location, a certain street near the Canal Saint-Martin. She would walk there, through the Jardin des Plantes, crossing the river at Austerlitz. She glanced at her map, settled the general direction, and went by instinct down and across a tangle of streets that did not have her purpose. An old freedom revived in her, the years fell away, her body matched its step to her spirit that now she could believe had never altered. Men noticed her, she saw the glad acknowledgement in their eyes. She felt her own appeal again, and its poignancy. The gardens – she hit on the almost secret entrance Puits de l'Ermite – came near to overwhelming her with their late abundance. She idled off-course, visiting, touching; sat for a while and watched an ordinary autumn morning going its accustomed way. The veil of familiarity evaporated in the sunlight off all things great and small. It seemed to her she could see more nearly perfectly than ever in her life before. Leaving, she heard sirens; but they were elsewhere and remote. She paused over the river, the astonishing potent body of it, ducking through bridge after bridge, tawny under a blue sky. She followed the canal to the place of its disappearance at Bastille; then followed the streets that covered it to the place of its reappearance, at Valmy and Jemappes.

Alice wished to locate her fictions in real places. The beloved wife had appeared on the gable end of a tenement in a large and beautiful mural, to advertise an Elizabeth Arden product. After her death, new building had been abutted on to the old, obliterating her. The faithful husband, having calculated carefully, purchased one of the new apartments and began to scrape through the wall, to the vision of his dead wife. Alice wanted some such violent marriage of the old and new, and was soon in luck. Perhaps the very one! She viewed it from a bridge over the canal. She sketched, she photographed, she scribbled notes. An old man came and stood beside her. 'Why are you so interested?' he asked. Alice told him. She told him the whole story. As it came back to her, the language made her candid. She was rich in words, fluent in them, the story, in her telling, moved her greatly. Such manic persistence in the widower! To see her again, to sleep up against her image... The old man wanted to keep her talking, he eyed her, he could not make her out.

She found somewhere for tea in the Passage des Marais, sat there nearly an hour, writing up her notes, nobody bothering her. For that ordinary bar, for the *quartier*, for the fiction she was pursuing, she filled with an intensely personal love and gratitude. Then she felt the evening coming on. She was tired, a vague apprehensiveness passed like a chill across her shoulders. Still, she would walk a little way, for the particular experience of fatigue. She consulted her map and made for Métro Belleville. The sirens again, nearer.

At the mouths of the métro stood the police, two or three together on either side, the riot police in black, overseeing everyone emerging and descending. As Alice reached the steps there was a halt, the beginnings of a crush; then release and rapid descent again as they removed a North African. The hurry of everyone else felt like relief. Police on the platform at either end. Boots, truncheons, handcuffs, pistols; the authority, the licence to stare into faces. The journey was under the sign of the CRS, the mood in the carriage was subdued. A beggar girl, a gypsy in blue and gold, went the length, keening softly and holding out a polystyrene cup.

Alice gave, a few others also, averting their eyes. Fear and pity moved them.

More police at Denfert-Rochereau, a pair standing together on the top step, so that the ascending throng had to part around them and, lifting their faces, be scrutinized.

At the hotel Alice almost asked were there any messages, then remembered there could be none. She took a shower, lay naked on the bed and dozed. She was near the surface in her little passages of sleep, dreaming nervously. When she woke, she watched the news. She saw a correspondent on an aircraft carrier, a middle-aged man in a suit and a flak jacket, beside himself with glee like a ten-year-old. He was patting, stroking, and rapping on a slung-ready bomb and explaining its nature and expected deeds. No word came into her head except: pornography. Next – some intelligence must have intended it – there was footage of what it is like to be on the ground two miles below the aircraft when they fly away. Dwellings made of earth, the colour of the burned earth, now returned to the earth as a tumulus; or concrete dwellings, built to withstand earthquakes but not bombs, not even accidental bombs. There was lingering, almost tender, photography of goods and chattels, rags of clothing; and, most affecting, the lovely crook of an arm, its shoulder and its gesturing hand still buried.

Alice dressed, went out to eat. She was first there, the *patron* turned the television off. She drank a glass quickly, tried to think to some purpose. Her volume wanted at least another woman, black preferably or Arab, francophone from the margins, a woman managing to live in this bitter city. She thought of phoning the children, but feared her voice would betray her. So she wrote cards instead, cheerful as possible, to their two independent households. She went to bed early, lay in the dark listening to the noises. Sirens, always sirens, but far off.

The soft blue sky next morning between, above and

beyond the waking tenements filled her with hope again; but as though time were short and a sky of that peculiarly poignant beauty could not last. She seized on her project. Breakfast arrived on a clanking lift from far below. Over those keen tastes she re-read the story by Maupassant, set chiefly around the Opéra and in Montmartre. The subject was a married woman from the provinces who, after years of dreaming about it, comes to Paris deliberately to experience vice. She takes up with a famous writer for one afternoon and evening and night; drives in the Bois with him; drinks at his café; accompanies him to the theatre; dines among his friends; and finally, what she most desires, shares his bed. The last act of the adventure, vice itself, grievously disappoints her. Café, theatre, restaurant were all named, and the writer's lodgings precisely located in the rue des Abbesses. Alice wished to examine these realities. She took the métro to 4 Septembre near where, in an antiques shop long disappeared, the married woman, summoning up her courage, had initiated the brief liaison with the famous writer. The police were in position and on patrol. Alice bowed her head, passing through them, keeping to her own harmless designs. The day passed agreeably. Taking tea in the rue Etex, she wrote up her notes. Then métro to boulevard Saint-Michel. She had in mind to look in the bookshops and ask after new writing at a literary café she remembered from way back; but there were police in great numbers all around the *place*, as though something very bad had happened or was about to. They were quite still, idling in the sun near their vans and motorcycles. The crowds too seemed to hush as they came into their presence. Alice bowed her head, not wishing to let any one of them look her in the face. She walked quickly to the Luxembourg and there in a low sun, sitting near the Orangerie, she read the story again. The woman was a fool of course, her longing ridiculous; but Alice sided with her against the disappointing world and saw the last page through a rush of tears.

They were bringing the trees into the Orangerie for winter. The ornamental trees, orange, lemon, pomegranate, oleander, were being lifted in their boxes by a little fork-lift truck and borne with infinite care and patience down the long *allées* into safekeeping against the cold. Alice had never seen this ritual before. The trees shook delicately in their carriages and were received in the great glass hall like household gods. The day and the year were ending. The usual melancholy of that lingering termination had in it now, because of the distant war, an edge of dread. She thought of treasures, all of a country's heritage, being stowed away in cellars, in caves, in a hollow mountain; and not for a season only but for the foreseeable future. Her little project, her very life in its advancing years, seemed to have reached a place where they lay at the mercy of what would annihilate them. Or her courage gave out; having reached so far, it gave out, the faith lapsing. So peripheral she felt. Nobody knew where she was. Her children were gone and thriving without her. Her husband had his mistress in her bed, a girl half her age and his. Easily as goods and chattels she might be replaced.

Alice stood up, walked away quickly, envying the trees brought in like fabulous animals to a sanctuary and tended there by men and women whose love and skill could be counted on in a job that was absolutely necessary.

First item on the news that night was a bomb in the city, in Belleville, among the immigrants, so that the motive and the culprit were hard to be sure about. There were several bad injuries, but only one death. Perhaps he was the bomber himself, dying by accident and maiming his kith and kin. Perhaps. The explosion had destroyed a flower stall, the spattered flowers lay all over the place. But the camera caught and held on to (or could not wrench itself away from) in particular a severed hand. The hand lay on the pavement in a chalk circle. It was a dark-skinned hand, a man's but delicate, palm upwards, the fingers open, severed bloodily at the wrist but otherwise without blemish, almost peaceful. This hand seemed likely to become an icon in the present troubles. It was being shown again in the restaurant when Alice went to eat. The *patron*, shaking his head, turned off the set and came over to serve her. He seemed to think it his duty to protect her spirits. He sat by her for a while in silence.

Alice's third location, in a story by Nerval, was the Catacombs; but she shrank from the visit and walked instead to the Fnac, rue de Rennes, to collect some catalogues and look along the shelves. She searched for women writers, black or Arabic; bought two recent collections; and chatted about her project to the young woman in that department, who was knowledgeable. This fortified her. At the same time she noted how unsteady she had become. Must there always be friendly people to advise her and give her strength? She knew how easily she engaged a stranger's sympathy. It had always been a gift or grace in her. The world was disposed to think well of her, to treat her kindly. Now, to assert herself, she resolved to visit the Catacombs after all, and set off at once, on foot.

Nothing happened, nothing bad, perhaps it was only that she was tired, but at Denfert-Rochereau, in sight of the entrance to the Underworld, Alice gave up for the day, turned irresolutely in the little park, bought a sandwich and ate it on a bench near which a school of drunks were bawling and splashing. What to do? She was heading back, to lie on her hotel bed all afternoon, but saw the cinema and turned in there instead, a thing she had never done in her life before, alone, early afternoon, she paid and went in, barely noting that she had heard of the film, it was directed by a woman, it was said to be beautiful to watch. She saw no one in the dark, the place looked quite empty, the film had begun, she sat in the middle of a row towards the back. The seat was plush and deep.

The film showed men in uniform, soldiers of the Foreign

Legion. At once Alice felt a knot of anxiety in her belly. Sooner or later there would be some violence. The landscape was harsh as hell, the men fitted it, they were so lean, reduced to the necessary muscle and ability, functional like their weapons. It was the beauty of perfected fitness, their training was choreographed, they achieved the unison of a machine. So the senses of a person watching were at one and the same time delighted and repelled. What was the purpose of this perfection? Killing. Surely soon then they would kill. The violence was ready, as in a tuned machine. It rippled through the corps. Everything worked and fitted, command and comradeship, the love of men together, all their differences sunk in a function: killing. How beautiful to watch, not an ugly man among them, all lithe, supple, strong as steel, all dancers, for the act of killing. Luxuriously seated, Alice watched in delight and dread. At any moment must come the execution.

Somebody came and sat next to Alice, on her right. Not that the place was filling up. The rows before her were still empty. Had he just entered? Perhaps he had been there all along in the dark somewhere behind her. She glanced at him. He was young, North African, no older than her son. She stiffened, clutched at the arm-rests, making to move away. But his eyes in the half-light were wide and afraid, staring at her. And how young he was. She felt he had fled to her. Should she then flee from him? She turned to face the screen again and before long sensed that he had done the same. So they sat side by side as though they had arrived together or met there by arrangement, watching the woman's strangely, beautifully troubling film. Alice sank again into the dread that at any moment something would happen that she would not be able to avoid seeing or ever rid her mind of afterwards. And all the while she felt the boy close by her, staring fixedly ahead and trembling. She sensed, she could even smell, his undiminished fear.

Three people came in: a middle-aged couple muttering in

English, they sat two rows behind her, away to the left; and an oafish young man who made for the front row, far right, and there sat with his legs out, scoffing popcorn. Then the Arab boy next to Alice took her hand. It shocked her, it went through her heart as though the violence, long expected, had been done at last in a way her anxious attention had not foreseen. She gasped, she almost screamed. His hand tightened on hers. And again she felt his wide eyes on her face, imploring her to allow what he had done. She allowed it. Perhaps he had not fled to her after all. Perhaps his trembling and the smell of his fear were due to the risk. He had perhaps premeditated and was carrying out a thing that terrified him. She could betray him, she could denounce him, the police would drag him away for a terrible punishment. But three people would testify, if he appealed to them, that he and Alice had been sitting together when they came in. Why sit together in an empty cinema unless both wished to? Was that a calculation in the Arab boy's frightened act?

Alice allowed it, she became complicit, she let him retain her hand in his, and after a while, feeling how he trembled still, she took the boy's hand into her lap and between her two hands stroked and soothed it. So they sat, watching the film. The popcorn-eater suddenly chortled, the English couple tut-tutted. Alice sat quietly with the Arab boy's hand, like a small animal, in her lap. It was a hand no bigger than hers, fine and supple and moist with the sweat of fear. The film showed a landscape wholly of glittering salt, a lake evaporated generations ago and now only a vast bowl of frosted salt, the queerest shapes, white encrustations around dead wood and the bony remnants of perished animals. A lick of salt is necessary, and the taste of it when the tongue caresses the skin of the beloved man or woman is a subtle and acute delight; but there on the screen, filmed lingeringly, was a world of salt and only salt, all drinking water, all watery sustenance, all the pleasures of water had long since gone and nothing remained but the unremitting thirst of salt. Alice pressed the boy's hand into her lap. The darkness was sweet to her, the darkness, the closeness, the snuggled pressure of an unknown human's hand were a delicious resource to her against the white horror of the salt. She wondered again had he fled to her or screwed up all his courage for an intimacy. How docile he was. His hand, unlike any other man's she had ever known, made no demand, merely rested where she had pressed it, fitted into her lap as she desired. This realization of his docility excited her profoundly. She began to tremble, the darkness seemed threadbare and events on the screen now seemed to be moving towards a frightful punishment. One man who had authority over the rest was ordering them to expose their comrade to the world of salt. The violence would be of a lingering kind. They obeyed, as they were sworn to. They began to rope the culprit. Abruptly Alice stood up and moved to leave the cinema, tugging the Arab boy to follow.

The daylight affronted her; or she seemed an affront to it. An old prudery! You went to the cinema in the evenings, you came out in the dark. Here she was, mid-afternoon, in the sunshine. She walked away quickly. At the park gate she halted; as though from nowhere the boy stood by her, shaking his head in a decided fear. Two policemen, friendly enough, were clearing the worst of the drunks out of the park. Alice looked at the boy, he had the eyes of a starving kitten, wide, black, beautiful in his scared face. His clothes were thin, they seemed got together out of bare necessity. She saw with a little tremor around the heart how much better he would be to look upon rid of them. He said, 'Vous venez demain?' As though his life depended on it. Alice nodded. He turned, ran through the traffic like a born dancer, across the road towards the entrance to the Catacombs. Alice watched until, with a portion of his terror, she saw how watched by others she might be herself.

She walked away quickly. Once clear of the scene she bought a paper, sat in a café in the rue Hallé, tried to look the innocent part. On the front page was a photograph of the hand. A little doctored, it lay on its back in the chalk circle, the fingers open, as though to give or receive. In big letters the caption said, 'Is this the bomber's hand?'

At the hotel she showered, lay naked on the bed, watched the news. The bombing continued. There was footage of take-off, an almost desperate lumbering; and then the grace, the triumph of it, the lightness of all that weight on the unsustaining air. A spokesman with a long stick indicated the hits. He denied that one was a pharmaceutical factory. He admitted and regretted that one was the wrong village. He promised they would rebuild it better than ever, earthquake-proof. But the main news was of increased security in Paris. People already on lists were being taken in. People who should have been on lists soon would be. People in neither category could rest assured. The atrocity in Belleville was discussed. The hand, its very signature, was shown again. A spokesman for the Muslim community said that the decided view there was that the hand was a victim's hand; the bomb by the flower stall had been aimed at peaceable Islam, the bomber had walked away unharmed, leaving many horribly injured and some dismembered. A spokesman for the police said they were keeping an open mind.

Alice switched off the television and lay on her narrow bed high up in the vast rumour of the city. Sirens, always sirens. Now she allowed herself to think about the Arab boy, his scared and beautiful face, his urchin clothes, his docile hand. How quiet his hand had been there between hers under cover of darkness given sanctuary in her lap. The thought of his docility made her heart race. She desired to be back again, holding his hand, contemplating the landscape of thirst, feeling in the place below her belly that quickening, rising, self-asserting fear. Where was he? How did he live?

Where did he hide? Strange the commingling of desire and fear. She desired some entry into his world of fear. She stood up, crossed to the full-length mirror on the wardrobe, appraised herself. Lay down again, stared at the ceiling, gave herself up wholly to thinking … 'Vous venez demain?'

Alice approached the cinema through the little park. The smells of autumn in it took her by the throat. A drunk was lying placidly in the sunshine on the grass. How could he lie on his back like that showing his face to the world? Did he not fear stamping on? The boy was nowhere to be seen. Alice bought her ticket. Behind the glass the man knew her again. He nodded in acknowledgement, discreet. Alice went in. Half a dozen people, widely scattered, none near her yesterday's seat. The film had begun. She saw an individual beauty in every soldier's face, shining through the frozen glaze of discipline. She became absorbed in the detection and appreciation of particular beauty. Then the boy, like a wraith, materialized beside her. She took his hand.

Alice lay naked on her hotel bed and watched the news. A young man, an Arab, had run full tilt at the steps of the British Embassy. He was waving his arms and shouting 'God is Great'. When he would not stop, the guards shot him dead. They supposed him to be a suicide bomber but he turned out to have been only insane or incensed. Alice switched off the television and lay wondering what, if anything, to tell her husband Rob.

Alice decided not to tell Rob anything. She wrote in her notebook: '17 September. I hope I will keep to that decision when he asks. Easy to imagine the dialogue if I don't: What dress were you wearing? The light blue one that buttons down the front. Did you leave your knickers off? Yes I did. So you had decided what you were going to do? Yes, I suppose I had. Who started it this time? I did. I took his hand. Then what? Nothing for a while. We watched the film again. Then what? Nothing for quite a while. I played with his fingers. Your right hand, his left hand? Correct. Then what? Then after quite a long time I put his hand in my lap. I opened my legs a bit and fitted his hand in between. And what did he do? Nothing. He waited. But you could feel his hand? Yes, I could feel his hand. Then what? I left his hand there. In fact, I squeezed my legs together to keep it there. Then I reached over and felt for him. Go on. His trousers were very thin. He didn't have anything on underneath. I could feel him at once. Was it stiff? Yes, he was stiff. And that excited you? Yes, I undid his trousers. It was buttons. I undid three or four and got my hand in and took hold of him properly. And then? He was wearing a very loose t-shirt. I pulled that down over what I was doing. And what was he doing? Doing to me? Nothing. His hand was perfectly still. So then? So then in the end I unbuttoned my dress and put his hand in through the gap. And then? He still did nothing, only rested there quiet as a mouse. So I opened my legs as much as I could, pushed his hand in and tried to press his middle finger in the way he should. And then? Then it was nice just sitting there in the dark watching the film. His finger stayed still. Were you wet? Yes, I was. But I didn't want him to do any more. Not really. It was nice the way it was. I played with his cock. I made the end of it very slippy between my finger and thumb. And then? Then nothing for quite a while. We watched the film and each was doing what I have said. Then? Nothing for quite a long while. Then I got frightened. I took his hand away, I took mine away, I buttoned my dress. Then I left.

There is nothing about the film in this account. Rob would not be interested in the film. At least, not until later, not until after; then he might. Nor is there anything about my fear. He might be interested in that, but chiefly as an ingredient in the sex. Am I doing him an injustice?

Afterwards I guess he would be – so to speak – more rationally interested in my fear. We watched until the salt again. I felt there was a sort of combat between the absolute dead dryness of that terrible lake and the wetness of my fingers and the boy's. Yes, the terror was in what we were doing, that we would be found out, that the film would suddenly cease, the lights would go up, the police would enter down the aisles and drag us away. But my dread came mostly from the film. They brought the victim to the sparkling white shores of the lake and their captain ordered them to tie him to a tree that had itself been turned to salt. I could see how dry his lips were, they were already cracking with the longing for fresh water. Then I could not watch and we left abruptly.

Years since I underwent one of Rob's inquisitions. The couple of times I had anything to confess I played the game with him willingly enough. We lay in the dark side by side and he said, And then? And then? He kept his voice as level as he could, but sometimes it would catch on what he was asking. Catch and sob. I whispered the best, the worst, into his ear. Or even, at the end, into his open mouth. Afterwards, perhaps a day or so afterwards, I rather wished I hadn't. I felt that it, whatever it was, didn't belong to me any more. Rob calls it sharing, and would always tell me his side if I asked. Years since I asked. He wants me to question him minutely about Lisa; but I haven't and I won't. I tell him it is his business. He doesn't like that. He fears one day I will say to him, That is my business.

I couldn't see any police in the little park so I crossed from the cinema and went in there and stood at the far side looking away at the traffic. After a while the boy stood at my side. We looked at one another. His fearful wonderment seemed to kick me in the womb. I said, Tu viens demain? He nodded, he ran from the park, the iron gate banging. I watched him dance though the traffic. I watched him out of sight beyond the Catacombs.

I look at my writing hand. I think of his small hand, how biddable it was.'

Next day Alice arrived down the rue Lalande. She had some notion she would be less visible that way. But it was a bad mistake. Turning right to the cinema she did not see the police until she was at the *guichet* buying her ticket. They were in the foyer. The man behind the glass seemed to want to warn her. But by then it was too late. They asked to look in her bag. She opened it, she held it open, one rummaged inside. She felt his colleague seeking to look her in the eyes. She would not let him.

Alice wrote: '18 September. Inside I took my usual seat. Few people, the film already well advanced. I was shaking with fear. I feared the boy would do as I had done, commit himself without looking and be confronted by the police. How I wanted him – and prayed hard in my godless heart that he would see the danger and stay away. I dared not leave to warn him. I sat in the worst fear of my life, watching the film. It was the salt lake already, the binding of the victim had begun. No transference of my fear was possible. There was no diversion or relief. I saw the soldiers complete their task, salute and march away. With the victim I watched their lingering progress out of sight. They marched in single file across the dead lake, their boots crushing the crystals. Astonishing that the fluids of their bodies did not dry and harden as they marched. Their blood and water oiled them, they continued moving, they trod in line through the harsh and beautiful salt. The shapes around them, stiff and fantastical, looked like predecessors who had tried and failed. The sun was white hot. When the comrades had vanished like spectres in a trembling haze, the woman's camera turned on the victim's face, and there she rested and her delicate hearing picked up the rasping of his breath, the puffball efforts of his tongue and the cracking of his lips. His face was splitting open like those pods of seed that require a fierce sun to detonate their next year's life. I was sick with fear and parched in the mouth with longing for the boy, for his moist hand in mine, for the obedient pressure of his hand between my legs. But he did not come. And when among my fears and my desires the worst at last was to know what had become of him, I left the man on the screen, whose face was no longer a face but a red wound offered up to salt, and emerged out of the dark into the daylight. The police stood aside to let me pass, the man behind the little window, complicit, nodded goodbye. I crossed to the park, still in their view, crossed again at the lights and only halted when I was sure they could not see me, withdrawn into the entrance of the Catacombs. I stood there looking out, where he might be, where he might come from if he was still at large. Strange, he materialized from behind me, as though from underground, but that could not be so, it is only an entrance, not an exit there. He must have pressed in with a crowd of visitors, hiding among them. Where had he been watching from? I gripped his hand, but let go at once, fearful. I have no nerve for these things, I am ignorant, unpractised. I would desist and flee, except that my desire is the equal of my fear. All I could say to him was, again, Tu viens demain? He nodded, waited, questioningly turned up his hands. I could think of nowhere but the ground we stood on. Here. Then he vanished. At once I had this thought: You have to learn, and there is very little time.

I went back to the café in the rue Hallé, sat quiet until I felt the world had forgotten me. I could do as I liked. But I must harden my nerves. I wrote up my notes, invented a story, made a list of questions. Then I phoned Marie-Giselle. She asked was I in Paris but I said no, in London, at the library, doing some work on my stories. Ah, she said, your stories. Yes, I said, but now I'm trying to write one of my own and I'm stuck over some real details. Then I asked my questions. She thought them very amusing and we giggled a good deal. She said she hadn't any idea herself but Luc might know – the swine – he was coming round in half an hour, she'd ask him for me, could I ring her back?

I left it an hour or so and in that time rode the métro nowhere particular. I wanted to face the police, accustom myself. I saw a pair of them beckon a black girl out of the crowd. One nodded at her bag, the other, as she opened it, inserted his black truncheon and forced the opening wider. Then they nodded that she was free to leave. I watched her face, she lifted it, looked them fully and calmly, first one, then the other, in the eyes. Then resumed the course of her own life. I watched for the fearful too. These days have sensitized me towards them. I see their bitten nails, their little repeated gestures of hopeless apotropaic magic. But how brave the beggars are, the unlicensed buskers, the hawkers of smuggled cigarettes and pirated CDs, the ebony black vendors of bright jewellery who lay their bundles open wherever they dare risk it. To live like that! Always on the look-out, always about to flee. And there was a blind girl, just where a tunnel opens on to the platform, a place where the CRS like to position themselves, there she stood, lifting up her naked face for all to see, and singing. People put coins into her open palm.

Then I phoned Marie-Giselle again. She said: Luc says he's not so sure any more, those days are over, but try the rue Garancière, near Saint Sulpice. I'm in London, I said. It's for a story. Yes, yes, she said. Luc said your hero should try the rue Garancière. And how do you know it's a place like that? They're ordinary hotels to look at, with a little notice on the door. And yes, they're quite nice nowadays, but he doubts if they take Visa. And you book it by the hour, best to get the number and do it by phone in advance. Thanks, I said, that's all very helpful. I mustn't make a fool of myself in things I am ignorant of. She asked when I'd be in Paris again. Soon, I said, very soon, I hope. I'll give you a ring.

It was 5 o'clock. I took the métro to Saint Sulpice, walked up and down the rue Garancière. There were four hotels, three looked too respectable, I stood at the door of the fourth, a woman at the reception watched me through the glass. There was no sign. Then I thought: Nobody knows where I am in this vast city. I went in, I asked for a card. The woman said nothing, handed me a card, surveyed my face, and nodded. I walked back through the Luxembourg, they were closing the gates. Gently, very gently, the lingerers among the trees were being shepherded out. On the boulevard Saint Jacques, at the Elizabeth Arden shop, I bought some hand cream, and in Monoprix a packet of condoms. I have never bought condoms before. Then I phoned the little hotel in the rue Garancière. It was the same woman, I am sure. The voice exactly fitted her demeanour. Beyond tact, beyond discretion, it bespoke an absolute rather weary complicity in whatever, in the world of love and sex, any human being might wish to do. She elated me. I booked a room in my maiden name. Then I went to my restaurant. The *patron*, his name is Maurice, sat with me for a while. He told me again that he longs to go back to Perpignan, he is weary of loneliness in the big city, would like to re-marry. I smiled. He bowed his head and let me be.'

Alice watched the Arab boy's arrival. He skipped, side-stepped, flitted through the traffic like the genius of a dangerous game he had invented. Then, all smiles, he stood before her in the entrance to the Catacombs. She wanted him at once clasped tight in her arms. She caught her breath in a sob on the desire for him. She took his hand, imprisoned it hard, let go, and set off, at a fast pace down the boulevard Denfert-Rochereau, past the Hospice des Enfants Assistés and the Asile des Jeunes Filles Aveugles. Fast as they went, a girl sped by them on rollerblades down the smooth pavement under the dying-golden vanishing lines of trees. Her hands were lightly clasped behind her back, she strode and leaned, gliding away in a paradisal easy confidence, freedom of movement and command of speed. Hurry, Alice thought. There is very little time. But in the Luxembourg, breathless, she halted, turned the boy towards her, touched his cheeks with the backs of her two hands. Still she did not dare to kiss him and the helpless wonderment of his look and the poverty of his clothing – his bare arms, his thin wrists – twisted tighter the knot of desire and terror under her heart. It was a Sunday. There were hundreds of people in the spacious gardens, all seemed easy, cheerful, tolerant of every diversion open to humankind. She took his hand, in this precinct she felt the intimacy was allowed.

Between the gardens and the chosen hotel there was very little public street, but Alice let go the Arab boy's hand and his fearfulness also suddenly increased. He hesitated, looked about him, looked to her as though for some reassurance or explanation. Really, she had none. She saw that she must be determined enough for both of them, and carry him along. She clutched at his thin shirt, led him like that, more a captive, as it must seem, than a lover. On the hotel steps she felt their appearance to be lamentable. How the street behind them, all eyes, must be sniggering. But so far in, desiring him and because of the terror of retreat, she must go through with it. She pushed on the glass door, gently shoving him ahead of her.

The woman was playing patience at her desk. Barely glancing up, she handed over a key, with one finger pointing to the lift, with four then raised in a gesture almost like that of blessing she showed which floor. There was a form, a way of it, this world had its own decorum. Now Alice felt freed and licensed to please herself, her terror lapsed, her desire overran it in a triumphant rush. In the rickety lift, no bigger than a double coffin, she held his hand and looked down at his shoes. They were cheap trainers, soiled and splitting. Her hand shook unlocking the room door. Her last fear was of a sordidness she would not be able to bear, but the room was clean, so uncluttered, so stripped to function it had a sort of decency. Only the lampshades made a gesture towards sentiment, two by the bed, one over it, they were faded yellow like an old parchment, printed with roses, a candle, a quill pen, black lines of verse in an old-fashioned hand. The sun was streaming in.

Ignoring everything, the Arab boy crossed quickly to the window. There he stood in silence with his back to her. Alice took it for a sort of discretion, that she should see to herself while he looked away. She remembered a story – who by? – in which a prostitute had squatted with perfect indifference before the client and soaped, rinsed and towelled herself while he watched. Alice undressed and did those things, hardly knowing whether she wished the boy would turn her way or not. But he did not, only continued at the window staring out. Naked then, dropping the towel on the bed, she went over and stood behind him. Her breasts touched his back. He shuddered. With her fingers she marvelled at the black curl of hair on his brown nape. His skin was as smooth as a girl's. He was trembling like a frightened animal. He would not turn to her. Instead, he nodded through the slit of tenements to a glimpse of the towers of Saint Sulpice and said, 'That's where I live.' 'What a nice *quartier*,' she said. 'I live in the tombs,' he said. She had no idea what he meant. Then he turned round to her, his eyes flung open wide. 'Let me undress you,' she said. He raised his arms like her son as a child and she drew up the loose t-shirt over his head and off. She kneeled on the boards, undid his laces, held each downtrodden shoe by the heel while he stepped out of it. Still on her knees she reached for the buttons of his thin trousers. He let her, trembling. His stiff sex came at once into her view. She slid his legs bare, he stepped clear. She had hold of his sex, she was making to take it into her mouth but he prevented her and said, 'Please look away.' She stared out at the thin section of Saint Sulpice, the window glass was cool on her brow. After a while she felt him materialize against her back. He was damp from the warm water. She felt for his arms, clasped them around her from behind, and held him so that he touched her down all his length. 'Je vous aime,' he said. Alice blushed. She felt with her forehead for a cooler place on the window pane. 'What did you mean about the tombs?' she asked. 'That's where we live,' he answered. 'We get in under the church.' 'I see,' she said. 'My name is Alice,' she said. 'What are you called?' 'I was called Mohammed,' he said. 'And now?' Still looking away, Alice felt him shrug. 'Jeannot?' he said, in an interrogative tone. 'I'll call you that,' she said. Then she turned, took him in her arms, looked him in the face as though to match his features to the given name, and began at last to have the kisses she felt she had been denied. The sun poured in, the room was as much in sunny daylight as any room behind its windows ever can be. They stood, kissing. Then she remembered something, went childishly immodestly over the bed on all fours after it, reached down to the floor and brought her bag up before him sitting on the counterpane. 'This,' she said, taking out the expensive cream. 'Give me your hands.' He cupped them for her, she filled the palms with a scented coolness and shared it with her own. The four hands, being lifted, turned and worked and wrung at the liquid in their common grasp. The wrists ran with it too, she daubed the excess on his belly and on her breasts and when her hands and his could absorb no more then she resumed in daylight, unafraid, what she had lacked the courage to go on with in the cinema, in darkness, faced by images of desolating salt.

That evening in the restaurant, sipping wine and before her meal was served, Alice wrote up her notebook. Two or three other regulars were eating, any conversation was quiet and occasional. Alice wrote:

'19 September. I have remembered what our hands reminded me of – chicory leaves, the way they fit and lie and overlap. And mine seemed as white as inner chicory. But Jeannot's are a lovely brown, as small as mine, as supple with the cream. For a long time all my excitement was in our hands.

He is still very shy, or passive, or docile. The sun was pouring in. I lay back on the bed, opened my legs, took his hand and put it where I wanted it to be. But he was too timid, or respectful, or ignorant. When I teased him he looked unhappy. I asked him had he never been with an older woman before. He said he had never been with any woman or girl before. Nor with any man? Nor with any boy or man. Then I sat up and leaned against the pillows. There was a mirror, of course, on the wall opposite. I watched myself showing him, with the tip of the middle finger of my left hand, exactly how to beckon on my clitoris. The sun lit up the gold of my wedding ring in my black pubic hair.

I will remember everything exactly.

When he could do it, when he was becoming almost skilled at it, I lay at ease with him on my right side, I felt his wet cock hard against my thigh, his nervous right hand between my legs delighting itself and me. The sun was on us, it was all in broad daylight, the parchment lampshades were lit up from the outside in the sun. I turned my head to read the poem there. It was, Mignonne, allons voir si la rose …Later I asked him to read me what it said on his. Remember, never forget, his puzzling voice reading out the lines of verse: Amour me tue, et si je ne veux dire/ Le plaisant mal que ce m'est de mourir… The line of his back as he lay turned away from me to read.

He was ashamed when he had to dress in his poor clothes again.

I gave the woman at the desk the exact money. She was playing patience still. I reserved the room for tomorrow. She wrote us in her book and nodded au revoir.'

The *patron* stood by the table with Alice's meal. He begged her pardon, nodding at the notebook. 'You're writing,' he said. 'A poem? A story?' 'Only my notes,' she said. 'Things I don't want to forget.' 'Bon appétit,' he said. She thanked him, ate with relish. She decided she would not use the condoms after all. It was a year or more since she had needed any contraception; and a virgin lover, even one living in the tombs, must, in respect of health and hygiene, be at least as safe as her husband. She reasoned quickly in favour of what she wanted; dwelled on it then, so that she was quite elsewhere when the *patron* came to ask what she would like for her dessert.

Alice lay naked on her hotel bed and watched the news. Things were getting worse. Too much to report: a small massacre of Palestinians; a grenade attack on an Israeli settlement in Gaza. But the bombing itself, a spokesman said, was going very well. No losses to report. They played and played again some footage of the missiles striking home. It was like a funfair. The spokesman pointed modestly with his white stick. Next came an interview with a Muslim cleric. He said the West was doomed, for its assault on Islam and for its sexual depravity. Alice thought of Jeannot. She made larger and larger plans: to move where she could sleep through the night with him, to rent a room and live with him for a while.

Next morning Alice got up late – she had hours to pass – and went shopping, for Jeannot. In Monoprix, boulevard Saint Jacques, she bought him some underwear, two pairs of jeans, half a dozen t-shirts (thinking of their soft colours against his skin), trainers, socks. At the till, watching the items appear on the girl's screen, it came to her like a quickening that she loved him. She said it to herself under her breath, she wanted her tongue and lips to commit her by forming the words. She was entirely abstracted, or entirely present in the *sotto voce* saying of the words 'I love him'. The girl had to break in on her, with the receipt to sign. 'Madame, s'il vous plaît, madame.' Alice took her card and the bag of purchases. 'I love him. What shall I do?'

From her café in the rue Hallé she phoned Eurostar, cancelled her reservation, changed her ticket to an open return and paid the difference with her card. Then she phoned Rob. As it rang, she thought, 'This will surprise him.' But he set in at once. Where on earth was she? He had phoned the usual hotel. They had no idea where she was. He had phoned Marie-Giselle. Her story baffled him, made him look very foolish indeed, not knowing where his own wife was. 'I've been out of my mind with worry,' he said. Alice had appraised his tone. Worry was not its chief ingredient. 'I'm sorry,' she said. 'I had to tell her a fib. I didn't want to see her. There's so little time.' 'You're home on Thursday.' 'No, it won't be Thursday.' 'When then?' 'I can't say yet.' 'What about my proofs?' For a moment Alice did not understand the word 'proofs'. She had a little gap of puzzlement. And when a meaning did materialize it shocked her as a mark of how far she had gone. The word lay dead, like an archaeological curiosity. But she collected herself and said, 'Perhaps Lisa could do them. She's still there, I suppose?' 'She's not as good as you,' Rob said. Then, his tone changing, he asked, 'What is it anyway? What are you up to? Marie-Giselle said you were asking her things.' But Alice did not want to be questioned. Her voice stopped him. 'Only for my stories,' she said. 'You and your stories,' said Rob. 'For one of my own,' she said.

At a cashpoint in the avenue du Général Leclerc she took out the maximum from their joint account, to pay cash again that afternoon. Then there was nothing to do but idle and wait. The thought of the literary café off the boulevard Saint Michel wafted into her consciousness as out of a previous existence. Though she had no intention of going there she let herself drift that way. Outside the Luxembourg Gardens a vendor was selling t-shirts printed with the icon of the severed hand. The dark-skinned hand, open on a background white as a bedsheet. She saw a girl take one, hold it against her breasts, turn to her friend for his approval. He grinned, he nodded, they went off with it into the gardens cheerfully.

Back in her room that night, after her meal, after the news, Alice wrote in her notebook: '20 September. When the boy and girl bought the t-shirt with the hand on and went off into the gardens together I was thinking of Jeannot's hand, how I have taught it what to do, and I must have been in a trance, thinking about that, because the noise of the demonstration had become quite loud before I realized what it was I was hearing in the background of my thoughts. They were leaving the rue Soufflot, coming out into Saint-Michel. There were drums, very steady, like a determined demand, because of course they want the war stopped, they were marching against the war and against the attacks on immigrants in this city. I know so little, not nearly enough, I must write it down. Oh Jeannot! They were all manner of people, linking arms so they took up the width of the street, then widening when they came into the spacious boulevard. Linked like that, behind the drummers, they looked unstoppable. They were students, but old people too, and whole families, with little children, even babies, every kind of occupation, I should say, and many blacks, and many North Africans the lovely colour of Jeannot, all arm in arm. Age, class, colour, so mixed, they seemed to me all the more powerful because they were mixed, I thought the mix must bind them and make them invincible. My mood was high, I am fragile, utterly open, because of Jeannot. I hugged the bundle of clothes I had bought him in Monoprix. After a

while, because I had time before I must go to our hotel, I
stepped in among the marching people. I have never been on
a demonstration before, my bundle embarrassed me when I
linked arms with my neighbours. On my left there was a
Frenchman of about my age, in overalls, he looked to have
come from work. On my right there was a black girl, a
student, she smiled at me: T'es bien entre nous! Oh how
elated I was! We were some way back from the drums, among
the banners, the placards and the shouts for peace and
fraternity, and behind us somewhere there was a jazzband.
Jazz is the best demonstration, isn't it? That joyous mixing,
that allowing of one another. At the bottom of the boulevard
I stepped out, to make for Saint Sulpice. They were heading
over the bridge, I suppose towards Belleville. I stood on the
corner, watching them pass, many hundreds, growing, they
would be thousands soon. The police were there, also
watching. Then the bad thing happened. Surely it was an
ambush. Did the police not know? Did they let it happen?
Down that street, rue Danton, into the boulevard, actually
brushing past me, came a squad of the National Front at a
run, not very many, fifty maybe, but in a phalanx, all looking
alike, hard, like one thing, all in black, with bare arms, shaved
heads, army boots. And they had clubs and coshes. I am
ignorant, I have never seen hatred close up. They lifted their
arms and smashed into the body of the demonstration. In it
they broke up like a cluster bomb. They were shrapnel,
entering and maiming. Whoever stood, they clubbed.
Whoever fell, they kicked and stamped on. The drummers
had gone out of hearing. The jazzband, at that very moment
drawing level, was overthrown, the players fell, their
instruments were trashed on the asphalt. Then it was
finished. Did it even last three minutes? The men in black
passed through and disappeared. The fraternal mix of
citizens kneeled or lay among the shattered banners. I saw
the clarinettist in a sort of wonder over his instrument's

broken fingering. Ambulances arrived as though forewarned. The riot police, many of them laughing, pushed in among the bystanders. I felt outlawed by the powers they stood for. I fled to our safe house in the rue Garancière. The city terrifies me.'

Alice knew the boy would not go into the hotel without her. She began to watch for him as soon as she neared the street. All her thoughts and feelings were set on seeing him again. So for a while she could hold off the horror of the violence at the Place Saint Michel. But she arrived and there was no sight of him. She must walk past the glass door and the old woman at the desk who had surely noted her. She walked quickly to the next crossroads, rue Saint Sulpice, turned and very slowly retraced her steps, hugging her bundle and willing him to materialize behind her. And like her shadow he did so, joining her as a shadow would if the sun were suddenly lifted to vertical noon.

The woman looked up from her cards, reached for the key, and again lifted her hand in a sign that was almost a blessing. Same floor, same room. And in there too it was the same. He stood at the window, averted, while she undressed and made herself ready. She knew he would not turn to watch, and she was glad of that. She came over to him naked; kissed the nape of his neck where the soft hair curled; he raised his arms like a child to be undressed; she knelt again for his battered shoes and thin trousers. He left her at the window looking out. The ritual steadied her. This time her trouble was almost greater. The first time she had been troubled by conventions, by the strangeness, by her ignorance. Since then she had admitted that she loved him. She had said it *sotto voce*, to herself. That added new fear to the old. She was shy of him. She was more than twice her age. What must he think? She heard him approach, and halt. Then, for the first time, he said her name: 'Alice.' So strange it sounded in his pronunciation. She shivered at it, as though a finger of ice had traced the length of her spine. She turned. He was standing on his side of the bed, his hands crossed below his belly in a childish shame. So serious. Must we always be so serious? Solemn, staring at her in a fearful wonderment. The room was as sunny as before. How daylit they were, so shown to one another. Then he leaned over and turned back the sheet for her. How thin his wrist was, and lovely the small dark hand against the white.

In his arms, in bed, in the locked room, in their safe house, Alice abandoned her self-defence and wept. She saw the men in black again, their boots and clubs, their purposefulness, the hard certitude of their violence. And afterwards the police, smiling. She wept and wept. Jeannot kissed her eyes, enclosed her hands in his, murmured her name, begged her to tell. After a while, lying next to him, tightly holding his left hand in her right, looking up at the parchment-seeming lampshade with its roses, verses and quill pen, she told him quietly, all of it, the rise of her feelings as she marched behind the drummers, and then the smash, her shock – the shock of ignorance – and her terror. He listened, held her hand tightly, reached over with his right hand to stroke her neck and shoulder. But he had nothing to say except, 'C'est normal'; and then: 'Pauvre Alice.' So Alice shifted a fraction nearer to his world and wondered at it on little waves of horror.

Alice sat up, and uncovered Jeannot, to look at him. He closed his eyes. She watched his sex, like a small animal, stir and slowly quit the snug shape on his thighs and turn, grow, stiffen on a new line over his belly, and only by the force of being looked at, her hands kept in her lap. She got out of bed, rummaged in her bag for the expensive cream. 'Give me your hands,' she said. He held them out, making a cup. When the liquid lay in them she was about to return to the bed, but saw herself in the mirror and left him waiting, holding up his cupped hands, while she drew off the silky counterpane and draped the glass with it, so they wouldn't be seen. Then she lay face down, and kneeling beside her he began to do what she desired him to do: go over every inch of her from under her hair to the soles of her feet with his slippy and scented hands. She closed her eyes, lay still. Once or twice when he seemed timid, she reached for his hand and directed him more decisively. After a while she turned over, filled his cupped hands again, and lay down. He went from her toes, which she thought as ugly as sin, to her forehead, which she thought too high and liked to hide under a girlish fringe. She let him anoint the stretch marks under her breasts and the skin on her belly where it was slack. She drew up her legs, he knelt between them, she let him acknowledge with his fingertips a black birthmark and the two or three places on her thighs where the veins showed through purple. Then when every zone of her skin had been visited and caressed by his hands, she reached up and brought his mouth to hers and his belly down on to hers and helped him with her hands, because he was maladroit at this new thing, to part her better and enter.

That evening at the little restaurant, as Alice arrived, first as usual, the news was just beginning. The *patron* made to turn it off, but she shook her head and stood at his side, watching. They showed the demonstration, the faith and hope and cheerfulness of the people arm in arm as they swung on to the boulevard. The jazz band was clearly audible. Then they showed the ambush, or at least its aftermath: the debris, the broken instruments; an elderly woman cradled by her husband, all bloody; a child lost and crying; a young man lying absolutely still. The *patron* shook his head, Alice was shifting in her feelings from grief towards rage. 'They knew,' she said. 'They let it happen. The police let it happen.' 'Of course they knew,' he said. 'That's what it's like.' He switched off the set, led her to her usual table, rested his hand with all tact and gentleness on her shoulder, asked what she would like to eat, brought the wine and the bread at once.

Back at the hotel, sitting up in bed, Alice continued in her notebook: '20 September. He went to sleep almost at once, turning away from me, and I slept too for a while with my arm around him. He woke me with his bad dreams. Strange his bad dreams in that room. Doesn't love cast out fear? I felt his heart, it was racing like a tiny animal, and he whimpered and moaned. My comforting woke him and he was ashamed. I caressed him for a little while, his arms, his back, his skin like a girl's. *La peau douce*, my learning hands. But it was almost time to leave. Though I did not want to see him clothed I wanted him to have his presents. When I stood up for them his seed ran very coldly down my leg. I was glad, I exulted. The presents made him embarrassed. I chose among them for him and he put them on. The transformation almost wounded me. I uncovered the mirror for him to see himself. He blushed. I rolled his old t-shirt and trainers up in the trousers. Then it was time to go. But we stood at the window for a minute and I pointed to Saint Sulpice. I asked him, What did you mean when you said you lived in the tombs? Just that, he answered. They go under the city, we get in by the church. How many of you? Many. How do you live? We work when we dare. And we steal. I see, I said, seeing nothing. Then we went down together in the rickety lift. I paid cash, booked the room again. I was bold as brass. He had the Monoprix parcel under his arm. I took him by the hand. We ran away like children, it was getting dark. We hurried to the Seine, down the rue Danton, through the *place* where the march had been ambushed. It was full of people and seemed already forgetful. We threw his old clothes in the river from the Pont Saint Michel. I wanted him to eat with me but he said no. To be exact, he said not yet. But he would walk back with me as far as Denfert-Rochereau. The gardens were closed so we had to keep to the streets. These are the boulevards and the streets we walked along, Jeannot and I, hand in hand, often laughing: Saint Michel, Henri Barbusse, Val de Grâce, Saint Jacques, Port Royal, Faubourg Saint Jacques, Arago. Near the entrance to the Catacombs, which was shut and locked, he kissed me goodbye. I took his hand and pressed it against my heart. I said we were so sure of ourselves now that whoever arrived first should go up to the room and wait in there, not walk the streets. He pondered this, thinking of his fears, and said yes, he thought so too. He left me almost blithely, saying, A demain. I watched him dance through the traffic and out of sight.'

Waking next morning it occurred to Alice that she had only bought Jeannot light clothes, as though the warm weather would last for ever. That gave her morning some point. She went back to Monoprix, bought him a jacket and a lambswool sweater, paying by card. She commented on the beauty of the clothes to the woman serving her. She wanted to be asked who she was buying them for. Are they for your son? She wanted to say no they are for my lover.

From Monoprix Alice went to her usual cashpoint in avenue Général Leclerc, to draw out the maximum from the joint account. After that, she idled her day towards its decided purpose. Outside the Luxembourg Gardens she noticed the t-shirt with the hand on, still for sale, and another by it, black on white, a raised clenched fist. Around the Panthéon there were knots of police and a gathering of spectators, staring up. Some protesters had climbed to the balcony below the dome, and were attaching a banner to be read from the streets. Students in groups, mostly silent, eyeing the police. Further off, towards the University, there were loudspeakers, but unclear. Alice felt the excitement, the apprehension, but was ignorant. She felt that at any moment a crowd might come together, its makings were there and its opponents too, the police, might collect in an instant and become a hard mass. The young people looked quite unafraid. A few passed by with their lower faces masked, they raised the clenched fist. Others waved and cheered. The police watched. One of them began to take photographs. The students posed and jeered. Any moment … Alice felt the pull of it, but moved away. At the bottom of the boulevard she bought some flowers for the rented room, chrysanthemums, bright bronze-coloured. It was almost time. Then behind her, back where she had come from, she heard drums, chanting, sirens, the beating of staves on shields. She hurried away, to her safe house.

It was late that night before Alice could write in her notebook. Then: '21 September. He wasn't there, he didn't come. I was there a few minutes early with his new clothes and my silly flowers (the woman looked at them). I thought it would be nice for him to find me in bed already. All that time on my own undressed and waiting for him, so frightened. I watched the sun begin to leave the room. The lampshade above the bed becomes very dark. It looks as though it were stained with smoke. You would have to switch the light on to be able to read the verse again. Several times I went to the window and looked out. I suppose that is the street he must come along. I suppose there is no other way. I waited two hours for him, in the bed or at the window. Then I began to hear sirens, quite close. When I next looked out there was nobody at all on the street. Then there were police, motorcyclists, and the black vans they use for the CRS. Then it was like in the cinema and I had to pray that he would not come. But I wanted him, oh how much I wanted him. I got dressed and took my flowers out of the sink and went down with them and my Monoprix bag in the rickety lift, to pay the woman playing patience at her desk. I hoped she would not show me any sympathy. But I suppose my face was begging for it. She took the money, looked at me, and said two words: *Joli môme*. Then she shrugged. But that was enough to make me weep, like any vulgar woman. Then she raised her hand in that sign that is like a blessing but this time it was a warning because she could see the street behind my back. And she said: Remontez, madame. Attendez là-haut. So I went back up with the key again and stood at the window. It was getting dark. Saint Sulpice, the bit of it you can see from there, was illuminated very white. I opened the window a little. I could hear terrible noises from over there. Fighting, it sounded like, and explosions. Then there was black smoke, in the light of the white church dome. More police down the street, in great numbers, at great speed. I saw other people watching from their windows, in dim lights or no lights, shadows. After another hour, when it was quite dark, there was no more noise. I went down to the old woman again. I offered her money for the extra hour but she shook her head. She pointed to the right, up the street, away from Saint Sulpice. That was the way I should go. I thanked her very warmly. But she was looking down at her cards again. The street smelled of smoke and another smell – I suppose it was tear gas. I cut through the Place de l'Odéon, walking fast, to get to Saint Michel and the Seine. I had a silly notion that he would wait for me on the bridge, if it was safe there, because that was where we had gone to the last time. But of course he was not to be seen, and it wasn't safe there. I stood between two little groups of riot police and threw the flowers into the river which was flowing very fast and dark. One of the men in black shouted something, and they all laughed. Then I hurried away and got the métro back here. The city feels held down by official terror.'

The domestic news was bad, so bad there was scarcely any wish to get on to the international news, the war, which was going well. A police spokesman said, quite candidly, that in their general drive to improve security they were clearing out some of the more troublesome nests of illegal immigrants. He expected widespread sympathy in that endeavour. But by then some corpses, black and North African, had been fished out of the Seine, and big demonstrations of revulsion were under way. Alice sat three days with the drunks in the little park at Denfert-Rochereau, watching the entrance to the Catacombs and the entrance to the cinema. She thought he would be more likely to materialize there than at the hotel on the rue Garancière. She took along one of her authors but that was only to give herself a semblance of purpose when the police passed through. The weather turned wet and cold, she needed warmer clothes, but lacked the volition to go and buy them. In the evenings she ate at her little restaurant. Unhappiness had invaded her like a winter flood, extending totally and freezing. She saw her own misery in the *patron*'s gentleness. Once she phoned the hotel itself. Yes, the woman remembered her, no the boy had not been there. Alice asked could she leave a number, in case. The woman said there was no point. Alice gave it anyway, Marie-Giselle's, but did not think the woman would write it down.

Alice phoned Marie-Giselle and, putting off all explanations, asked could she stay with her a while. Would she come and meet her in the little park the next day? Marie-Giselle said yes to both. Alice said she needed to know everything possible about the Catacombs. Did they really extend under the city from Denfert-Rochereau as far as Saint Sulpice? Was it true that people lived in them, in hiding? Did she know of any entrance except the official one? Marie-Giselle said she knew some things and would find out more by tomorrow. Was it for her story? 'Yes,' said Alice. 'It's for my story.'

Alice paid her hotel bill with her Visa card. That evening she told the *patron* she might not be eating there again for a while. 'Are you going home?' He asked. 'No,' she said. 'I don't want to go home.' He glanced round the room, everyone was quietly occupied. He sat down at her table and said again, not having said it for some time, that he was tired of Paris, more than ever lately, the hatred, the violence, that awful business of the people in the river, and would surely go back to Perpignan very soon. That was all he wanted, but for his loneliness. Going back to Perpignan, he said, was less important than finding a wife and if he could find a wife he would go wherever she wished, or stay if that was what she wanted. He had a round and entirely candid face and thick black hair that was going grey at the temples. Alice touched his hand and bowed her head without speaking.

Next morning when she went to her usual cashpoint on the avenue Général Leclerc, to draw the maximum from the joint account, her card was refused. She collected her bag from the hotel, it was not heavy, and the Monoprix bag with Jeannot's warm clothes in it, and walked to the little park, to watch for him and wait for Marie-Giselle. The drunks knew her by now and saluted her gravely. She watched and waited. At 11, as arranged, the iron gate banged and her friend came into the park and sat on the bench beside her, kissing her and taking her hand. The day was cold, beginning to drizzle. Alice had a glimpse of what she must look like, which is to say how far she had come, in her friend's loving alarm. She gave her both her hands and Marie-Giselle chafed them for some warmth. 'Ma pauvre Alice,' she said. 'Raconte.' And Alice began to tell her, leaving her two hands safe and warm, but all the while spying to left and right, across to the Catacombs, across to the little cinema, for the sight of a thin boy in the clothes she had bought for him, a boy like a dancer, fearless in the murderous traffic.

Life After Death

Joseph went down on his knees. In his fist he had a bunch of brilliant yellow flowers. The words came out in a rush. 'Mother,' he said, 'she says she'll marry me, I've had the letter, she says she'll come over here and live, with the boys, as soon as I like, she says, the sooner the better as far as she's concerned, she says.' Early summer, the best day of the year in Joseph's view, best day of his life, best in the whole history of the best and happiest lives of the human race and the place where he spilled his news out the holiest on earth. He rammed the flowers into the ornamental pot. At once it seemed they had sprung up there, they burst forth, they widened, they were the little sunflowers that seeded themselves and you could get a fistful of in no time in the fields. He sat back on his heels, grinning, chuckling, he raised his open palms. 'Sooner the better, she says, to settle the boys in school and get the house straight how we want it before the winter. We shall have your room, you won't mind that, will you, and the eldest will have mine and Tom will have the spare room when I've done it up. They'll all need doing up. The kitchen's a bit dark, you said so yourself some days, I thought I'd put another window in. Then there's the loft one day. One day I'll floor it like I always said I would and think of the view you'd get from there if I put a big skylight in.' Sky, sea, all the little islands. The thought of the work his hands would do, the thought that his hands had it in them to open up such a perspective filled him with wonder and gratitude and he made a pause in his rush of speech and contemplated them. Then: 'And you won't mind, you'll be glad for me, it was a grief to you that it didn't happen sooner, but now it has, you and she would have got on a treat and you and the boys, but never mind, you're the first to know, at the post office they maybe guessed, but you're the first to know out loud, and here's the letter.' He patted the breast pocket of his red shirt. 'And don't be worried about the money. She's a great manager, Maggie is, she'll bake and sell things up the shop and we'll grow more vegetables. And that job clearing paths I told you about looks pretty certain now, so we'll do all right, we'll do very well, no need for you to worry.' Again, the faith, the wonder at so much faith for such a purpose, to such an end, welling up in him, in his sinewy body, welling up out of him in amazing abundance. 'Some purpose,' he said, 'that's what a man wants, a purpose, and I've got one.'

Her grave never needed anything doing to it. He was up there every day, talking to her. Often he brought flowers, childish brilliant flowers from the garden or the growing wild ones from the fields. He wanted it bright there under the headstone, under her solitary name. More often than was really necessary he renewed her flowers. Some of the other graves needed seeing to, and they were his job. The whole little churchyard was one of his jobs, to keep the grass cut and the brambles from creeping in too far through the granite lichened walls, and in that acre a few graves in particular were his special job when people who had left the island and couldn't get back very often or perhaps never came still wanted the satisfaction of knowing that their loved ones were in a resting place that was looked after, and they paid Joseph so much a year to do it, not much but something. The acre was his patch, he knew something about most people in it, about their fates and if their deaths were unusual generally he had the details. He even knew some people and some little thing about them where the stone had fallen and the name had gone or there had never been a stone only a wooden cross and that had long since gone and perhaps there was only a hump but even then sometimes Joseph knew a fact or two. The graves were on both sides of the church and behind it, three score or so all told but some, of course, with generations in. The drystone wall was hairy with one kind of lichen, grey-green, the ancient graves and the church stones themselves blotched golden with another kind. Wild flowers around the hem of the place where Joseph let them be. Airy, on the backbone of the island. You saw the church tower first thing coming home across the water if you ever went away. Nearly everyone was chapel but they gathered here together around the church when they were dead.

That day the letter came Joseph was so full of it even when he moved away and got the sickle and whetstone out, thinking to do the far corner, he continued talking to his mother, not in a louder voice as he moved away but in the tone he had always used that was tuned to her as hers been to him. There was the news, there were the facts, but that never took very long, and there were the different points of view if he were in debate with himself about a matter and wanted her advice; but the day the letter came the fact was single and luminous and nothing needed to be debated, but instead, released by the fact, there was a wondering appreciation of his fortune, and this seemed inexhaustible, more and more dawned on him, again and again he paused in his work, sat back on his heels where he was ripping at some couch grass, and shook his head and told her frankly he could hardly believe it, he could hardly believe his luck, so much good luck on one small patch of the earth in one man's body. He started to say aloud but simply did not dare because the words shone too much, they were too shining with holiness and splendour – he started to say: 'With this ring I thee wed, with my body I thee worship, and with all my worldly goods I thee endow', but after 'with this ring' he broke off and the rest shone before his eyes as though inscribed on the air. Instead, standing and stooping, feeling for the base of nettles and thistles with the sickle edge, he said: 'I'll get them a rod each for an arriving present. They'll come with me like last time but for a lifetime now. They'll be such fishermen when I've taught them all the tricks. And we'll get a little boat again and pots. We'll live like royalty, on mackerel and crab. I'll show them everywhere there is that's good.' This quiet-spoken man who never boasted about anything, who never thought he had anything to boast about, saw his own skills and abilities now, in great abundance, when he imagined how he would transmit them to a couple of boys who were dying to learn, and he felt an admiration of himself, almost as though it were another man, an admiration and a humility interfused, and out of that a gladness, a gratitude, the immense gladness of having something to transmit, hand on, teach.

He was in the north-eastern corner, in the far lefthand corner if you face in from the only road, as far from the road as it is possible to be in that small churchyard, stooping or kneeling, in a place that did, when he let it, get overgrown, where the few strangers were buried and the wholly unknown who had been washed in, and where the little memorial tablet had been set. He was at home everywhere in the graveyard, but if any corner ever made him feel uneasy or turned him towards melancholy then here where the buried dead were strangers and their families and histories were unknown to him. He imagined them young, not half his age, these few unknown sailors of the Wars, but couldn't put a name or a face to them and knew, as any islander must, that if they were a long time in the water even their own mothers would not have known them. Twice their age! But it was not how long you lived, it was purpose that justified a man in his life, a purpose and his works.

That being, so to speak, the churchyard's war corner, the Council had set an iron tablet there, among the strangers, flat on the ground, with the names on it, only a dozen altogether, of the men gone from home and dead in the first war or the second, and a sentence praising them. Joseph went round this with an old knife, spat on a cloth and was getting some bird dirt off the iron itself, muttering all the while, muttering to his mother that if he had three or four times as long a life as the poor boys washed in here or gone from here and dead abroad that still wouldn't be enough for all the happiness he and Maggie had in store for one another, when a voice behind him, in the air above him, a man's voice said: 'That's me there.' The man was close, reading down from his height over Joseph's shoulder. Joseph went white. The wrench out of his preoccupation and out of his own dialogue into one with a present person was severe. It was as though he had been torn from one zone into another too abruptly. He shivered, the hairs on his neck prickled, the shiver travelled down his spine. The man was so close, above him, dressed in black like an undertaker or an old-fashioned insurance agent, in a bowler, an overcoat, a suit, black Oxford shoes, despite the sunshine. He had a grey moustache, his hands, in gloves, were clasped over his private parts. He said again, in an accent that was not local: 'That's me. The one you're rubbing the bird dirt off is me: Percy Reynolds.' Joseph turned, sitting back on his heels, looking up: 'You're not dead then?' 'As you see,' said Reynolds. Joseph looked at the name, which was very clear now he had rubbed it. 'Says so here,' he said. 'Surprise to me,' said Reynolds. 'No wonder I couldn't find out where you were killed,' said Joseph. 'You asked, did you?' 'I like to know.' 'Where was Francis killed then?' 'Francis Mumford?' said Joseph. 'Tripoli.' 'And Lego Nance?' 'Over Berlin.' 'And Viv Lethbridge?' 'Kola, in the water.' 'You know your stuff,' said Reynolds, dabbing at his lip with a white handkerchief. There was a silence. Joseph had got his colour back. He was becoming quizzical. He sat on his heels, brown as a nut, bald as a coot, big ears, bright eyes, a shark's tooth on his bare throat for an amulet. He still had the rag in his hand, the tools for cleaning and clearing were strewn around him in the grass. And the grass smelled sweet.

After a while Reynolds said: 'You were talking to yourself.' 'No, I wasn't,' said Joseph. 'Begging your pardon,' said Reynolds, 'I heard you.' 'I was talking to Mother,' Joseph replied. 'I see,' said Reynolds. 'She's not here but you were talking to her all the same.' 'Yes,' said Joseph. 'She's not here the way you are but I was talking to her all the same.' 'Where is she then?' 'Dead,' said Joseph. 'I see,' said Reynolds. 'But you talk to her anyway.' 'Oh yes,' said Joseph, 'the way I always did. I tell her everything. No reason not to.' 'I see,' said Reynolds. 'When did she die?' 'Two years last Christmas.' 'I see,' said Reynolds. 'Yes,' said Joseph, 'I had some good news today so naturally I was telling her that and discussing the future with her, knowing she'd be pleased.' 'I see,' said Reynolds. 'Yes,' said Joseph, 'I'm getting married.' 'God help you,' said Reynolds. But Joseph in a rush, looking up at the man in the dark clothes, came out with it all again, about Maggie and the two boys and how things couldn't be better. 'Some people will make fun of me,' he said. 'I know exactly what they'll say: "Just in time, Joseph. Got yourself a widow, Joseph, just in time". But let them. I shan't mind.' 'Well, well,' said Reynolds, 'rather you than me.' There was a pause. They looked at one another: the standing man as though he'd come to pay out on a death, the other in that shirt and the sailcloth pants like a gypsy or a pirate. Then Reynolds said: 'How old would you be, if you don't mind my asking?' 'Forty-four,' said Joseph. 'And herself?' 'Forty-two next month.' 'Rather you than me,' Reynolds said again, and dabbed his damp moustache.

Joseph spat on the rag and rubbed at the names again. 'They're clean enough,' said Reynolds. 'Leave 'em be.' Joseph sat back, cocked his head. 'You weren't on the launch,' he said. 'No,' said Reynolds, 'I had a special.' 'Cost you,' said

Joseph. 'It bloody did,' said Reynolds. Then he asked: 'What did you find out about me when you were making your enquiries?' 'Nothing much,' said Joseph. 'Nobody knew very much. Except that you were dead. They all knew that. But where, no one could tell.' Reynolds took off a glove. The hand was plump, with hairs on. He raised it to the tight knot of his tie. 'They even got that wrong,' he said. 'Seems so,' said Joseph. Reynolds said: 'Nobody had a good word for me, I don't suppose?' Joseph shrugged. 'Dying for king and country, they thought that was pretty good.' 'I see,' said Reynolds. Then he added: 'They told you I was a home boy, I suppose?' 'Yes,' said Joseph. 'And you know what that means?' 'It means you never had one,' Joseph answered. 'Right,' said Reynolds, 'exactly, and they sent me over here and I worked like a nigger, and for what?' Joseph shrugged. He did not like to see the afternoon clouded by any man's bitterness. 'I'll tell you this much,' Reynolds said, 'I thanked God when the war came and I could push off out of here with Viv and Lego and Francis and the rest. Nobody here cared whether I stayed or went.' He broke off. Then: 'Except one. One did. And much good it did her, caring.' He took off his bowler, his crown was pink, but the back and sides, which fitted around the bowler when he replaced it, were silver-grey and respectable. The dome coming out, however, pink and damp, was strange, like something that shouldn't in the daylight. 'But you weren't over Berlin?' Joseph asked. 'No I bloody wasn't,' said Reynolds. 'Nor anywhere like it. Thank God.'

There was a silence. Joseph, told off for rubbing with his rag, played idly with the sickle, thumbing its blade. 'Nice thing,' said Reynolds abruptly in too loud a voice, 'nice thing coming home and seeing your name on a slab.'' Joseph shrugged. 'Good company,' he said, for a harmless joke. But seeing that Reynolds really did look aggrieved, he said: 'I'll tell them at the post office, shall I?' 'What do you mean?' Reynolds asked. 'I mean they'll tell the Council that there's been a mistake. They'll rub you out, I suppose. I should think you'll get an apology at the very least. I mean, if you're not dead it isn't right you being here, is it?' And he added: 'Besides, it's upsetting if you come back, as you say.' Reynolds wasn't listening. 'Forty-five years,' he said. 'I might as well have been. Honest to God, I might as well have been.' The hat was off again and circling though his hands. The bald crown beaded visibly. This agitation was upsetting Joseph, who rose and tapped at his leg with the flat of the sickle blade. 'Are you staying?' he asked. 'Pardon me?' 'Have you come to stop? Are you back for good?' 'No, no,' said Reynolds. 'Flying visit, that's all. To test the water, as you might say. And now this...' He gestured at the meagre little plaque. 'Shall I not say anything then?' Joseph asked. Reynolds seemed abstracted, seemed not to understand. 'Shall we leave things as they are?' 'Me among the dead, do you mean?' 'If you like. There's only me that knows you shouldn't be. I'll tell Mother, but nobody else.' 'You'll tell Mother?' 'I tell her everything. Always did, always will do.' Reynolds was sweating. 'Either way,' he said. 'Rub me out. Leave me be. Neither way's right. I might as well have been dead. But I don't belong there either.' He dropped a glove. Joseph stooped for it. 'You on the launch going back?' he asked. 'No,' said Reynolds, 'I've got my special.'

They turned away from the war corner. Joseph brightened up. 'This is all my patch,' he said. He explained the arrangement: so much from the Council, so much from particular families for looking after their loved ones. 'And next month,' he added, 'they're giving me the paths to do. All the island's paths, to keep them clear for ourselves and the visitors. With this...' He let the blade of the sickle, its silver edge, flash in the sun. 'More for house and home when Maggie and the boys move in. We shall do very well between us. She'll sell her bread and cakes up the shop. Everyone likes Maggie. She's nearly an islander already.'

They were walking to the gate, the longer way, around the south wall of the church, Joseph elated and loquacious, Reynolds bowed. 'This is Mother,' said Joseph, halting at a white headstone, tapping it with his blade. 'Mother?' said Reynolds. 'I see.' They stepped round, one either side, and turned, six feet from the stone, to face the lettering. 'Fresh flowers,' said Joseph. 'She loved them brilliant and yellow.' Such a fistful, a clutch of colour, the explosion of Joseph's happiness set down under the headstone as an offering when the words came tumbling out. Reynolds had gone grey, a dirty grey, dirtier than the silver grey of his moustache and back and sides. 'Catherine Goddard,' he said. 'You're Catherine Goddard's boy?' 'That's right,' said Joseph. 'I'm Joseph.' There was a pause. 'You look as if you'd seen a ghost,' said Joseph. 'Should have,' Reynolds mumbled, 'might as well have been.' 'Shall I tell 'em or shan't I?' Joseph asked again. 'Do you want rubbing out or don't you?' He thumbed at the sickle blade. It was an idle old habit. So beautiful the silver where it came out from the rust, so honed to a purpose, effective. 'Either way,' Reynolds was mumbling. 'Neither way. You'll tell your mother anyway. You tell her everything.' 'Always have done,' said Joseph. 'And such a lot is coming up she'll want to hear about.' Reynolds was eyeing him, but all askew. Joseph was grinning. He had a gap top left. 'Come home,' he said. 'Come and have a tot. You look as though you need one. The shock, I expect, seeing yourself among the glorious dead.' And he began to chortle, seeing the funny side. But Reynolds was stumbling towards the road. 'Must get my special!' he shouted. And: 'Might just as well have been!' And: 'Either way!'

Mouse and Bear

Bear died. They all came back after the funeral, for the Celebration; then they all left, and Mouse remained in the big house on her own. Of course, the children phoned, Julian quite briskly – 'Managing, are we?' – Paula as though she were consoling her youngest child. To Julian Mouse replied: 'Very well indeed, thank you'; and they were both pleased with the exchange. To Paula she said: 'But I'm not really on my own, dear. He is still with me. You needn't be worried on my account.' And there also each knew what she had to say, and both were satisfied. 'And you've got good neighbours,' Paula added.

Neighbours, the gardener, people from church, the priest himself, they all called. And although there might be differences in how they felt about her situation and her demeanour, still whenever two or three such visitors were gathered together and Mouse came up among them as a subject, the right thing to say was always obvious.

Mouse was a big woman, big and strong; not in the least beautiful, except, some said, in the spirit, and there radiantly so. To nurse Bear during his long incapacity she had needed all her strength. Lifting him, turning him, bathing him, wheeling him about the house and in the fresh air – he was a deadweight, an affliction. Some even said he was a monstrous deed against her. But Mouse withstood, she never complained, not once did she say he was a burden on her life, not once that his death released her. She prayed a good deal. Sometimes he opened an eye on her and saw her bowed head and her murmuring lips. Then he might say: 'Praying for me, are you? Pray your damnedest.' Perhaps that. His speech was greatly hindered by his throat and only Mouse could understand him at all well. If she had any bad thoughts she spoke to the priest. He it was who put the word 'radiant' into circulation.

Only after Bear's death did Mouse begin to be overwhelmed. Many ailments, so it seemed, had been in waiting; she had held them off by main force of her concentration on her duty to Bear. That discharged, the defences in her gave and the bodily ills assembled their powers against her. Truly, it was as though they had always inhabited the big house and she fell to them in turn now as she went from room to room. She developed allergies, particularly in what she breathed or ate. She could eat no bread, for example, the very staff of life. She dared not even risk swallowing the host but must eject it discreetly into her handkerchief, as soon as the priest had passed. She lived in a complicated struggle, enlisting homeopathy, praying. At times she seemed to be held alive, at some central point, by the force of all her ailments combating one another. Julian still said: 'Managing, are we?' And Paula said she hated to think of her in that big house all alone. But Mouse said yes she was managing very well, and no she was not alone, Bear was always with her still. The neighbours and the gardener thought the big house far too big and the priest asked tactfully after the children's domestic circumstances; but Mouse smiled her smile and said the children and the grandchildren had lives of their own to lead and she was in God's hands in the ghostly company of her dear Bear and there was no better place to be.

Mouse suffered a stroke. The gardener could get no answer when he knocked at the back door for his money; but he went away again, through the garage, the way he had been told he must come and go. Then Paula telephoned a neighbour. Would she mind looking in? Paula had rung and rung. Neighbour, police, ambulance. Mouse was on the bathroom floor, had been for two days and a night, her face much battered by the fall. After that, they must make some arrangements: keys with next door and opposite; alarms direct to the social services. Mouse stood up again, for a while she went heavily on two aluminium sticks. But she was in retreat, inch by inch she was being driven back. One morning she asked the gardener to look out Bear's old wheelchair from the garage. He found the wooden ramps as well, to move through the downstairs rooms to the lounge, the French windows, the view of the terraced garden. The stairlift had never been dismantled. Paula phoned the firm, they sent a man round, he checked it, got it going, said it wouldn't last much longer. Glanced at Mouse. Again and again the children said that money was no object. She must stay in her own house if she wished. Yes, she wished it. 'I'm more than ever in Bear's shoes now,' she said.

Mouse was on a roster, the carers called, they spoke into an intercom, the door buzzed and opened. The Council, for a sum of money, guaranteed her a parking space outside her own front door. The carers were glad of it; so might also an ambulance or her family be. But the street was crowded; jostlings and infringements were very common. Mouse telephoned, to complain. Her voice was level, insistent, righteous. In all her demands she was righteous, only that, only wanting her due. Her children declared her to be very *un*demanding.

But there were accidents, inevitably; and sudden, imperative anxieties in the long gaps, as they seemed, between the carers' visits. Then she must ring a neighbour. The gardener had stood too long in the kitchen, she could hardly breathe for the smell of cigarette smoke still lingering from his clothes. The priest had set down his shopping in a string bag on the table; one crumb of his fresh bread would give her cramps. People forgot. Who could blame them? The neighbour came over, to cleanse. Next the strap of her handbag, in which she kept a photograph of Bear when he was young, caught in the wheel of her chair, wrenched the bag from her hand and halted her violently. A good thing she had her mobile in her lap! The man from opposite knelt for an hour or more. 'Such a nuisance I am,' she said, beckoning vaguely down at his balding head in a gesture almost papal. In the end he said he had no option but to cut the strap. 'What a pity,' she said. Next came the death of the stairlift; she was stranded, neither up nor down, the carer saw her through the letter box. But the decisive accident occurred a month later, in July, nobody quite knew how, her memory perhaps distorted it. The gardener found the French windows open, her wheelchair between them, empty, her phone on the floor, herself on the grass half way down the garden, lying face up, eyes open, her sticks beside her like possessions in a chamber tomb. He did not know at first whether she was alive or dead, conscious or unconscious, and her look he described as creepy. But she said in her level voice: 'I couldn't get up again.' She was sodden, impossibly heavy. The gardener noticed that she had far more clothes on than usual. Fearing for his back, he let her lie and went to phone. Then he sat with her until the ambulance arrived, offered her a slug from his hip flask. She refused; but in a sudden confidence told him that she had been trying to reach Godfrey's grave and the summer house where she and Bear had often taken tea together, but had gone over backwards and had to lie there. She had been afraid only once, when young people, roaring and screaming, had approached along the road; but they passed and she lay patiently, seeing first the stars and a yellow moon, then cloud and feeling a sweet rain on her face and at daybreak hearing a robin and a blackbird very close. 'I was like Saint Francis,' she said. 'I was near to God.' They phoned Paula from the hospital. Paula phoned

Julian. In a day or two, as soon as he could, he drove over from Tunbridge, to sort things out.

Julian saw at a glance what was necessary. Scrap the stairlift, rise directly from the lounge into the upper rooms. He telephoned the firm. They could do a structural survey immediately and press ahead, all being well, at a price, within a week. But the lady would have to vacate the premises for the duration of the work, a fortnight perhaps. 'Yes,' said Julian. Then he addressed the question of safe access to the garden and the summer house. No problem there either. A descent from the patio might be rather abrupt, but out by the front door, under the kitchen window, through the garage and down in a sweep and a curve or two should be safe enough. Concrete all the way, walled either side with Cotswold stone. He would take advice and arrange it. 'You must visit the grave of Godfrey and sit with Bear in his den whenever you like, my little Mouse,' he said. Then he telephoned the priest. 'Mouse would like to go to Lourdes. For her ailments, you know, and because of building works at home.' The priest said he would move heaven and earth to get Mouse to Lourdes. 'Excellent,' said Julian. Leaving, he glanced into the garage. 'It will want clearing out,' he said. 'No through road at present.' And he volunteered his nephew, Paula's only son, who had been travelling. 'He'll be glad to help. He was always Bear's favourite, you remember.'

Of all the children – Julian's two, Paula's ten – only Patrick had ever gone with Bear to the damson hedge. He must have been nearly eleven, it was the year they sent him away to school, and in that year Bear took him twice to the damsons, first at Easter, early in the morning, to see the long, long hedge of them in flower, and again early in September, a sunny evening, at the very end of the holidays, to pick all the damsons they could carry and bring them home and make jam. In those days the street lost nearly all its traffic at a junction on the right and continued quietly for another few hundred yards and came to an end in fields. There was a gate of sorts, off its hinges, in a broken stone wall, and in at the gap you went, into the fields. They were an old estate, lying in a long reprieve, the mile or so of damsons making the southern border. Patrick would never forget the beauty of it that early morning, delicate as snowflakes, faintly quivering, a substantial ghost along the border of the dewy fields, and in his love for the big and clumsy man who had shown it him he would never falter. Threshold, promise, an opening up – and an abundance in like measure when the summer ended. Allowed for many years, the hedge had spread in places to be almost a woodland, a shade, a covert, friendly to birds, and the boy and his grandfather passed through to the southern side where the ground fell away over allotments and playing fields to the many square miles of motor works. There in the sun, all alone, they browsed along the bushes until they were swagged and burdened with bags of softly bloomed and darkly lustrous fruit. Bear carried a gigantic haul and Patrick competed like a man, beyond his age and size.

On both outings there was an alliance between the man and the little boy, against the wife and grandmother, the woman of the house. Patrick stood by him, even reached for his big hand in a childish way, and the man took comfort and strength from this comradeship. Later, of course, Mouse felt vindicated in her hatred of the damson hedge and she for one was glad when they grubbed it up. But that September why should she hate it so and punish the man and the child for their love of it? Patrick had no idea. He knew the fact, the hatred, the poisonous, acidic resentment, he knew the fact of the feeling, but he had no explanation. All evening, till it was late and Mouse had gone off without a goodnight to bed, he made jam in the big kitchen with his grandfather. They rolled up their sleeves, they washed the fruit in the sink, the water was solid with it, like a pack of hard spawn, they stripped off any lingering leaves, uprooted any stalks, cast out anything damaged or soft, it was all a delight, all the sifting and cleansing, up to the elbows in the black-bobbing water. Then solemnly Bear fetched in from the scullery a great gleaming copper that had been his mother's and from her book, putting on his glasses, he read aloud the familiar recipe, pausing at points for Patrick to mark them well. It was like an alchemy, arcane, ancient, half crazy. So little water for so many densely nuzzling damsons, but see them in no time soften over the flame and go to a mush and liquify dark-redly. Then – this was Bear's particular *manie* – to sift, squash, probe and fillet them for stones, to hoard the stones in a pot with shreds of hot flesh still adhering and force that soft and hard up against a sieve and scrape the emergent mess off with a spoon and return it, full of goodness, to the matrix. Then the sugar, its peculiar endeavour to sop up the juice, as though *it* were the body and purpose and the juice its large ingredient; then rapid defeat, speedy loss of its granular self, its sweetly liquid contribution to the rolling boil. The spattering, the popping bubbles, the coagulation round the rim and upper reaches, the staining of the stove. Few words were spoken and none at all that did not have to do with the making of the jam. A fierce concentration, time suspended, the common world going its own way in the night outside, and man and boy only waiting and watching for the moment they must on no account let pass, when the jam would wrinkle on a white saucer under the crooked testing little finger. The upturned jars were heated in the oven, too hot to touch, they were empty, full of heat. Bear's gloved hands set them upright on a board stained year after year by this sole ceremony. The jam was decanted in, it stood dark red, jar after jar, almost black red, but with a light in it, from the sun, from the snowflake spring of flowering, from the eagerness of their gazing, from their love. Then Bear said flatly: 'Better clean up or Mouse will not be pleased.' True, there were shades of the slaughter house in their paradise. They scrubbed and scrubbed and threw the stained rags in the bin. Pounds of damsons still remained, but that one evening was the most the adept and his novice might annex. Bear began carrying them through into the garage. He winked at Patrick. 'I have an arrangement with the gardener,' he said. The wink was an error, he could not do it well. He shrugged and exited. Patrick followed him, carrying the cleaned and gleaming copper pan.

Patrick recounted this to Rosa in a scrap of high surviving beechwood above the M40 where it violates the ridge and falls on Oxfordshire. They had endured their hunger for one another as long as they could, many miles, so saving up a space in time to dump the family car and leg it with their blanket and their bread and cheese and plums into the trees, to strip and feast. What hunger, after an absence after a summer travelling and loving each other so thoroughly that every hair and pore and inch of fleshly surface, being deprived, lamented, longed and pleaded for reunion. They were at that stage of hungry love, slim girl and boy, abundant enough to create another cosmos. It dawns on each that each is a universe, infinitely interesting and exciting. So Rosa woke hungrily listening to Patrick's account of a time nine years ago. 'I wonder if he ate it all himself,' he said. 'Or gave most of it away, and who to if he did? Mother gave me one pot to take to the school. I ate it with a spoon, crying my eyes out.' Rosa dwelled on that. She dozed. Then woke and sat astride him and leaned down for his puzzled mouth with hers. Again. Again and more.

When they had left the wood and found the car and reconnected with the foolish world Rosa teased Patrick for driving slowly and very carefully, more like a grandad than a boy of twenty. They were nearly there before she asked, 'Why did they grub the damsons up?' 'Because the developer wanted a wall along that edge,' Patrick replied. 'It's a very exclusive estate. You can't get in without knowing the code.' 'But Bear did what he did before that happened?' 'Yes, a few weeks before. About now in fact, when the damsons wanted picking.'

The space outside the big house had been taken by a thoughtless neighbour. Patrick parked where he could and standing with Rosa, struggling to emerge out of the sexual haze, he rang the bell. Mouse spoke, his shocked voice answered, the door received a shuddering buzz, it opened, they were admitted, a voice hard to locate continuing to direct them. They stood in the empty lounge like children, looking up. Mouse, enthroned over the hole, had been immobilised, the carer (God bless her) having left a little table in the way. The clever ray had detected it and countermanded Mouse's instruction to descend. Soon solved. Down she came, her hand, clutching the zapper, waving in mild blessing. She asked first had they been able to park outside her door. Next what colour the offending vehicle was. Swapped zapper for mobile, consulted a little notebook, and phoned the culprit. Her voice was level, righteous. 'People forget,' she said, when it was done. 'And who can blame them?' Then she addressed herself to welcoming Rosa. 'You must call me Mouse,' she said. 'Everybody does.' The antipathy between the old woman and the young was instant and palpable. Rosa would call her no such thing. 'Patrick, dear,' said Mouse, 'you are in your old room at the top. And I thought your little friend would like to be by me.'

After tea Mouse ascended again. Patrick and Rosa, via the ordinary stairs, joined her in her bedroom and seating themselves as instructed, Patrick on her right hand, Rosa on her left, they watched a video of her time at Lourdes. She had been very strengthened there, she said. The piles of discarded crutches had affected her particularly. She had learned to hope, and to count her blessings in the meantime.

The Golden Wedding was unspeakably ghastly, Patrick

said. All the clan assembled, all the women and girls. He was fetched out of school for it. By that time Bear could not be moved very far. He lay tilted back in the chair with a red bib on, dribbling constantly. Paula had baked a cake with a golden mouse and a golden bear upright upon it hand in hand. Whenever Bear made any particular sound Mouse told the company what he was saying. Altogether she spoke for him. His lids were nearly closed, but Patrick, standing by his feet, saw the eyes under the lids looking out like separate little intelligences in hell. Mouse held his hand, his great soft paw, its pinkish flesh. He was still not corpulent, only massive, massive and collapsed, a loose deadweight. His throat worked in spasms, as though trying to bring something up. His breathing laboured through a foul blockage. Mouse was radiant, Paula the same. Patrick noticed the familial likeness with a thrill of horror. He had been away, he was seeing things more clearly. The youngest girl recited the sweetest of Bear's little poems on the antics of the tomcat Godfrey. The three eldest, gathering around Bear's head, performed some music with their violins. 'Bear says thank you,' Mouse said. 'Bear says that was heavenly.'

'Put the light on again,' said Rosa. 'I want to look at you.' The bed was narrow, the ceiling sloped over it. She sat at his feet, looking down the length of him uncovered. 'Beautiful lover,' she said. 'My beautiful love. Lucky me.' 'I like this room,' he said. 'I slept here when I went to the damson hedge with Bear. Also it's like the room where I first slept with you.' 'She saw me, by the way,' Rosa said. 'She was sitting up in bed with the door open when I went past. I think she was watching the video again.'

Next morning, as they stood at a loss in the lounge, Mouse appeared in her chair above them, calling down. She told them to make themselves at home, to help themselves to breakfast, she would not descend just yet, she had not slept especially well.

They took an apple each and went out through the French windows. The garden, becoming autumnal, sloped down to a rather dank place under the wreckage of an orchard. There stood the summerhouse, itself decaying, and by it Godfrey's grave on which was carved: 'Press on, press on regardless,/ Keep smiling all the time/ As Godfrey did and you will be/ Immortalized in rhyme.' 'He was the miserablest old devil of a neutered tom you could imagine,' Patrick said. Once Bear was recumbent, Godfrey, who weighed a ton, would come and lie on him like an incubus. Mouse loved to see this. She said it was proof of the goodness of all God's creatures, and when Godfrey passed away soon after Bear she said that was a further proof and she was glad they were together, though it left her doubly bereaved.

The garage door was ajar, they entered from the garden. All the clutter and jumble! Patrick saw the copper preserving pan gleaming dully from under a heap of suits and shoes. Then with a harder look, combating a rising nausea and horror, he ascertained that most things in the place were Bear's or had to do with Bear. Rosa, watching him, took hold of his hand. From behind them, startling them, they were so remote in their own love and trouble, came a loud snigger. Even when they turned they could not instantly locate it. 'Only me,' said a voice. 'Be not afeard.' It was the gardener, hidden in a den among boxes and packing cases, enthroned on a commode, rolling up a magazine. 'Come to clear me out, have you? Extend the M40 to the summerhouse?' He had seen nothing like Rosa in the garage before. He admired her frankly. Bits of hair stuck up from his head and out of his ears and nostrils, the stuff of shaving brushes. He grinned a good deal, offered them from his flask. 'All for the tip, is it? So the lady said. Even the relics? Mind you, it's all relics. Start here if you like.' With his foot he shoved a cardboard box towards them, Patrick picked it up, the gardener's eyes fixed on him gleefully. Between them Rosa and Patrick opened the box. Inside lay a collarless white shirt dyed thoroughly a dirty brown with blood. On the shirt lay an open letter, its writing all but obliterated by spilled blood. On the letter lay an open cut-throat razor, the blade of it seeming rusted. 'I see,' said Patrick, all his colour gone. 'I found him,' said the gardener. 'I used to come in that way. I've met him more than once at this time of the year, picking his damsons, or in the spring just looking.' 'They never told me it was you,' said Patrick. 'They said it was a man from the development.' 'No, it was me. And I should have left him lying there. He made a very bad job of it but he would have got off in the end if I'd left him lying there. Instead, he lived to celebrate his Golden Wedding. But he made a bad job of most things, Dr Little did.' 'Not jam,' said Patrick fiercely. 'Jam, I grant you, he made very good damson jam,' said the gardener.

Patrick did not know what to do with the box. Rosa took it off him and laid it on the gardener's lap. Then they turned to leave. In the doorway Patrick asked, 'Why did she hate him going to the damson hedge?' 'She hated him doing anything outside of her,' the gardener answered, 'but she hated him going that way in particular.' He took out the letter, held it up in the sunlight slanting through the open door. 'I daresay an expert could decipher it.' Rosa led Patrick out.

Patrick wrote to Rosa: 'I am very bleak without you. When we were looking at each other on the bed last night I wondered if it would be possible to look so much it would get us through the few days without suffering. But I see that it isn't possible. I can't look enough on you. All day I've been driving to and from the tip with stuff. I hardened my heart as you said I must, except for the preserving pan and that awful cardboard box. And perhaps I will screw up my courage and dump them too. For, as you say, what do we want with all their deadweight? I keep thinking how light we were in France and Italy, nearly nothing on us really, and going from place to place as easily as gypsies in a fairytale. Poor stupid Bear. He should have run for it, if that's what old Priapus in the garage meant. But he was too heavy to run. We are so light, my lovely, we can fly. Say when, say where. In the evening my grandmother ascended again and I went up the common stairs and watched another video with her in the bedroom. It was of the Holy Father on a tour, in Mexico. He is so ill, he has to have a portable altar, like a zimmer with a shelf with the goodies on. I never saw anything quite so creepy. How I hate him. And yet without him I think I should never have been born. For who would go on and on with it the way my mother did, were there no pope? So I don't hate him after all because he got me into the world in time for you. But all the trash and deadweight sickens me. I had thought – when we were in that little place under the volcano – that there was not much point in going back and studying any more but we would move on as we liked and make love all the time. But I see we have to have knowledge if we are going to fight as well as possible and make a difference. How I love and thank you. My thinking is harder and more lucid because of you. I am getting free because of you. A real life is beginning in me because of you. This morning I got up early and walked to the end of the road to satisfy myself that every trace of the way into the fields and every last intimation of a damson hedge has been obliterated. Truly it has, by an ugliness so foul it cries to heaven. Oh my beloved girl, I kiss you from head to toe, I linger on your eyes and lips, your throat, your nipples, your belly button and your curly mound, I kiss you to the toes and back again. This lubricious imagining in the meantime, till the truth next week.'

Paula phoned a neighbour and asked would she mind breaking to Mouse the bad news that Patrick had been killed in a car-crash driving home. She said particularly to say that she, Paula, could see the good in this and that she was sure that Mouse would too. That was indeed the spirit in which Mouse, after a little while collecting herself in prayer, returned her daughter's call. The arrangements were already made. There would be a brief funeral and then, back at the house, a long celebration and thanksgiving for Patrick's radiant life. His chums from school were all invited. They would say how fondly they remembered him.

The police impounded the car, to check it over. They had returned its contents in the meantime. These were a blanket on the back seat; on the blanket a copper preserving pan; and in that the young man's few belongings in a soft cloth bag. Nothing else. Soon they concluded that the accident was very unfortunate. It had occurred in perfect weather on a particularly pretty stretch of the Dorking road. The young man was not in the least to blame. No drink, no fast or careless driving. But he was hit head on by a vehicle whose driver, an elderly lady, had suffered a heart attack. It was, the police said, all very unusually unfortunate. But with that verdict neither Mouse nor Paula could agree. It seemed to them indisputable that Patrick, homeward bound after doing good, had been taken up to heaven instantly. No grief then, only rejoicing and celebration.

Mouse said she would not trouble them to fetch her over for the occasion. She would sit quietly at home, reflecting on the dear child's life. Paula asked did she think they should inform his little girlfriend and invite her to the Celebration. Mouse thought not, it might be kinder not to. Paula agreed. Rosa wrote Patrick a letter, which they returned. She telephoned, they told her, in a tone of voice she could not understand, that he was dead. She lay face down for a week, inconsolable. Then, inconsolable, she stood up to the world without him.

Self-Portrait

When he had gone, I thought about it: what he had asked, what I had answered, what, in the end, I had volunteered, thinking he would want to know that as well. It seemed to me, when he left, that he was taking away the makings of a story.

It will be a pitiless story, and I shan't blame him. I can't use his pity. He only stayed one night. I don't suppose he needed longer than that. Perhaps he didn't even need to stay the night. Perhaps when he saw me on the station, that was enough. We could have had a cup of coffee while he waited for the next train back, that might have been enough. I saw at once what he saw me to be like. Writers are a pitiless breed. I mean, he is the nicest man, he would never say a thing to hurt anyone. Certainly not a woman. He loves women, his premise in any meeting with a woman is sympathy. But he is pitiless, like all his kind. So I saw in his look that I had not made an effort. I had let myself go, and did not make an effort, not even coming to meet him at the station, to look the best I could. I saw my hair. He used to admire my hair, like Ophelia's floating on the water. I saw my face. He always said he could see the native Indian in my face, finer than the women around me. And I saw my clothes, they reminded him that I used to make my own, to suit myself, often with an Indian motif, to show the old connection. Kindly and pitilessly he looked me over from head to toe. Had he left me then, he might have made up a story to fit a face, a head of hair and clothes like mine. And I should have believed his fiction and wept for the life of the woman he described.

Perhaps all he got by staying the night was background, my environment. He got the details. He says the truth of a fiction is in the concrete details.

I told him he hadn't aged at all, which was almost true. But when he didn't – couldn't – say the same for me but only smiled, I added: A bit whiter perhaps. And then: Thin as ever, at least. Worry, he said. What on earth does he have to worry about?

In the town he let me concentrate, he could see I was nervous. But as soon as we reached the turnpike he asked me about Florida. I had told him when he phoned that I was upset. Oh yes, my father… But before I could begin he said: You'll have to remind me. I realized on the train that I didn't know why your father was in Florida. I thought he lived on the reservation in Canada. Yes, I said. He sold his house and his land on the reservation in Canada and bought an apartment in a condo in Florida, and that's where he lives now, with my stepmother, who wanted to stay in Canada. This will be the last sad episode of my father's life. He will soon drink himself to death. I see, said my visitor. There was a silence, while we pondered it. Then he said: So you were upset by the spectacle of your father drinking himself to death? Yes, I said. Since he went to Florida I have begun to hate him. I say to him: You are killing yourself. That's what I want, he answers, the sooner the better. My stepmother watches him. If she had any tears left she would shed them all day long. Soon he will drop down dead, the money all gone, she will not be able to go back to Canada. And sadder than that, she loves him. I say to her, Marie, I'm his daughter and I've learned to hate him. Why can't you?

And that upset you? my friend, the writer, asked. That and the rest. The rest was worse. The rest was a new thing he suddenly came out with. Perhaps he saw in my face that I had begun to hate him. He was very drunk. You can see in a drunk's face when he comes to a decision. It is grossly obvious. He decided he wanted to hurt me before he died. He narrowed his eyes, he gave me a terrible leer. Hear this, he said. My stepmother ran out of the room. Then he told me he never loved my mother. She came visiting on the reservation. She liked the idea of native Indians. She fell to him. He said he and his friends used to laugh at her.

What had I thought before he told me this? I thought what she told me often and repeated just before she died. That she and my father were helplessly in love, I was their lovechild. They married, they struggled, they did their level best. They tried setting up home in Oswego. But it didn't work out. He pined for his life with the tribe across the lake in Canada. But he loved her and she him, always. And not until she died would he marry again. But it wasn't again. He never did marry my mother. He never loved her. I see, said my visitor.

I wonder does he see. I wonder how he thinks it matters in a woman turned fifty who has had her chances like everyone else. Perhaps he will think I was lucky to have had such a helpful illusion along the way. I wonder what he will decide when he has mulled it over.

We were a long time getting home. The traffic was bad. I told him I was on the highways at least three hours a day, getting to work and back. Why don't you live in Springfield? he asked. I like where I am, I answered. It was late afternoon when we got there, nearly dark, so he could not see much of the estate. But I saw him looking from house to house along the road. Some of their outside fairy lights were coming on, and the big coloured screens inside. In the cold wind we heard the wind-chimes chime. I showed him where he would be sleeping. It's where I work, I said. All your books, he said, glancing along the shelves. Among the books he must have seen his own. Then I took him upstairs, showed him my bedroom, the big double bed, so much of my stuff in boxes still around the walls. And the even bigger room next door, empty except for my sewing machine in its case on a table and a box of patterns by it on the bare boards. He looked and nodded. I was thinking later what that look of his is like. I could more easily say what it is not like. He does not look round a house as though he were thinking he might buy it. Nor as if he were judging the arrangements, the decorations, the owner's taste. It is a look quite peculiarly dispassionate, and forensic. I suppose it's the mark of what he is and does: I'm interested to see how people manage in the time allowed, he says. Downstairs he noted the big television and my stacks of videos. Yes, I said. I record things and don't get round to watching them. Truth is, if I did nothing but watch, I'd hardly get through them all now. And I go on recording. But let me show you the basement: a vast, cavernous and very warm place. The stains on the carpet are from when the boiler burst. And the insurance quibbled and wouldn't pay. Lastly, there's the cat. She lives in the basement. She was over in the far corner, as usual, anxious. I got her from a refuge. She had been abused. She won't let me stroke her yet. Does she go out? he asked. She's frightened, I said. She went out once and I think something must have bitten her. So now she stays in, down here. But I hope she will let me stroke her before very long.

We stood side by side at the kitchen window. It was dark outside. I let down the blind. I was ashamed, I wished he hadn't come, I did not see how we would get through the evening. And yet he was kind, I could feel the affection he had always felt for me. Then he put his hand on the bird book and then on the binoculars on the working surface by the sink. I saw again – little shock of recognition – how small and quite ugly his hands are, the nails all bitten. He has a way of touching that is not in the least like a claim or a move to possess. It is more like a thought, or a question he won't even ask aloud if you don't wish him to. Yes, I said, I have taken up birdwatching. Lovely birds come here. You'll see them tomorrow: cardinals, blue jays, golden finches. The loveliest creatures. They come out of the woodland to the bird table. You'll see in the morning. They are quite unafraid. At the weekend I watch them for hours. I know a lot of their names. Now and then I add another one. I saw a male rose-breasted grosbeak a couple of days ago.

Do you hear from Edward? he asked. Not often. He is very unwell. He retired long ago and nobody visits him. Still married? They are still married and they are the same. He writes that they have done all the harm they can to one another and now they sit in silence face to face. He can hardly walk. Sometimes they drive to the University Parks and she pushes him in a wheelchair for an hour or so. Then I warned him the evening meal would be nothing special. I've rather lost the knack. I get home so late, and never have people round. You get in late, eat quickly and watch one of your videos, he said. Not just, I said. Some nights I read. And I am learning Spanish. I do my homework for a class.

He offered to help, but I told him to sit in the living room with a book. Then I got on with things. I was nervous. I poured myself a drink. That steadied me. After a while I took a glass through to him. He was in my big chair, under the lamp, a book was open on his lap. I thought: What a pleasure this is! A guest in my house, a dear friend. I've brought you a glass of wine, I said. His face, when he looked up, looked older by ten years. I had forgotten his capacity for showing sadness. Is that what he means by worry? It had always been a shock, almost like an indecency, to see his face when something saddened him. I was reading about the Indians, he said. I don't know enough, do I? No wonder this country is the way it is. All that murder at the outset. Drink, I said. They are very silent in my classes when I tell them about Wounded Knee. Drink. Come in and talk to me.

We stood by the stove. He was asking me more about my father. Is Florida as bad as everyone says it is? Worse, I said.

At first, when my stepmother was trying to make the best of it, she would tell people they lived by the sea. But they're a block away from the sea. All they can see is condos like their own. True, their condo has its private bit of beach. They have a key. They go through a gate and sit between two fences. Except they don't. My father never goes out. My stepmother fetches him the necessary and he drinks it. He shouts a lot, she sits and watches him.

Not true this meal will be nothing special, said my friend. I agreed. Suddenly I was persuaded. I left him setting the table, I decided I would change for the occasion after all. I went upstairs, took off my jeans and sweater. Looked at myself. I found a dress in the wardrobe from way back. It had a Mohawk pattern through it. I saw what it did to me, how it showed very well how I am now. And I knew he would see what I saw. He might as well have been standing by me in my bedroom in the mirror. I ran down to the kitchen and watched his face. Just so.

You and Edward, he said. I remember you used to go and watch the badgers in Swinford Woods. On summer evenings, or very early on summer mornings. I've often thought about that. Yes, I said. He knew the places. And that is what we used to do. But it was only one summer, one late spring and early summer. Oh, said my visitor, the way I remembered it, you watched them summer after summer, it was your tradition. No, I said. It struck me then that when I call him pitiless, I mean, besides the obvious, that often he imagines things better than they ever were, and when he tells you them you wonder is he right. Did I tell you about the dawn chorus? I asked. No, I don't believe you did, he answered. That was the best. We left our two houses very early, long before it was light, and cycled to the woods our separate ways. I met him at the gate, not the main gate, a little one, nobody else seemed to use it. I arrived in the dark, just my bicycle lamp. He was there first, though I couldn't see him till I got off my bike and was pushing it along the bumpy track. Then he appeared out of the dark and we left our bikes and went into the wood together. He knew the way. He took his lamp but we hardly needed it. He knew the best place for listening to the birds when they woke up with the light and began to sing on a May morning. When I think of it now it seems to me that we never spoke. I held his arm and we went along quietly until we came to the place he knew. Then we sat on his coat under a tree, a pale beech tree, in a grove of them, tall pale trees, and we waited, and soon the singing started, like the beginning of a downfall, first a few drops, then more and more, until it was copious and we were drenched with the singing, it was dewfall and summer rain, we sat under the beech tree and the hesitant light arrived and we said not a word, only sat close and listened with upturned faces.

Yes, said my visitor. And of course if Edward told his wife – even if she elicited from him, by questioning, the bare fact that you met in the dark by the gate nobody uses and went in to a place he knew and listened to the dawn chorus – that fact alone would be sufficient to torment her mercilessly. Some facts, in half a dozen of the plainest words, are quite sufficient to do that, wouldn't you say? I smiled at him. He is very male sometimes, very male and teacherly and pedantic, setting it forth. I continued for him, so he should see himself: And suppose she were ignorant – I never enquired – the thought of her ignorance is just as terrible, like something growing that might at any moment burst and infect her fatally, body and soul. In such circumstances, another person's happiness is an unbearable pain, and will never be assuaged, not even by my unhappiness ever since. Wouldn't you say?

I've never forgotten the moment he knew he loved you, and couldn't help himself. I often think of it, my friend, the writer, said. And I think perhaps you told me because you knew I would never forget. Yes, I said. I was in my office in the museum. I was cataloguing a new acquisition. It was a loom, from North America, and I had to describe it, for the Acquisitions Book, and then précis my description, for the public. My door was half open and Edward came in behind me. I was concentrating, I didn't hear him. And that was it, my visitor said, he saw you were concentrating, he was fearful of intruding, he felt clumsy at entering, but the sunlight through the window was on your hair, and he couldn't help himself. And the first I knew, I said, was the touch, or really the entry, of his hand into my hair. He lifted it, in the sun. I was not very shocked. I imagine it is like being woken out of your sleep by someone you love, you are not very shocked, however deep the sleep, it is as though you expected it, deep down. But Edward, when he dared to do that and when I looked up at him, he was like a boy caught doing something wrong. He blushed, he couldn't speak. He looked at me, still with my heavy hair uplifted on his hand, and the light of the sun on it. That was when he knew, when he was – so to speak – cornered in the fact of it, helpless, nowhere to turn but towards you, who were the cause and the thing itself that had moved him inescapably into the fact of love.

Soon after that the swifts arrived and Edward began to watch them. They come every year, to the same nesting boxes high up in the tower of the University Museum. For decades they have been closely studied. Individual birds are recognized and welcomed back, from Africa, across the Sahara and the sea, to our museum. They meet their spouses from the year before. Their cosy domesticity can be observed in close-up, by means of cameras cleverly positioned. The hungry young appear on a screen. But most beautiful, I always thought, is the way they have of sleeping on the wing. They trust themselves and slowly spiral down towards the land or the water. Asleep, they trust themselves until, by a mechanism in the brain, they are woken, refreshed, and can climb again and resume their journey through the air. I loved that most of all in them, especially as Edward spoke of it. His voice was inspired by wonder at that gift of theirs, that grace and ability, the sleeping in falling spirals, full of faith.

When I came down next morning my friend was writing in his notebook, in my big chair. Two books were open on the floor. Still reading about the Native Americans? I asked. I was, he said. Then I went for a walk. And where did you walk? Up the street and down. And what did you think? But he asked me, by way of an answer, who lives here. I told him, so far as I knew: a policeman, a post-office supervisor, a warehouseman, that sort of employee, with their families. And they all vote for Bush? And they all wanted the war? But they are nice enough. My neighbour helped me when the boiler burst. A man I had never spoken to came and cleared the snow off my drive. I saw that my friend was appraising me in the context of my street: a single woman, childless, never smartly dressed, an old car, no flag. And she lives in a house like theirs, a family house. But I saw one lovely thing, he said. Gave me quite a shock. Something I *knew* but had never seen before. My glasses, that I wear first thing before I put my contacts in, lend my face an owlish and a wondering look, an owl in daylight, the look of a creature rather at the mercy of the day's coming phenomena. Tell, I said. Walking up my street and down again, you saw a thing you already knew and had not seen before. Like Adam, I thought, this visitor of mine is like Adam, he dreams, he walks abroad in the early morning on a very ordinary street, and finds that what he dreamed is true. Only the birches, he said, nothing to you, you see them every day, but a shock to me. Tears came to my eyes behind my big glasses. Don't hurt me so, don't say that anything you find true and beautiful is nothing to me. Don't cast me out, don't leave me lost among the lost. I couldn't get into your woodland, he said. I couldn't find a way. But I could see the birches, silver-white, a shining silver white against all the other trees that are still dead and look too dead ever to come back to life. They were beautiful like that, but that was not the shock. The shock was seeing the ones that are bowed down to the ground and cannot rise. It was an ice-storm, wasn't it? You must have had an ice-storm and it weighed the birches down so that even in the spring they won't get up again, they'll always be stooped and bowed, whatever else around them lifts towards the sky. That poem, he said. Remember? Poems are true. And all the truths in poems lie in wait for you, scattered in bits and pieces like splinters of ice, all over the phenomenal world, and at any moment you might come across a piece and know in the world what you already know in the lines of the poem in your head and heart. Then it was like playing chess with him. He lifted up the open book and read:

> Often you must have seen them
> Loaded with ice a sunny winter morning
> After a rain. They click upon themselves
> As the breeze rises, and turn many-colored
> As the stir cracks and crazes their enamel.
> Soon the sun's warmth makes them shed crystal shells
> Shattering and avalanching on the snow crust –
> Such heaps of broken glass to sweep away
> You'd think the inner dome of heaven had fallen.
> They are dragged to the withered bracken by the load,
> And they seem not to break; though once they are bowed
> So low for long, they never right themselves…

And he watched my helpless face in its big spectacles, he is pitiless. He was watching to see would I make the answering move. And of course I remembered. I could almost have quoted it. But I took the book from him, to be word-perfect, and I read:

> You may see their trunks arching in the woods
> Years afterwards, trailing their leaves on the ground
> Like girls on hands and knees that throw their hair
> Before them over their heads to dry in the sun.

Then we were standing at the kitchen window. No birches are

visible from there. My lawn goes over into rough grass and the woodland. Nothing that morning looked to have any hope of spring. The winter is like that here: it lasts, it looks final. But in among the trees, which were the colour of all the dead things you could think of, the birds flitted and perched. Little starts and sightings of crimson, electric blue, jet black and rose. And their visits began, to one or other of the feeders and the tables. My house and my arrangements seemed a trustworthy offering to the birds. They came out of cover – in which they were audaciously visible – crossed my trim lawn, and fed and displayed themselves. It seemed a fair exchange between them and me. And I was proud that I gave my visitor something to marvel at, before he left. Exotic creatures, the primitive primary colours of the earth and the sky, not yet subdued. I was sure he had seen nothing like them before, except perhaps in books. And the deer come out, I said. I've seen them in the early mornings, so delicate. And once in the snow, a small family of them. I had come in here to look at the snow before I went to bed. They were standing on the lawn, which had been joined by the snow to the rough grass and the woodland, they stood there absolutely still and looked at the house, the way we look at animals they were looking at the house and at me, the owner, appearing in the window, as though I were a wonder. And one morning a bobcat passed, clear as anything, that way, from left to right, along the border of the wood, glancing at my house without much concern. And once, in broad daylight, bold as brass, a bear shambled over and reached for that feeder and carried it off. A bear, on my suburban lawn! The woods must be very deep and extensive, said my friend. I see why you might want to live here, looking this way.

A week or so later I had an email from him. He was back in England. He thanked me nicely, but then got down to business. He listed the things he had noted about my street – the fairylights, the yellow ribbons, the flags, the three-car garages, the large yellow signs to left and right that said 'Dead End', the alsatian wearing a red kerchief – and asked me had he missed anything very characteristic. The silence had struck him, of course, the absence of any walker but himself, only a car cruising by very slowly now and then to the busy road below. Also, the curious isolation of the big white houses from one another, even though they stood on open lawns. Anything else? I mentioned that the owner of the alsatian wore a similar red kerchief, and barked back at the animal when it barked. Then sadness got the better of me, I gave myself up to it. I wrote that I had not been entirely honest with him, I wrote that for him to know the truth about where I lived I must add that the woodland the bluejays and the cardinals came out of was sold and condemned and would be cleared before the fall and a street of houses would go up the slope much like the one I lived on whose characteristic details he had noted. The deer, the bobcat and the bear would move away, further away, and would move and move until there was nowhere left for them to go. One last question, he concluded. Could I give him the names of the exterminated tribes that had lived where I lived now when it was all a wilderness? Yes, I could. I typed them out, I had them by heart. They were the Weantinock, the Quinnipiac, the Niantic, the Anasazi, the Hohokam, the Susquehannock.

That night I went down into the basement as usual, and tried to induce my rescued cat to come closer to me. She would not – not quite. But I saw for certain that she will. Her courage is increasing, the makings of faith have begun to collect in her. When I had got undressed for bed I sat for a while in front of my mirror, which I never do. I took – so to speak – a splinter of ice into my heart and tried to say exactly what I look like now in my long hair. My hair, so long and copious that, as Edward once said, it clothed me almost modestly when I sat up before him and he sat back on his heels in a wonder, admiring me.

Visiting

The church is still there, or it was last time I visited. It used to be black, now it's whitish. I suppose they built it when they built the big houses along the old road. I never thought of that before: just a church and the wealthy families, and fields on either side.

We lived this side, in a Sunshine House, built on the fields. All the fields have gone. Such a garden we had. There was a lawn and flowers and vegetables and a wild bit at the bottom left for us. And where our garden ended, easily we got through into the gardens, the stables and the yards of the big old houses. They were ours as well, to trespass in. The millionaires had long since gone and their mansions were flats or nursing homes. One was a blind home. We climbed over the wall and trespassed there like ghosts. The inmates couldn't see us. How Cousin Mikey would have liked our territory! But he never visited. We were the ones who did the visiting.

It was all allotments on the other side of the road. That was the way we went when we went visiting, through the allotments to the railway line and along by the railway to where the old terraces began. The allotments were a lovely world all of their own. I could show you where we went in, at a little gate behind the church, and I could show you more or less where we came out, but everything in between, the terrain itself that I love like a bit of paradise when I think of it now, all that has gone long since under the new estate, under other people's lives.

They got their Sunshine House in the Blitz by a lucky chance. The terrace where they used to live was bombed. Night after night the bombers came up the railway line, looking for the docks, and hit the old terraces, perhaps by accident. Then the mother got a Sunshine House and waited in it for the father to come home. And he did, by lucky chance.

So we grew up in a decent semi with a toilet inside and a bathroom, bay windows at the front and gardens front and back in a drive among scores of drives and avenues on what had once been fields. And our back garden ended under the trees of the vast old mansion gardens gone to rack and ruin. But still we crossed the old road and, behind the church, went through the allotments and along the railway, visiting. You might say we belonged over there, in a sense. But Dad said: 'Who needs an allotment now? We can grow all we want at home.'

Cousin Mikey's was the end house on the street. It had gone last time I went back there, all the end of his street had gone, to make room for the motorway, and most of the railway had gone as well, under the traffic of the motorway. Mikey's street was a grove not a street. They were all called groves round there: Birch Grove, Maple Grove, Ash Grove. And not a tree in sight. We had all the trees, where the millionaires had lived, but Mikey had the railway line. In his bedroom – his with a big sister and a bigger brother who was never home – you were as near as you could be to the railway line and still be in a house. Now and then a brick fell out of the gable end, such a roar and a shaking the big locomotives made as they belted past into town or, faster and faster, out. Mikey said one day there'd be a hole right through and we could watch them from his bedroom standing on the bed.

We watched through knotholes in the fence. There were holes at different heights. There was one for our Lizzie when she could be bothered to watch, and one for Mikey's big sister, but she hardly ever came. Mikey and me stood more or less equal, more or less level, at two planks side by side and squinted down the track. We knew the times when the big trains came and stood there well before, waiting. Oh the sight of one head-on at the limit of your vision down the dead straight track! The mean slant of its windshields and the swept-back mane of steam! There's been nothing like it since. The roar, the airless gasp, it sucked the breath out of our lungs, we saw the fire at the heart of it, and the shock, the long noise following, beat us back from our spyholes aghast at such proximity. Nothing like it ever since. The whiff of the hot smoke through the creosoted fence and the look we gave one another with flung-open eyes, holding one another tight by a scrag of clothing at the neck.

Crossing the old road Mum and Dad held me and Lizzie tight by the hand. Look right, look left, look right again. Through the macadam you could feel the cobbles and the buried tramlines. We crossed in a row of four, us two in the middle, safe. After that, in the allotments, going in at the little gate, how safe it was and altogether lovely. Me and Lizzie dawdled behind and ran ahead and dawdled behind again just as we liked. Sometimes they turned to be sure that we were following. I saw things then I haven't seen properly till now. They seem to have lasted on the retina till they could be understood. His left arm was aslant across his heart. Her right was linking it. Man and wife, they stood together, smartly dressed. He looked – or he looks to me now – as if he thought that things needed holding on to very tight. As if they had only come to him by a lucky chance, and he must deserve them. I think of him saying: 'Don't make mistakes. Don't lose it. Do what's right.'

We were all dressed up when we went visiting. We could see our faces in our polished shoes. My socks were pulled up straight, my trousers had the crease in, our Lizzie's frock was spotless. In summer, or even in spring if the day was sunny, I could go without a tie and wear the collar of my white shirt open on the collar of my blazer. But Dad wore a collar and tie. Mum wore a long skirt and a hat with a bit of a veil. She had a handbag on the arm not linking Dad's. But at Mikey's they never bothered if we got our white things smirched. We had made a good impression when we arrived, when we knocked the knocker and stood down off the step to be let in.

Between trains me and Mikey ran down the cobbled alley under the washing slung from back to back. There was a works at the end with water cooling in small reservoirs. We gripped the railings and stared at the wraiths of steam. Mikey said his brother could piss into the middle but we got nowhere near that when we tried. We crept into the yard and spied on our Lizzie in the toilet. We listened to her talking to herself. Or she sat there trying to whistle a tune. We fell over laughing. When she came out she said: 'It smells in there. All your house smells, Mikey, and you smell as well. Your mum's the only one who doesn't smell. And she smells posh.' I hated our Lizzie, I shoved her, me and Mikey ran away laughing. Outside was best, the creosoted fence, the companionable knotholes, the tremendous locomotives.

The rag-and-bone man came round Mikey's streets but not round ours. He halted with his horse and cart. 'Ragbone!' he shouted. 'Ragbone! Sambone!' Then the women ran out for a brownstone to do their steps. Mikey's mum didn't do the step. Mikey's mum was lovely, like a filmstar. When she bent down to kiss you, you could smell her lipstick and her powder and her hair and all her other scents. There was a scent in her bosom when she hugged you tight. Her look was not like Dad's. 'How's Jess?' he asked. 'Not so bad,' she answered. Then she shrugged.

Our mum had gone through to say hello to Uncle Jess. He was in the back kitchen by the range. Summer and winter they always had a fire. Otherwise it was dark, as I remember it. Some light came in from the yard, but nothing much. Uncle Jess was by the fire, winter and summer, holding out his hands to the flames. 'How are you, Jess?' Mum asked. 'Not so bad,' he answered. He had very bright black eyes. His hair was black as well, in little curls. But his forehead was white, with little drops of sweat on it, and they looked as cold as raindrops. He said hello to Lizzie and me. His face was as white as her frock, but not a nice clean white, his cheeks went in, he coughed, he spat in the fire, it hissed, his breath had a thread of whistling in it. Aunty Evelyn was in the doorway, Dad stood by her. They were alike but he had a different look. He looked determined to be different. We were all looking at Uncle Jess. His long white hands were up against the flames. He wore a navy waistcoat and a shirt without a collar. He turned his face away. One hectic spot, like rouge, otherwise all the cheek was dirty white. The clock, the dying sizzle of his spits. 'Run and play,' Mum said. 'Mikey's in the alley,' Aunty Evelyn said. Me and Lizzie ran out.

We were at the fence, Mikey, Lizzie and me. It was sunny, you could smell the pitch. We were waiting to see a train. I was at my spyhole, Mikey and Lizzie had sat down. Then he said to Lizzie or to me: 'Does your dad belt you ever?' 'Yours does,' Lizzie answered. 'I bet yours does. I bet he belts you on the bum.' I said: 'Shut it, our Lizzie', but turned from spying down the track to looking down on Mikey. I saw the tidemark round his neck. The wool of his jersey was unravelling. He said: 'He takes our pants down and belts us on the bum.' Lizzie asked: 'Does he do your Shirley too?' 'Not now,' said Mikey. 'She's too big.' 'Train's coming,' I said. 'I want to hear it in your bedroom,' Lizzie said. 'Stay here, Mikey,' I said. Lizzie ran off, Mikey ran after her. A minute later the train came, on the near track, leaving town, faster and faster, already faster than any one before. It thrilled the fence, a brick fell out of Mikey's gable end, but I stood my ground at the spyhole, shaken through and through, and watched down the length of the departing carriages and all their rapid diminishing to the very last.

Mikey wasn't there. I mooched into the yard. I went on my belly like an Indian but couldn't see any feet under the toilet door. I went on past the coalhouse on my hands and knees. I rose at the kitchen window, quiet as an Indian brave. Aunty Evelyn was in the doorway, all dressed up. She had a hat on but it didn't have a veil. She looked like a filmstar. Mum and Dad were side by side. They were holding hands, even though it was somebody else's house. Uncle Jess was at the fire, holding his hands out to the flames. But his face was turned to Aunty Evelyn standing in the door. He had finished speaking, but his face continued in a ghastly aftermath, already like his own reproachful ghost. Silence. I saw the terrible black silence among humans in the grown-up world. Aunty Evelyn shrugged. I crept away on my belly like an Apache.

Mikey and our Lizzie were at the fence again. They were grinning. I hated them. 'We heard the train,' she said. 'I saw it,' I said . Then she pulled me down and whispered in my ear. Mikey blushed. 'She asked me to,' he said. 'She said she would as well.' 'I never,' Lizzie said. 'Liar! Smelly liar!' She stood by me, she reached to hold my hand. Mikey was white now. 'Don't tell,' he said. 'He'll belt me. Our mam's going out. He'll belt me if you tell.'

At the back door they were looking for us, to leave. All in the kitchen, in the dark after the sunshine, we stood around the fire to say goodbye to Uncle Jess. 'Hope you'll be better, Jess,' Mum said. She bent and kissed him on the cheek. Dad took him by the hand, right hand to left hand, held it, slowly let it go. 'Say goodbye to your Uncle Jess,' Mum said. Lizzie said goodbye and gave him a little kiss. But I said: 'Mikey showed our Lizzie his willy and his bare bum.' 'I never,' said Mikey, white and his tears coming. 'He did so,' I said. 'She asked me,' said Mikey. 'She said she'd do it too.' 'She never did,' I said. Aunty Evelyn giggled. But Uncle Jess said: 'Well thank you, son, for telling me that. He knows what he'll get from me for doing a thing like that.' And he gave me a smile, the best he could manage in the way of a smile. He nodded at me, as though he recognized my qualities. His eyes, black eyes, were burning bright. I understand now that he was very pleased with me. He was thanking me for giving him something he could do.

Aunty Evelyn left her house with us. She bent to kiss me goodbye, I smelled her scents. She was the only one smiling when the company broke up. She went off down the street on her noisy heels. Mum and Dad stood watching her. Dad seemed to be deciding there was nothing he could do. Then we entered the allotments and were heading home. From there the high spire of the church is visible at once. Beyond the church were all our trees, and all the ruined gardens to trespass in. Me and our Lizzie ran ahead, holding hands. When we turned for Mum and Dad they were facing away, still at the gate, hiding their faces, hiding their trouble, I suppose. They turned, looking very decided, but stood for a moment as though for a photograph, against the gate with the old terraces behind them. Then they followed me and Lizzie towards our Sunshine Home.

The Afterlife

She knew a hotel. I suppose you knew it too. Sitting up in bed there you could see the Acropolis, like a lantern at night and blanched, like a shell, like a lingering husk of moon on the blue sky in the day. But the first thing I saw next morning in the rush of daylight was not the temples lifted up but, when I reached for my glasses, Lou herself naked between the curtains she had just flung wide. I noted the little hollows either side of her spine low down. Then she turned, praising the view which she entirely blocked. She stepped to the bed-end and pulled off the sheet. You are very white, she said. But nice. Your skin is very smooth. She clambered over, like an urchin trespassing.

Then we sat up side by side looking through the window at the Acropolis. People had begun to climb the long slope to the Propylaia and the Parthenon. The sky was a whitish blue, as though veiled with lime. The day looked hot already and the climb arduous. Raised up above the city, in its own large precinct of trees and scrub and ruins, the site looked alien and heroic; it had the spectral holiness of whitened relics beached and stranded in modernity from some remote elsewhere. At that remove, the small black figures climbing had the air of pilgrims.

She asked would I mind if she went and saw you. I had known she would ask and I knew what words and tone of voice I wanted for my reply. The words came out – Of course not. Why should I mind? – but the voice was odd, so substantially odd it seemed a third thing there between us, a queer third creature we were both a bit ashamed of. Still it would have to do. She would have to act on it. I watched her leave the bed. When she was gone into the shower I watched the pilgrim figures slowly ascending to the Parthenon. She came out busily drying her breasts and between her legs. I thought: She won't smell of me. I watched her bend and rummage in our bag for some brief underwear and a sleeveless dress of washed-out blue. She stood between the bed and the window, clothing. What will *you* do? she asked. Wander round, I said. The Kerameikos is nice, she said. Not many people go there. There are trees over the tombs, scented, sweetly dusty, shady. To and fro you can walk among the broken monuments and sarcophagi. I got out of bed. Again she praised the whiteness and the smoothness of my skin. Truly, she said. Don't you believe me?

Leaving, with a sudden hopefulness, she asked one more thing. Shan't we all meet up and eat together? She said she knew you would like to see me again. I had not rehearsed for that. I doubt it, I said. I must say, I said, I don't specially want to see him. Aren't we fine as we are? You and me. I turned away. I could not bear the look of myself in her eyes. He likes you, she said. For a coffee even? For a drink? Why shouldn't we? She was like a child, very winning and disappointed. I shook my head, which felt massive and stupid. I thought: I am so ugly she will keep me on in charity for a while, then let me fall, in loathing. Lou shrugged, she kissed me lightly on the cheek. Don't forget your hat when you go out, she said.

So she left and had you asked her she would have been honour bound to deliver my refusal. You would have known I did not want you in my day.

I left soon after. I did not forget my hat. I had no idea what to do. Wander around. I knew I needed to counter her day with mine. Some act, some absorbing interest, to be able to say: this is what I did. I might take a bus to Sunium, come back very late and full of it, the headland, the temple, the sunset, all my doing. Or find a quiet place in the Zappeion and push ahead with my reading of the *Iliad* in Greek, 200 lines, double my usual pensum. But I was already on the street, without my text and pocket lexicon, and no idea where the bus to Sunium went from and no will in me or wish for anything but torment.

The street gave out, it had been dug up and a section of the city's innards – its pipes, cables and conduits – had been exposed. That was my first shock: the sight of the rusty earth beneath the streets and women in high heels stalking over it. There was a smell of sewage, gas and grilling lamb. Mistaken traffic had rammed together in a blaring mass, except for the scooters which bucked along the broken pavements. All human utterance was a bawling or a screaming. The din, the heat and the light made one elemental force. I thought: Leaving me to stew, she will have flitted through all this joyfully. The more it roars and tangles itself up, the more she will have loved her speed and freedom. So she leaves me. I imagine a last glimpse of the pale blue dress, which she must have thought you would admire her in, and feel the burden of me falling from her shoulders and her desire running ahead to you.

There was a sort of shape to my day, or to mine and hers together. I could not see it then but I can write it to you now. I think of her certainty of purpose. Typical of Lou. She will go and look you up. Will I mind? She will go whether I mind or not. And you will be there in your office in the Museum, behind the Mycenean rooms. It is a normal working day. You will be at work as usual and somebody in reception will phone and say, There's a young woman come to see you, Alexandros. Typical of her. It must be nothing less than an astonishing surprise. She will make a heavenly intervention into your quotidian work. With all my heart I admire the beauty of it now, the very idea, her certitude, the certainty she lives in that her life again and again will be a shaper of miracles. She turns up unannounced in your cool museum and of course you are there and can come and go as you please and the day is yours and hers, at your disposal. That certainty, hurrying ahead in sandals, a straw sun-hat and a sleeveless dress, consigned my day to a helpless chaos, but the two together made a sort of shape, as I recollect it for you now: a point, an aim, a passionate desire, passing through chaos like a lovely comet. I suppose there must have been other purposes in the city on that day, there must have been other people fixed on doing something good or bad, hurrying to an occasion, set on making an event, but I thought only of Lou and hers and of how, all unbeknownst, you were there waiting to be taken up into it, to make up its abundance, the two of you.

I was near Thissio, where the electric shows and goes under and shakes the ground and you know it is burrowing through aeons of the city's life, all the shards and bones and splinters of marble and the stains of iron and bronze, all the strata, all the generations trampled down. And on the concrete there, diagonally across from the beginnings of an excavation of a temple of Aphrodite Ourania – the beginnings, abandoned, so it seems, to the slime, the leaks of sewage, the rising waters, the ebullient bullfrogs, the tossed-in empties and the blown-in scraps of news – diagonally across from that abandoned uncovering of the ancient worship, on the soiled concrete I was mooching with the drunks, the beggars, the cripples, the fleabitten mongrels in all the junk, thinking of her in her sweet cleanness hurrying to find you in your vestibules and marble halls among the statues and the lovely vases, all the craft, all the shapeliness, the exact fashioning, all the garnered, catalogued and safely harboured knowledge, and how she would arrive and pluck you out, beyond all measure pleased with herself, arriving like a heroic challenge to take you by the hand and hurry you away, back into the heat and noise and savours of the streets and bid you find a room – you would surely know a room – with a view of the Acropolis where she would stride as she always does and fling the windows open and marvel like a child aloud, before she turned and stripped.

What stuff they lay out on their rags of blanket, carpet or an old tarpaulin, what a presentation it is of bits of trash and debris and odds and ends of other people's finished lives. And the idlers looking thoughtfully down, as though at any moment Hermes the Joker might whisk it all away and challenge them, on pain of horrid death, to remember a thousand and one of the million different items there displayed: a bayonet, a family photograph, a rusty flat iron, a coin with a hole, a fireman's badge, a hank of scarlet thread, a wreath of plastic flowers, a wad of old pornography, a little silver hand-mirror void of glass… I saw a gypsy woman there. She had some pretty lace for sale. She wore a dark blue dress, blue-black like midnight, all spangled with golden moons and stars, her skin was very dark, her feet were bare and dusty. She looked completely self-possessed. People might stare at her if they wished and despise her or admire her and buy her lace or not. What did she care?

Lou once told me she thought you liked men better than women. I wondered whether she said it to make us more brotherly, so I should be less fearful. But I thought of her trying all the harder to make you like women better than men, and of your cool, minute and fine appraisal of her trying. Or I thought she was mistaken, or telling fibs.

Such an abundance she is, in her sole self. And a lover with her, another body, raises the abundance power by power into infinity. Two people in love, when they lie down together, are far more than twice the bodily delight of either one. Coupling, they are infinitely pleasureable, from head to toe and fingertip to fingertip, and the mind playing over all, devising and delighting. I remember the shock, always the shock, of seeing her unclothed – and 'remember' is not the word, it thumps me in the heart again, flings open wide my eyes, raises my hands in a gesture of worship that I would fashion for a statuette in clay, if I had the skill, and you might excavate it out of the earth in some far distant future incarnation.

Did she tell fibs? She might, little white lies, for convenience, for a quick prevention, for a kindness. But we had an understanding – I don't suppose you ever demanded any such thing – that if I asked her she would always tell me, and I would too, if she asked. So it was equal. Except that I had nothing to tell, only the circles of my hate and shame and the intricate developments of my want of faith to go through yet again. Loving her, the body and the soul between the sheets enjoyed an infinite abundance of delights. But in my fits and lunes, when the tide or the wind or the moon of my humours turned, then she was infinite in the power to torment me. Because of our compact she would always tell. Question by question she would answer truthfully, every dot and cross, and always there were as many details still to come as there are dead and burning stars in the fleeing galaxies. So I lay in the dark or walked in the daylight side by side with an infinite capacity to harm me, whenever I asked for it. She might stall or fib for a while, in a sort of pleading on my own behalf, but as soon as she saw in my face that there was no reprieve, then, by the compact, she submitted to torturing me. A strange way to know you more nearly. I fed on you like an addict, and she supplied.

At Monastiraki they seemed to be rebuilding the station while the life of it went on the best it could. I was above ground, watching the piledrivers. Noise and sensation were as one, in the chest. The milling of people was like what you get if you kick an anthill, that frenzy, which might be purposeful but looks like panic, so many creatures pullulating. They were struggling into or out of the hole in the ground, fast. Streets alive like a wrecked anthill. I shrank as though it was maggots revelling in rotten meat. In those parts – I don't expect you frequented them – there is an infinite reproduction of articles for the tourist trade, there are millions of replicas of the best-known pieces in your Museum, the Youth of Marathon, the Artemesium Poseidon, Aphrodite and Pan, and any number of ithyphallic satyrs, on plates, bowls, cups and cloths and done in tin or brass. And a like quantity of Christ, the Virgin, God the Father and all the saints. Syrtaki by the ton; worry beads, sandals, headscarves, woven belts; skewers, with the heads of heroes. All reproduced. There must be heroic magic trees somewhere that seed the various artefacts down the wind in abundance year on year. The weight of it, the accumulation, surely they will be a discernible stratum in the geology to come. And they disperse abroad like debris from creation's first explosion, all over the world, the souvenirs. I saw two Mycenean vases of that kind at my aunt's in Salford only the other day. Her son, a cousin I never knew, brought them back from the Boy Scouts Jamboree in 1966. She was very attached to them. He was killed on his bike soon after he came home.

I once asked Lou why she loved you. She shrugged. Could she really not think of any particular grace? It was after your exploit at Delphi, but she did not say she loved you for your bravery. Perhaps she was sparing me the plethora and, for once, I did not call her to the compact and insist. Myself, I should have cited the quickness of your hands – or of your hands and eyes and mind – that day I saw you sorting a heap of shards, the Geometric, the Protogeometric, Mynean, Minoan, Mycenean, so quickly, all in their styles and phases. I noted your unbitten, femininely attractive nails. Also, in London and Oxford, your foreignness, your being on the margin and belonging there, so that I thought – was I right? – that even in your mother country the aura of it would cling to you, from being some years abroad and on the margins.

Your careful language, your dark skin, round head, black eyes and neat moustache. And because I asked, because she was honour-bound to tell me, I know about the rest of you also. With the mind's eye, with the mind's exploring fingers, I know you perhaps as well as she did in the flesh. Helpless as a weathervane, I swung from torment to a queer delight when she spoke the skills and graces of your body into my gasping mouth. I know why she loved you, in every detail. Still, she was right to shrug when I asked her why. She was indicating an excess over everything that I, only a questioner, could ever know.

I've often waited for her to finish teaching. I'd arrive a few minutes early or she would go on a few minutes late and I'd sit on the chair outside her room, and wait. I never minded. I'd hear her speaking Italian in her room. Then the door opened, her students came out, and Lou, at her desk under the window with its view of the river, would smile at me through them. But the day I first met you I was outside waiting on my chair and I heard Lou's voice and yours speaking Greek. It was a shock. I knew she was learning it but I hadn't known how far she had got. I waited – a bit longer than usual perhaps – and when you came out she said, Oh sorry, Ian, this is Alexandros, stressing the second syllable very pointedly, as if to teach me. And there you were, courteously appraising me. She asked: Will you mind if Alexandros comes to the pub with us? And I said of course I wouldn't mind, and I liked you at once and we all three got on well, so it seemed to me. Then I had to leave. You and I shook hands and Lou kissed me on the lips and before I reached the door I heard your conversation resuming in Greek. No, I didn't mind.

I taught myself Ancient Greek from a variety of courses, primers and readers I picked up for next to nothing in secondhand bookshops. They were old public school texts and they presupposed a knowledge of Latin grammar, which

I didn't have. But I plodded on. Soon I read some Plato. I copied out the Greek in pencil and wrote a literal translation of it word by word in ink on the line below. That was my system. I loved making the letters, though I could hardly say them aloud as words. I'm almost ashamed how many great works of your literature I have read like that. Much poetry, and never able to say it. I bought the *Iliad* and the *Odyssey* in four neat volumes, and Crusius's pocket Homeric Lexicon in an English translation of 1853, that had once belonged to someone at Charterhouse.

When we got to Greece, I was pleased how much of the language – how much Plato, Euripides, Homer – I could recognize in print, whilst never quite knowing what it meant and understanding scarcely a word of it in speech. Lou managed everything that had to do with our getting around, all the rooms, the restaurants, the boat-tickets. She shopped at local markets. She was a joy to watch, which is what I did: stood by and listened and watched. Wherever we went she chattered to all and sundry, revelling in the tongue. Often I watched their faces, the men teasing and flirting, the women glad of her as though she were an ally or a famous daughter. What joy she gave them, speaking their language. By that language she was in the midst of life, which I loved and admired her for. I was towed along, it was delightful. But left to myself I found a quiet place somewhere and laboriously read my hundred lines of the *Iliad*, mouthing the words almost aloud, trying to fit them, in my head at least, to the rhythms of the hexameter which, so I had read, had the lovely repetitiveness and infinite variety of wave upon incoming wave of the wine-dark sea. I was some way into Book XII and the Trojans' breaching of the Achaean ramparts by that morning when she asked would I mind if she went and found you in your room in the Museum.

I always wondered at your ability to do without one another. Such long stretches, the odd postcard, never even a proper letter, a once-in-a-blue-moon meeting if you happened to be in London or Oxford, and on her trips to Greece. Sometimes I thought that perhaps it was no very great thing between you after all; but mostly I thought it rare, radiant, so sure of itself it could exist with none of the usual human need for proofs and signs. Her certainty that you would be there when she came looking for you unannounced was a part of that.

At Delphi we were the last to leave the site. We were on the highest terrace, alone in the stadium. Such a place that is, above the pelt of olives drawn up the slopes from the sea at Itea. We were above the city with its temples and statues, under the snowy mountains, the eagles, the blue ether. Lou sat still, I paced out the stadium with a guidebook in my hand, trying to locate important points exactly. After a good while all alone up there we heard the custodians hallooing from below. They were climbing to evict us from the domain. It was then that Lou told me about your exploit. She said she had been trying to work out exactly which cliff it must have been. She said there were photographs in the newspapers, of the helicopter and of you with the frightened child. She decided on a pinnacle so precipitous I shook my head at it in disbelief. But she said yes, that must surely have been the place. Later, of course, back in England, I believed her. I could make my own heart race by thinking of the climb. She said the child was odd in some way, agile as a monkey but perhaps autistic. He escaped his mother, climbed to where he could neither continue nor get down, and stuck there gibbering. For you, apart from the difficulty of the climb itself, there was the problem of his panic and unpredictability. He might have clung to you fiercely and toppled you both to your deaths. You soon decided, so she said, that you could not risk conducting him down. So you sat up there hushing and diverting him. He was a beautiful boy, but quite alone in his bouts of super-confidence and terror.

Then at last the helicopter arrived, strange phenomenon in that archaic holy place. You saw him harnessed and winched aloft and lowered like a gift from the gods to his sorely tormented mother.

The indoor market is a famous place. I was in it without thinking, not by choice, not out of eager curiosity, I was washed in or sucked in through the lower bourg of buying and selling that spawns and proliferates from it like a polyp. The streets around there are like dry riverbeds that want a spate to cleanse them. The shops are like caves of every human specialism or every possible miscellany. Every noun that was ever in Babel must be in them somewhere, sorted with its near relatives or flung in the common grave. Then I was in the belly of the place, the emporium of edible Creation. True, people go there to buy. They cram their bags and carry the foodstuff home to devour it in greater privacy. But for its size, its ribbed and echoing hollowness, the market is like a belly, working to evacuate what it has ingested. The floors are slippy with blood and other liquids. The bare light bulbs act like blatancy. So it is, so we are. Behold! And the roaring, the shrieking, the sounds of sluicing, flailing, beating, cleaving, chopping. Close your eyes, this is Pandemonium. Close your eyes and sniff. It is blood, roes, marrow, lymph, flesh, soil and flux and salty ice. Most unlike us are the fish and crustacean things, fetched out of their element into ours, where they must die. How long the crabs and lobsters take to die. Even piled up in a tub the topmost at least finger slowly at the air. What must it be like below, under the equivalent of tons of their own kind. If this were a heap of humankind, that faint groping and feeling and the bubbling at a vent would excite either a coup de grâce or a shout of the will to rescue. I saw one or two on the wet concrete itself, making a hopeless bid for the distant sea. In that they are like us, in the will to live. But their appearances are very foreign, their shapes, their colouring, the number and dispositions of their members, their eyes. Squids like a rooted boil, narwhals, steaks of leviathan. The animal meat is closer. It had warm blood in it. Some, when it had legs to stand on, was capable of nuzzling affectionately at a mother or even at one of our hands, feeding. Now look at it. Hoisted up beheaded, flayed, eviscerated and opened wide. How naked and glistening a lamb looks without its fleece and skin. I gawped at the hanks of intestines, the blobby mountains of liver or kidney, the unstable slopes of tripe, the slop of sweetbreads and lights. There is a neatness and an order as in a factory or an extermination camp. Hearts here; tongues, trotters, brains and pizzles there. But over all a chaos, a frenzy, a desperate hurrying to sell and eat before it rots and stinks and breeds the sort of life we cannot live on.

There are dens underneath this place where butchers, carters, buyers and sellers go and eat. You would think the liquids might seep through the ceiling. There are beggars on the steps, showing their stumps, shaking with a biblical palsy. I pushed between them, went down the steps and peered in. There they were, my fellow humans, feasting. The noise was much as it was in the place itself, but stifled in the small headroom. They were drinking rapidly, and forking and spooning the platterfuls in as though to stoke a furnace. Many were in their bloody coats and rubber boots. I did a strange thing: I went in. I blundered to a table like a sheep evading slaughter. A glass and bottle were set before me, then a bowl that had an eye in it that surfaced through a film of fat and ogled me. I drank the resinous wine and swallowed whole the eye. I left a sum of money large enough to cover ten such trials and punishments of my cowardice.

Outside I vomited by a tilted container of carrion, near a nest of spindly cats. The eye passed up unscathed. Somewhere later, I made a wordless but successful transaction and paused, facing away, to sweeten my mouth with fruit. I thought – if I thought anything – that I would go

back to that hotel and sleep for a while and then go out and
wander around a while longer. On no account to be there
alone and waiting for Lou to return from seeing you. Always
the fear she never would return. But at reception – a
cluttered desk – the amiable man said, The lady is already
upstairs. He said it in Greek, which I did not understand,
then in a sort of English, pointing up through the ceiling and
grinning. The door was shut, I knocked softly, Lou opened.
Her blue dress lay crumpled on the floor. She had been
sitting up in bed, naked, and went back there, tugging me by
the hand. We had perhaps half a minute in silence. I could
not read the expression on her face. I matched it against what
guiltiness might have looked like, or embarrassment or a
reluctance to cause me pain, but it was none of those. The
window was open, she looked away at the Acropolis, then
back at me and said you were dead, of leukaemia, in three
weeks from the point of diagnosis, at Eastertide. I have never
seen anything sadder than Lou's smile when she finished
telling me that. As for me, she always said she could read me
like a book. She shook her head very slightly and put the
fingers of her left hand on my lips. I think it was to stop me
spilling over in self-disgust. I stood at the window with my
back to her. The noise of the streets was constant, like
something you might get used to and be able to sleep to, like
the sea. The Acropolis was beginning to look ghostly in the
late afternoon. Then Lou said: Undress, will you. Come to
bed. I did as she asked, conscious of my whiteness. When I
kissed her she began to weep. She wept and wept. She made
a copious libation of tears for you, Alexandros, all the while
gripping me into her as though I were her hold on life in the
spate of a drowning grief. I can feel her fingertips on my back
still and in anguish the sudden pointing – like an unsheathing
– and the imprint of her nails.

Afterwards we were sitting up, watching the people
descending from the Parthenon and the Propylaia. At that

remove they had a lovely solemnity. Easy to believe they had freighted their lives with a lasting seriousness. Lou said she had gone through the cool rooms of the Museum, among the vases that she thought of as yours, to the very door of your office. Almost, she said, she had entered without knocking, so sure she was of your presence and the welcome. It was an elderly man inside, who had known you well. He watched her face in much concern over the shock. She talked in a low and level voice from deep inside her sadness, so that, shoulder to shoulder with her, sharing her view of the white Acropolis, I seemed only to be eavesdropping. She said you were buried in the little village above Patras, where your mother still lived. I said we should go there if she wished, visit your grave, perhaps speak to your mother. Lou said not. She said she had walked from the Museum to the Kerameikos, she thought I might have gone there, at her suggestion. She walked up and down for a while among the broken sarcophagi in the dust under the sweetly shady trees. You taste of oranges, she said. I was thinking, while I listened, that you have been dead six months, unbeknownst to Lou, and between the people climbing up to the Acropolis and their coming down again the fact of your death has come alive to us and you are with me now and I weep for you and ask forgiveness, now it is too late, that I would not let you share an evening meal with us, nor even a cup of sweet black coffee nor a glass of wine. I sent her to you with a refusal when you were dead and already beyond her loving invitation and my fearful want of courtesy, my friend.

Sleepless

She wished hard, like a child: That it would be Italy when we went out. Adding in a softer voice: And a great big bed. If the Angel had answered: One or the other, girl, I'd have urged her to go for the second, easier, but the Angel said nothing and we went out for both and needless to say got neither. Hope for the first had rested on nothing more than the fact – which she knew, she is writing a guide-book – that in the church the martyred saints had been done by painters come all the way from Italy.

We had the codes and the keys of a couple of beds but they were forbidden and we trailed the streets for several days in a state of sleeplessness. I never knew where we were going next or what was likely to happen. It is a noisy city and much of what she said I didn't catch and much of what I did catch was unintelligible to me because often to perplex me or as though I wasn't there she spoke in the language and often, I believe, in verse. Once or twice or even three or four times it seemed to me that she suddenly bethought herself or made her mind up. Then she seized me by the hand and dragged me away in a contrary direction and my heart raced and I felt certain she had remembered or had been shown in a vision where there was a bed and where it would be allowed. I am such a fool. We left the sunlight or the pelting rain and went down the steps into the underground. She hurried, dragging me. There were women on all the steps selling lilac, lilies of the valley, roses, baby tortoises, puppies, kittens or themselves, old women, young women, one all in sequins like a fish, but we went down past them quickly to the escalators. Seeing the depth and the tilt and the queer pale lights and the almost opalescent marble walls I felt more and more certain that if any citizens, living or dead, wanted to sleep together and were in difficulties this would be the place to come. The lamps were set at such an angle and looked so like candles it seemed you should take one as the staircase carried you down, to light your particular way. But no sooner were we down than we came up again, past men on the steps selling watches and pornography, into the daylight where it was raining or sunshining.

Perhaps having her wishes thwarted made her cruel. On the square near the place of execution she showed me a cathedral built by a famous architect whom an early Butcher in the long line of Imperial Butchers had blinded immediately afterwards so he would never build anything better as long as he lived. We were in a fast-food place having a cup of coffee in polystyrene cups, we were the only ones, wherever we went for a cup of coffee we were the only ones and the staff dressed in the Stars and Stripes would lean on the counter and watch us fall asleep and listen to our sleepy language that they could not understand. I was developing an idea that the architect had his revenge by lying awake at nights with pains like terrible migraine in his extinct eyes imagining cathedrals, palaces, pleasure domes and hanging gardens compared with which the edifice in the square was a shit-house and a pigsty. Also that if he ever showed himself in the daylight with his empty sockets the common people ran to take him by the hand and guide him wherever he wanted to go, but nobody ever took the Butcher by the hand, not unless he threatened them with blinding or amputation – when she suddenly launched into a defence of this horrible person and said that he knew his own mind at least and did what he liked and had a sense of humour. After that I vowed I would watch my tongue and be altogether more circumspect, but for vows of that sort it was much too late.

She knows everything there is to know about the city, which is why they have asked her to write an up-to-the-minute guidebook that will be a help to foreigners. Nowhere on earth perhaps are such gross and rapid changes under way, but she has sworn she will always record what was there before and also what was done. For example, a sparkling gold and white cathedral has come up overnight on what used to be the Public Baths. But the baths themselves had been sunk into the destruction of an ancient nunnery so that in the changing rooms you might suddenly feel your nudity stared at by a bride of Christ and through the incense now if you open your eyes when you are praying you will see the families of grey swimmers drift. The city is full of ghosts and it seemed to me she knew most of them. Without her guide-book you would probably take the place of execution for a bandstand and hope for some innocent music on a sunny evening, but once you have heard from her even a few of the many and unusual ways of killing you would feel uneasy seeing the instruments, I imagine. Later – we were in a sparkling new gold and silver shopping-precinct that had appeared overnight in a vast hole in the ground, we were deep down in there drinking coffee in beakers of starspangled polystyrene, alone needless to say and all the staff were watching us: she recited a poem by the nation's favourite poet telling of a gallop through the night and the fog, into that very square, which was soft with the corpses of his executed friends. I don't speak the language, not a word, not a syllable, and she mumbled her translation, but I think I got the gist of that famous poem. Then – I think it was then, it was then and on several other occasions – by her look she seemed to be asking me to show her the pity she would not show herself. But we are two of a kind – unkind – and I asked her as we rose in a transparent lift, as though to heaven, as though to question the angels: was it true the dead from the latest provincial war were unburied yet, and where were they kept, in what cold places, the forty thousand? And though I made no comment she saw me note a soldier-beggar with one leg and a girl with both but the foot of one turned up impossibly and exposed like a pudendum. She watched my face, to see how I took the things the city pressed into my eyes.

It occurred to her that it might be food we needed more than sleep and we hurried to a place she knew, pretty far away, for which she had the keys and the necessary codes. All I remember is the notice on the lift. Friend, it said, when these doors open do not step into the lift unless the lift is there. Now I will prepare you something typical, she said. But afterwards my spirits lapsed, the mood turned sullen and the cruelties returned. I was at the window, looking down, and began to tell her about a man, a poet, whose love of women went hand in hand with his terror of them. Love and terror, I said, the double helix of him body and soul. She was staring away, asleep with her eyes open I shouldn't wonder, never answering a word and besides I was talking to myself and might have gone on like that for ever and a day, when suddenly it rained. That woke her up. The sky opened and slanting across the sunlight sheets of rain slopped on to the roofs and sluiced the windows. That animated her. There was lightning, some thunder, and rain in sheets, a strange flopping of water. She stood next to me at the window, she even took my arm, she said: Now everything will be green. It was only a week since the river unfroze, but what a river, not worth unfreezing, but after that small disappointment she had turned her desires elsewhere, to the gardens, such as they were, the public parks and the heroic trees. Now everything will be green, she said. It wrung my heart to hear her uttering her desire for green, but I did nothing and said nothing and only looked at the water, how it streamed off the roofs and tried to enter the gutters and the downspouts but they had come away or were blocked and the water overran and dashed its brains out on the pavement never less then several hundred feet below. That was a specatacle, rash and troubling. After it there was a rainbow for a while. Then nothing.

We were hand in hand, asleep on our feet, waiting for a procession of the Old Guard to pass, when I began to tell her about a boy I knew, called Ben. I think his name was Ben. He thought very ill of himself and to show it would burn his arms with a cigarette. Nothing anybody said could make him like what he was, and one day he moved with his cigarette from his arms to his eyes. Don't, she said. Not really his eyes, I said, only the lids. He went into the toilet and when he came out... Please don't, she said.

We were on the kerb, the gutter like a brook. She said: It seems that all you see is horrors when you close your eyes. Now why? I ask myself. If we were waiting for a gap there never would be one. She said: I suppose you think I'm used to soldiers with no legs and women selling themselves for half a dollar? I suppose you think I'm used to it by now? I was ashamed. She seized my hand, we jumped the cheerful water. There were six lanes of traffic, fast as falling headlong. We'll take a trolley bus, she said, but halted a car, any car, and told me not to speak or the price would rise.

We had come to view a curiosity in an old part of the town. It was a house in which a famous poet of the eighteenth century had spent a night with her lover, half her age. I say a house but the house had gone and only the facade was standing and very uncertainly. They were demolishing it, she said. Then a foreigner told them what had happened there. Behind the facade was the rubble of the rooms themselves and on the rubble, upside down, like a dead cockroach, a car. Her face wore the look it wears when she is noting something important for her guide-book. The Mayor has ordered a plaque to be put up, she said. But the wall will fall on a drunk before they do.

I was still ashamed. I gripped her hair, I held her pale face steady between my hands, I looked her in the eyes and praised the sky. I praised the flowers being hurried in from somewhere distant where there must be fields and market-gardens. I praised the dignity of an old comrade with so many medals on his chest they shingled him, he looked like a scaly magic fish. I praised the amber, the delicate white bone, the fossil ivory. Go on, she said. The girls, I replied, their clear skins, their extraordinary clear beauty. Hard to believe they are the daughters, impossible to believe they are the grandaughters of the heroically ugly women on the trolley buses. They're not, she said. But I was developing a hopeful idea according to which, after years, after centuries, after an entire Holocene of concrete and atrocity, these clear beauties were coming through, after the rain, under the rainbow, in unstoppable abundance. We could try eating again, she said.

I was at the window, looking up and down. Silence, silence, silence, the tap dripping. To change the subject and to test her I asked when the place was built. 1951, she said. It is the ugliest building in the world, I said. It is the biggest lie and the most dispiriting brutality ever built by man. There are another six, she said. The Butcher was so pleased with the first he ordered the architect to build him another six. Silence again. I wondered what I could wish for that would make it feel better. Then a man came into the yard to do the bins. He shoved the hooded crows aside. He rooted thoroughly. He had a decent rucksack on his back which I suppose he must have stolen since the rest of him was trash. Some things he found he fed his stomach with at once, in at the mouth, intently. Others he found a plastic bag for in the bin. Perhaps a thousand people at their windows on the many floors, a thousand tenants and the guardians were watching him, but he took his time, he made the corbies wait, he browsed and gathered, he ate the little titbits and stowed the rest into the rucksack which was of new black leather with shiny silver buckles. Then he wiped his hands on his jeans and left the yard. He was very purposeful. The crows resumed. They are not fussier, only better at it. Then a wife came out and slung her garbage in. Soon after her another. I began to develop an idea according to which you were always in with a chance when you did the bins, they were always replenishing, there was no point in hurrying or scheming, it was always possible to be the lucky man, and if not here then elsewhere, there are so many bins. Then my mouth dried up.

She was at the table, I went back to face her. Silence, the dripping tap. How to explain about her face? I felt we were taking advantage of her sleepiness. I mean she let me look. I was looking at her but she was watching me. She was watching how I looked when from off her face, because of her sleepiness, because in a sense (perhaps she told herself) with her eyes wide open to all intents and purposes she was asleep, when from off her looks the veil of prohibition fell away. The tap, the silence pressing on the pulses of my head and against my heart. If I can say of a face that it wore a look then I can say that now it was divested. Because my mouth was dry I stared at hers. She watched me becoming certain that her mouth was not so thick with drouth as mine. Sleeping, she allowed herself the ghost of a smile. By ghost I mean what has been and what might be, I mean the memory and the wish. But when I inclined to that, the wish, the ghostly foretaste, she shook her head, but only a little, so very little I will swear it meant not only no, perhaps not even no, but also, even, wonderingly, yes.

I drank a couple of handfuls at the tap. That tap, I said, I'd never sleep with the tap dripping like that. We never will, she said.

Now I don't know where she is. She turns away, I see the sparkles of rain in her black hair, I see her stepping into the lanes of traffic. Perhaps she lets the Angel and the cars decide. If I get through, if I get across, I will. Then she heads for the Metro, fast. I follow her. The women offer her their flowers and baby animals, she pushes past, down into the hall so jostling with people I am fearful of losing her. The escalators fill me with apprehension, like an imminent waterfall. We shall topple, we shall have to dive, the height, the depth, is at least a thousand feet. But she steps on never hesitating and the fast treads take her down.

There is nobody else. When I get this far the place is empty, the whole vast public place has emptied of everybody else. And but for the treads, the rapidly clicking treads, and the wind, the moaning of the wind in the tunnels far below, there's never a sound. The marble is cold and faintly luminous, the torches rise, one after the other, the pale electric candles rise towards her right hand. I see this whenever I like if I close my eyes and the question every time is will she turn, and am I following?

Under the Dam

Their first home was under the viaduct. Seth found it. His train slowed and halted, waiting for clearance into the station, and he looked down on the rows, the smoking chimneys, the back alleys, and imagined being down there looking up at a train strung out along the arches in the sky. Next day he went in among the little houses and soon found one to buy for less than it would be to rent a room in nicer places. He fetched Carrie at once, as though this opportunity were a glimpse into the heavens and might at any moment close. The back bedroom had a pretty tiled hearth but Seth was at the window craning up. The arches climbed higher than he could see, the track lay on an upper horizon out of sight. Okay, said Carrie, in a loving wonder at this renewal of his eagerness. A train crawled heavily over and away. The house trembled.

Now began a good time for both of them; different for each, but equal in its fullness. They would look back on it, separately, and marvel: that was us then! The house was solid; or if it wasn't, they never worried. The sashes rattled under the heavy trains, once a slate came loose and slithered down; but they only laughed, Seth with a kind of satisfaction. The house was never light, not with daylight, at least – how could it be? But they made it cheerful with lamps, candles, coal fires, bright paint, and with lovely things they had collected on their travels.

Carrie advertised, and got two or three pupils for the fiddle or the guitar. They came to her and played or listened in the front room, always lit and scented, under the viaduct.When a train passed overhead, they paused and smiled. Seth kept on his job at the art school, only a few hours but just about enough. In his free time he did his own work, still trying for a true style, he said, but with some hope that, if he trusted, he would feel his way. He worked, and looked about him with a lively interest, to see how the things were that he must try to answer.

Under the arches, where the little streets ended, were strange dens and businesses. Seth and Carrie had a scrap man for a neighbour. He lived behind a wall of old doors, corrugated iron and barbed wire. He was black as coal, except for a grizzly head of hair the colour of ash. He had lost the power of speech. His clients were humped old men pushing bicycles and handcarts. They brought him rolls of lead and lengths of copper piping snapped like the limbs of insects, stuff ripped out of a vacancy before the Council came to board it up. Seth sketched them from his window as they passed. They were like gleaners on the slag heaps. When Carrie bought a big brass bed and several knobs were missing, Jonah hunted out the exact replacements from a drawer. When she asked what she owed him he raised his arms and tucked down his head, to mime a fiddler. She fetched her fiddle and played him a jig. He capered like a bear, on and on, until she feared for him and paused. Then the energy left him, he slouched off into his shack. Carrie glimpsed his primus stove and mattress. Seth marvelled. The man lay smack under the tracks!

They were mostly old people under the viaduct, or who looked old. The young left if they could. The Council accommodated difficult cases there; and one or two incomers, like Seth and Carrie, lodged or settled by choice. A pub had survived very easily, a couple of corner shops by dint of bitter struggle. Carrie soon got the feeling that they were welcome. Their outlandishness was engaging. She felt people look at her and Seth with a sort of hope. Seth did a sketch of the landlord's little girl, for her birthday. Then one or two others asked him. He did it quickly, for free. They marvelled, and forcibly he had to quell in himself a rising pride. Likeness, however exact, was not enough. He saw the hands of the old miners, the broken nails, the blue-black fragments of the job inhering under the skin like shrapnel; he saw the flaky cast, like talcum powder, over their puffy faces. Then he knew his uselessness and averted his eyes.

Seth did some research on the subject of the viaduct. He learned the weight it was built to bear, and the weight that nowadays it must. He gazed up, wondering at the difference. All those blackened bricks, arches like a Norman cathedral, the iron road, the thousands of oblivious people travelling north and south. In the pub he edged the talk towards catastrophes.There was one in 1912, coaltrucks, the last two in a long line somehow derailed and hanging over the parapet, emptying. Street next to yours, somebody said. Coal through the roof, coal on the bed. Then the iron. The Company rebuilt the houses, paid for the funerals, let them keep the coal. Seth wanted more. He had read of a suicide, a man dangling from the parapet on a rope, discovered in daylight, a crowd of citizens gazing up. All night there, trembling under the trains, tolling in the breeze. Carrie watched his face becoming helpless under the pull of his wish to know. She tried to cover for him, to veil an indecency. She feared for him. But that night, thrusting a poker into the congealed coals and letting the flames out, their warmth and dancing light, he said in the story of the derailment it was the richness that overwhelmed him, the too-sudden, too-abundant giving of the fuel of life. She pulled a face, shook her head. Then he said: We'll get an allotment, they're dirt cheap, we'll grow what we like.

The streets, yards, rooms were not entirely dark. In summer the morning sun slanted in very beautifully; in fact, like a peculiar gift and grace. There were early mornings of nearly unbearable illumination: sunlight through the rising smoke, a blood redness being revealed in the substance of the arches, through a century of soot. But the allotments, higher up the dip the houses were gathered in, enjoyed an ample and more ordinary helping of daylight. Seth was given a plot on the slope facing the railway embankment, just below a ruined chapel and a few wrecked graves, just before the viaduct began its stepping over the sunken town. There was an attempt at terracing, almost Mediterranean, he said. He went up there whenever he could and Carrie joined him. He watched for her climbing the path from the houses into the allotments among the sheds and little fences. She brought a flask and a snack. Then they worked side by side. Palpable happiness, real as the heavy earth, as the tools in their hands, as the produce. So it was. She said to herself: Nothing will obliterate this.

One of Carrie's pupils was a boy of seventeen or so. He was called Benjamin and had no home to speak of. He came to their house under the viaduct, said he wanted to learn the guitar, but had no money. Could he do odd jobs for them instead? Carrie said yes. He spoke a thick vernacular. He had black eyes that seemed to be seeing things he hadn't the words to utter. Seth saw how it would be and to all that he foresaw, like Carrie, he said yes. Soon Benjamin was in love with her, muffled and bewildered by it, but with the steady helpless gaze of a passionate certitude. The best he could ever say, including both of them, but turning back helplessly to Carrie, was: You're not like people round here. Seth watched Carrie shift so almost imperceptibly in her feelings that at no point was there reason enough to halt. From pity for the incoherent child – he wrings my heart – she passed through the troubling satisfaction of being loved by him into loving him, in her fashion, in return. Seth came home once and saw them in the music room together. Benjamin was making his best attempt at the accompaniment of a familiar song. He was bent down and away from the door, anxiously watching his own fingers. Carrie was singing, and watching him. Seth saw how far along she was in the changing of her feelings. She met his eyes and knew that he knew. Afterwards she said: It doesn't make any difference. I know that, he said; but felt a difference, of a kind he could not fathom. And she added: Whatever you ask, I will always tell and whatever I tell you it will be the truth.

Seth had been planning to restore the kitchen range. It should heat, like the back boiler, from the open fire, and once would have cooked and baked for a family.But all its intricate system of flues and draughts was blocked and useless, one door hung loose, a cast iron hob below it was cracked and tilted. For weeks Seth had been brooding on his project with a secret satisfaction, as though it were the promise of a breakthrough in his drawing and painting and he must bide his time, gather his energies, make a space, and finally set to. It was all his own, all his own dreaming, that he would act on when he chose. It amazed him therefore, one afternoon when Benjamin came in from the lesson, that without thinking he took him by the arm, stood him before the hearth and said: Know anything about ranges? Benjamin blushed. Here was a large opportunity. Aye, he said. Same make as my mother's. I always did hers till my stepfather moved in. And he went on his knees before it, opened the loose door, rattled gently at the damper. No worse than you'd expect, he said. He looked up at Seth, then quickly away. In the firelight on his looks Seth saw clearly how Carrie must love him. He said: I had a mind to get it working again. You could give me a hand. His project, disclosed, shared, made over to someone else. Suddenly he was deferring to the boy, who was local and knew about these things, knew better. He tested his feelings for regret and could find none. Benjamin was rolling up his sleeves. No time like the present. There should be a rake somewhere, and wire brushes. They're out the back, said

Seth. In secret he had been making his preparations. He fetched the tools, a dustsheet, a tin bucket, overalls for them both. Soon he was taking out a pail of rust and soot. Thinking Benjamin had already left, it shocked Carrie to see him in Seth's overalls, crouched close to the fire, intently working at the blocked airways. Seth came in. We've made a start, he said. Feel. She put her hand into the open oven. The warmth was coming through. A long way off baking bread, but a start. Like cleaning a spring and the water beginning again. Ben's the man, said Seth. You both look the part, said Carrie, bringing tea, their filthy hands closing round the mugs, eyes whitened through a faint mask of soot, eyebrows, hairs on the wrists lightly touched up with dirt. She felt her own cleanness like an attraction, almost too blatant. She said: Why don't I go and ask Jonah for a new door? It's the hinge, Benjamin said. The door's okay. Well, a hinge, said Carrie. Why don't you? said Seth. And to Benjamin, as she left the room: She likes asking Jonah. Five minutes later Carrie was back, with Jonah himself. Couldn't remember the make. Thought he'd better see it. His appearance in their living room was astonishing, as though an order of things had been undone. He bulked much larger, blacker, more grizzled, more indifferent to any usual manners. He glanced and nodded, tapped the cracked hob with his boot, nodded again, departed. It's sunny out, said Carrie. Strange irrelevance. Under the viaduct they seemed to be making a life that would be all interior, by lamplight, intimate. Their feelings wanted sleet and hail, early dusk, the long nights. The fire would roar, the oven would heat up tremendously, Carrie would bake a batch of loaves, there would be a kettle whispering on the hob.

They were in a hurry to finish, but it took some days. Seth would only work at it with Benjamin, at which Carrie smiled. She went to Jonah for the hinge, he had found a likely hob as well, also a battered kettle that might polish up. He beckoned her into his shack and pointed to a can of WD40 on the table. There was a notepad by it, to do his talking. He scrawled: FOR THE RUSTY NUTS AND BOLTS. And after that: YOU PLAY ME A TUNE? His oily hand had smudged the cheap lined paper. Carrie kissed him on both cheeks. A baker's dozen of tunes, she said. In town she bought the substance necessary for loosening rusty nuts and bolts, and a tin of the proper stove paint, glossy black.

Seth and Benjamin were at work, kneeling on the dustsheet side by side. Your mother must have been glad, said Seth. Why ever did he stop you? Benjamin shrugged. Whatever I liked, he put a stop to it. And after that he started thumping me. Your mother let him? Couldn't stop him. Didn't try? Little by little let the boy go, for the man, reneged on everything, betrayed him utterly, crossed over, stood against him with the incomer. Stepfather said he was a pansy, queer. Unbuckled, belted him, left him curled on the hearthrug swallowing his own snot. Then joined the mother in the room above, in the marriage bed. Benjamin said again: You're not like people round here.

It was Seth's birthday. They declared the kitchen range open for use. The burnished copper kettle boiled for tea. By evening the house smelled of bread. Red wine and brown ale shone in the firelight. Savorous things, all manner of plates and dishes, it was all their travelling gathered in. Jonah came, grinned, tapped with his dirty knuckle on the shiny iron. From somewhere in his throat came up a cheerful clucking. Two or three others were invited. Carrie played her promised thirteen tunes. After dark they went out into the yard. The arches stood supreme and along them, elongated, lay a halted train. The lights shone like scales. Nothing above until the infinitely distant constellations. When the others gone Benjamin came to Seth and Carrie by the fire. I got you this, he said, handing Seth a thing in a plastic bag. It was the shape and weight of a bible, but cushioned to the touch and a lovely dark green and the thousand pages, closed, made a

block of brilliant gold, and on the cover, ornately and
goldenly inscribed, the name: Shelley. Benjamin was anxious.
Okay or not? I wouldn't know. He shrugged, sorry on many
counts. Seth looked from the gold to Carrie to Benjamin and
bowed his head over the gold again. You've got no money, he
said. It's only Oxfam, said Benjamin. And anyway I nicked it.
Seth kissed him and left them by the fire. He wanted to be
outside for a while, under the viaduct and the Plough,
holding the book of poems. Carrie said to Benjamin: Don't
go. We want you to stay.

2

In Rhayader they went first to the solicitor's, to sign. Seth had
insisted that it be in Carrie's sole name, so she signed. He
cradled the baby in his arms and watched. The man was
polite, punctilious; if he found a client odd he would never
show it. Seth felt as remote from him, fellow humans though
they were, as one star is in fact from any other. All people in
professions, decently dressed, decently doing their jobs, they
were moving further and further away from him. He bowed
his head over the sleeping child. He prayed his wife would
never go from him into the icy distances while he lived. The
estate agent's was a few doors along. They collected the keys.
The man was jolly, heartily wished them both good luck,
extended a little finger to touch the baby's cheek. Was there
anything in his manner which said he was glad to be shot of
the place and rather you than me?

Rhayader looked a nice town, simple on the axis of a
clock tower. The waters felt very near, and the cold breath of
the hills. Carrie remembered it well enough and they
shopped quickly. It was late February, the daylight would
soon give out, they wanted to arrive before dark.

Seth drove. Carrie held the baby on her knees, on the
open map. The road climbed the river, which was rising, they

heard it roar, the tyres hissed over sheets of running wet. After a while they must take a junction left, out of woodland and across the narrow reservoir, a sinuous long water whose lapping edge they clung to. So far so good. The lake seemed to double the light of the clear sky, giving them more time, a reprieve. Then, sharp right, the thin road took up with another river, doubling it exactly. Carrie opened the window. Such a din entered, the river hurtling in excess of the course at its disposal. The hills, streaked white with headlong tributaries, opened and were revealed on either side, very beautiful, terribly exposed. Seth, as so often lately, viewed himself and his enterprise with fear and pity, like a spectator. As though from high above he viewed the cumbersome white van, in which was everything he owned and loved, crawling forward at the mercy of the universe. He admired the three of them, loved them intensely, wished for their safe arrival; but remotely, as though they were fictions, actors, a lively dramatisation. Carrie was in doubt. She had begun to wish it should be dark before they arrived, that he saw the place for the first time in a fresh daylight. She felt answerable, the onus on her felt as vast as the opening hills. Not that he would not like it, but that he would like it too well. Was she not siding with him against himself? Was it not a conniving in his destruction? The daylight lasted, they were far west, the stars appeared on a sky still white.

Then the road ended, they were at the dam, up under it, up against it. A stream came tumbling off the hill, the hill came steeply down in rocks, and there in the angle, between rocks and sheer black wall, on a platform reached by a raddled track, stood the house. Carrie shook her head, wondering over herself, appalled. But Seth had jumped out and stood marvelling in the cold air. He took the baby from her arms, helped her down. Home from home, he said. Well done! He was radiant. He seemed shocked back into proximity. At once he had energy, the spirits, the courage for anything. She unlocked the door, it needed a heave to open it. Never to be forgotten, the first breath of the place, the soot, the damp. The electric, he said. Can you remember where? She could. They had lights. Now for a fire, he said. I saw a wood pile. She followed him out, stood by him. He turned with his arms full of logs, faced the sheer black wall. Beloved wife, he said, I shall work here. Under the stars they lugged their brass bed from the van.

Craig Ddu was a dead end. The road stopped there, it was for Midlands Water and the few tourists. A carpark, a public toilets, a phone box, all like a failed outpost. And from under the massive wall the original river set forth again, ignominiously. True, in no time at all, fed fresh water by the free streams off the hills, it had recovered and rattled along with the dam behind it like a fading nightmare. The house itself, older than the dam, a survivor of the colossal works and shoved by them into a new relationship with the world – the house itself wanted living in. There was an acre around it and forty more vaguely up the hillside and a little way downstream. But the wall was so close and towering it seemed to Carrie that at the least diminution of their resolve they must lose the contest and be overwhelmed. Again she wondered at her choosing it for Seth. Was it vengeful? But Seth went from room to room and paced the territory blessing her name. He said his love and gratitude were as vast as the backed-up waters behind the wall. So she was reassured, but still with an anxiety that his exaltation, her doing, was itself a precipitous and dizzying thing. But they had days full of appetite and savour and at nights their love was like a miracle at their disposal. The house warmed. They owned a copse of twenty or thirty shattered firs, fuel for ever, so it seemed.

Carrie drove into Rhayader, to stock up. They needed blades, paint, sand and cement, as well as food. Seth watched her out of sight, a long while. After that, with little Gwen slung on his chest, he continued to discover how rich he was.

He found a damp place in the very angle of rock and wall, a lighter green and lit up with celandines. It was a spring, and only wanted cleaning. In a stone barn he found a collapsed tractor; and a scythe, a rake, pitchforks, all wormy wood and rusted steel, that he would surely mend and put to use again. He fed Gwen, laid her down for a sleep, sat on the boards and leaned against the cot, dozing. He felt fuller than the rivers. He must have slept for a little while soundly. His face was wet with tears when he woke. Only grasp it, even a small part of it, make even a little of it able to be seen! Joyful commission, courage to come up to it! Gwen was waking. Together they went and sat in a mild sun, to watch down the length of the river and the road for Carrie coming home. Scores of rabbits browsed and scurried below them over their ragged estate. Benign neglect.

It was a week before they climbed to see the lake. They might have gone down through the carpark to the road which served the dam ordinarily; but they had seen, with a shock, a steep path, almost a stairway, starting behind their house, near the celandines and the newly discovered spring. That was the way they must go, arduous, secret, starting from their own ground. So cold, so damp – more than damp, the hillside oozed and trickled and spurted with more water than it could hold. The rocks were soft with moss, tufted with the ferns that, in their fashion, luxuriate in chill and wetness. Seth cupped the baby's head and steadied her against him, against his chest, in the warm sling. They were in an angle, almost a chimney, close into the join of dam and hillside, hard up against an unimaginable body of water behind its engineered restraint. At first, for about half the climb, they were in a shadow akin to darkness at noon, eclipsed. Seth turned whenever the stairway allowed it, for Carrie to come up. Over the bright scarf on her head he took in their new home and beyond that the river, its recovered force, its intrusion and insinuation through the resistance of the hills.

How slight and at the same time vigorous and cunning they were, to climb an intricate and precipitous stairway under a deep reservoir of water, the child pressed against him felt as brave and tiny as a wren, he felt her pulse to be infused into his own, married in, blood into beating blood. The day had grandeur, like a heroic expedition, like a myth. Then they were in the sun, the low sunshine of the dawning of the spring, it warmed and illuminated the greens and the tones of gold, they climbed with a faint warmth on their backs, felt for it with their faces when they paused and turned, like a whisper of earthly everlasting life, a breath, an intimation, infinitely delicate and poignant against the immensity of the immured waters up which they climbed.

Their arrival, a last steep haul, landed them in a grave uncertainty of feeling, with no words. It was like surfacing: there lay the level water. Come up through the depths they were level now with miles of length and breadth, the far reaches winding away invisibly in many bays and inlets and the inexhaustible hills continuously contributing. The total bulk exceeded comprehension, like a starry sky. From the far head of the lake, or rather from off the hills and harrowing softly over the face of the lake, came a cold breeze. The water lapped steadily at the ramparts under them, the water came on and on, without end, hit against the stone, each wave that ceased in its particular self being at once renewed and replicated. Somewhere in the distance, out of sight, was an infinite spawning of waves against the dam. Quite suddenly their little human enterprize seemed futile. They became anxious for the baby, the necessary energy was lapsing out of them. There was a watchtower halfway along, locked and boarded up, but they hid in its lee, saw to little Gwen and settled then without much regret on the ugly and ordinary way to climb and descend, the waterboard's metalled road. Clouds were driving up, such hurtling clouds, you might stand and watch the world occluded in three minutes.

What are you thinking?

About the dam.

Don't.

Not badly, I wasn't thinking about it in a bad way.

What way then?

Only about the water. How it naturally wants to be level.

Not there it doesn't.

No not there. There it wants to go headlong, and be level later. Real lakes are different. They're serene in comparison. When it's too much, they overflow. That's very gentle. But the water up there, even when it's still, all the weight of it doesn't want to lie like that. It wants to be headlong.

Stop it.

Can't stop thinking. I was thinking about the waves as well.

Kiss me instead. Love me. I want you.

Carrie was feeding the baby by the window. Such a view from there, away from the dam, downstream through oaks and rowans towards the little hidden town. On the draught through the sash window she could smell a bonfire. Always a bonfire, so much to clear and burn. Seth came in, went upstairs, she heard him rummaging, floorboards and ceiling were one and the same. Peaceful feeding; the quiet view, the scent of smoke. Sometimes she dozed as the baby did. Seth went out again, she glimpsed him, what was he carrying? She dozed. Then it broke in on her. Oh no! Oh no, not that! She ran out, her dress undone, Gwen's eyes flung open wide.

He held a portfolio open on his left arm and sheet by sheet he was feeding it to the flames. Carrie halted, clutching the baby tight. He was like a man on a ledge. Should she snatch at him or quietly, quietly talk him to safety? Seth, don't, she said, soft as the small rain. He turned, his face was rapt. She hated to see it. Grief, despair, would have been easier to view in him, not rapture, feeding his work to a bonfire. No harm, my love, nothing wrong, he said in the voice of some peculiar wisdom. I see my way, I see I have to begin again. Seth, for my sake, stop it. She saw sketches and drawings, beloved likenesses, herself in the little churchyard above their allotment, a warm and vivid picture of their hearth, the burnished kettle, the rug, the glossy range. I have to, he said. One folder lay on the earth, wide open, wholly empty. Soon be over, won't take long. Then we'll begin again. They're ours, she said, they're not just yours. When they're done they belong to both of us. Herself in her sixth month, peaceable. The baby newborn. How can you? There was Jonah, seated at their kitchen table, manifestly content. And again and again, there were the heroic arches of the viaduct, striding across the town. Everything? All of it? He would not be talked into safety. Carrie made a grab for the portfolio, dislodged it from his arm, spilled out the remainder on the ground. Pictures lay under the sky, half a dozen of Benjamin. Seth's face jolted and altered, as though from a stroke. Bitch, he said in a voice like a ventriloquist's. Bitch, you are in my way, you and your bastard you are in my way. And he reached for the pitchfork, newly mended, wrenched it from the earth, raised it, stabbed and stabbed at the images and rammed home all he could of them hard into the fire. Gwen was screaming. Carrie went on her knees, scrabbling together what few sheets were left. Seth leaned on the new handle, worked the prongs free, and stood back. He saw her breasts, her weeping face, what he had done.

Listen to the rain.

So soft.

And the streams, can you hear the streams?

All of them, near and far.

It's gone again. I'm better. I feel you have forgiven me.

I love you. Nothing else matters. I will forgive you anything. Except the one thing which you know about. Do that and I will haunt you day and night in hell.

Where is he, do you think?
Who?
Benjamin.
I don't know.
Does he know where we are?
How could he?

Gwen woke. Seth went naked to her room, reached down into her white cot, lifted her warm and snuffling against him. Carrie sat up, reached for her, all in the tranquil darkness. The baby's whimpering became a focussed hurry; then she settled into the blissful certainty of satisfaction. Seth stood by them in the dark, Carrie leaned her head against him. The baby had her hunger exactly answered. He went to the window, parted the heavy curtains, looked down. He could make out the water, like the ghost of the milky way, a soft luminance in movement. He could almost believe that the dam was a natural lake that has no wish to topple but in a measured fashion gives into the valley. Across the cold room Carrie said:

I suppose he visits his mother.
Did he say?
He said he always would.
He is very loyal. You could write to him there.
I suppose I could look for that address.

Seth came back to bed, obliterated his face against her, dozed, woke when it was time to carry the sleeping child back to her cot. Like a little boat, he always thought, a safe little ark, into which he laid her, in which she drifted safely on the waters of her sleep, returning, calling out in the dark when next she needed a reassurance of the close connectedness and safety of her world.

The van tilted, rocked from side to side. The descent always did look perilous. Carrie, watching, was glad when he reached the girder bridge and the start of the road. There he paused, got out, waved, blew her a kiss, departed. All the way out of sight she watched him travel. Then she went indoors to prepare the house. As for herself, she made an abeyance. She feared Seth's changes. They were the abyss. Now he was marshalling events the way she most desired. Or the way she dreaded most. Or both. And between her and him, one flesh, it was never certain whose proposal they were following, either might serve the other for the self's obscure desires. She knew that much, but it appeared impenetrable and induced in her a passivity and a fatalism, under which, like a spring making for daylight, ran the irrepressible force of self-asserting life.

In the late afternoon Carrie and Gwen went down to the bridge and the junction of the little stream with the river creeping out from under the black doors of the dam. They were less in the wall's shadow there, the sunlight lingered a while longer. The rabbits fled; watched; soon resumed their trespassing. At the waterside Gwen was absorbed by all the babble and movement. A yellow wagtail flitted over and stayed close. Carrie lost her consciousness almost wholly in the child and the bobbing, darting soft-coloured bird. Her particular complexities were postponed.

At the waterside she heard the motor but could not see it. The rhythm was unfamiliar, the arrival might be somebody else, though scarcely anyone ever came so far. Having no wish to see a stranger, she took Gwen in her arms and climbed the track home. The engine still approaching made her nervous, like a pursuit. Not till she was on the level, at their usual viewing place, did she turn. The vehicle, an old estate car, long as a hearse, was riding grandly over the bridge and embarking, with great caution, on the rocky track. Seth and Benjamin. Where's the van? she asked. Seth was pleased with himself. Sold it. More seats in this. Carrie said: What about our bed, if we move? We're not moving, Seth replied. Here we are now. First job tomorrow: improve our approaches. Benjamin stood to one side, smiling, very uncertain. An army surplus haversack seemed to be all his luggage. Again that gaucheness, again his black eyes seeing more than his tongue could utter. It lurched under Carrie's heart. So here we are, to stay. Again; anew; as before; wholly new. So be it.

Then began a good time for the three of them; for the four of them, since Gwen among the childish grown-ups continued in gaiety and satisfaction with only little bouts of fret. That very evening, in a lingering daylight, in firelight and candlelight, Seth begged their forgiveness and explained as clearly as he could what he must try to do in his drawing and painting henceforth. He said: I look at you. I look from you to my hands. I can make a likeness of you but it will not be enough. It won't be what it is truly like. So my premise is failure. My axiom is that whatever I *can* do, whatever my hands *can* make, will not suffice. Carrie was anxious, wanted to halt him, she saw him raising the precipice. No, no, he said. Through what I *can* do, its manifest failure, I will feel my way towards what I should do, always by failure, I'll know what isn't right, what manifestly will not do. Carrie stood up and stopped him softly with her fingers on his mouth. We haven't had enough music lately. She fetched the guitar for Benjamin, the fiddle for herself. Benjamin shook his head. You men, she said. So fearful. Start, it will come back. Listen to this.

Seth said he would go and stock up. Food, and we need a sledge hammer and a pickaxe, he said. Gwenny's coming with me. Back for lunch. Carrie strapped her carefully in; leaned over her, kissed him on the mouth, feeling for his tongue with her tongue. Benjamin stood in the doorway.

A bit uncertainly, Carrie first, Benjamin hanging back, they came out of the house, to greet him. They were like children, he laughed at them, how he loved them, he laughed aloud over them and him, he exulted, the life there lifting up before his very eyes filled him with a wild glee. Guess what, he said, handing Carrie the sleeping child, guess what, or perhaps you knew, and he kissed her lips, perhaps you knew already when you brought me here? What? She asked. Such a shop I did, food and alcohol for a fortnight and tools for eternity. He was handing the plastic bags out to Benjamin, overburdening him. What did I know already perhaps? Carrie asked. Shelley's down there, him and Harriet, under the second reservoir. They were alive down there and planning a thorough revolution of our ways of being in the world, in the summer of 1812. They came up here for picnics. It's all in a book, I bought a book, it's in that bag Ben's holding with the cheeses, five different cheeses. Truly, there's no end to this place. He faced the towering black wall. That wasn't here then, of course. It was a high valley with the little river hurrying down. He cupped his mouth, tilted his head and shouted at the dam. Back came the clearest sound of craziness imaginable – the sole name: Shelley, fracturing and chiming. Gods, said Seth. Did you know that as well? No, said Carrie. Benjamin stood like a beast of burden with the shopping, watching Seth and Carrie as he had under the viaduct when they appeared like an enchantment on his life. Shout, Ben, said Seth. Shout out who you are. Echo it to Rhayader that you're here. Benjamin looked called up for an ordeal. Shout, said Carrie. Stand where Seth is and shout your name. First time no sound came, none from his mouth at all. He licked his lips, raised his head, called out his name. The echoing fell away in a cadence that was utterly forlorn. Carrie ended the game. Food, she said. Then work, said Seth. Work and pray. Work and play. But work first, the chain gang. Anchor me with a ball and chain, don't let me float away.

That afternoon, with pickaxe, sledge hammer, shovel, wheelbarrow, in boots and heavy gloves, they worked at smoothing a way from the girder bridge to their platform under the dam. Parts had become like a riverbed, from frost and sun and torrents, and it was with some reluctance that Seth made them carriageable. He worked next to Benjamin, or parting and returning as the tasks required, almost without a word, in the intimacy of a shared hard labour. At first Benjamin was shy, watchful, but Seth won him over, slowly and surely into something akin to his own present state. By four the job was half done. Enough, he said. The sun was behind the dam. They went indoors, made tea, sat at the table in a too early dusk. Carrie was at the window with Gwen. Not far down the valley lay the sunlight still, the shadow advancing very slowly over it. She felt the haste more characteristic of Seth. We must show Benjamin the water, she said.

All they had seen so far cried out to be seen again, to be seen and shown, and he was the only fellow human they wanted for the revelation. The climb was eerie, chilling; the wet trickled on them as though night and blackness were exuding an icy dew. They felt the cold of the body of water through its concrete shield. But all the while, as in a seaside town when a street heads at an incline for the sea, Carrie and Seth were expecting the enormous light over the brink and treasuring it like an imminent gift for Benjamin. At the last they sent him ahead and waited, looking down over their own chimneys to the pool of sunlight on the woodland very far below. Then they joined him on the rampart of the dam. The breeze; but gentler, warmer, a zephyr if there ever was such a thing. And sunlight dancing, a shattering white radiance further than they could see, more than they could bear to contemplate. They drifted apart, drifted together, gauche and ineffectual, brimful of love and joy and their mouths silenced with shyness.

So their days rose, whatever the weather, they had work to do, they played like children, were passionately companionable. Benjamin went back to the echo, he became the master of it. He positioned Gwen on the ground to listen to the names returning strangely. He invented birds and animals, he brought them forth for her, as though from an ark.

In the evenings they read or Seth painted, Benjamin withdrew as far as the room allowed, turned his back on them, strummed softly at the guitar and in an undertone, barely audible, hummed and mumbled some words of his own invention. Seth said aloud: Nantgwyllt went under the water in 1898. The Shelley Society lodged a formal protest. The Welsh were evicted from their homes, where they had lived for many generations. Carrie went for her bath. The clock ticked more audibly. She came in naked and kneeled on the hearthrug between her husband and her lover, bowing her head, towelling her long hair, the curve of her spine in the lamplight. She sat back on her heels, the firelight on her knees, her belly, her breasts. She slung her damp hair forward in one hank over her left shoulder. What else is under the water? she asked. The house of his cousin Thomas Grove, where he stayed in 1811, wondering what to do, when they had sent him down from Oxford for professing free love and atheism. Nothing under our dam here? Some sheepfolds, one or two cottages already given up and the ruins of a chapel at the very far end with a holy well, a hermit lived there in 1300, he had moved further and further into solitude and come this side of the hills from the Cistercian community at Strata Florida.

They trekked over hill and bog and down through woodland to a vantage point over the second reservoir from where, closely comparing Seth's old maps and the reality, they believed they must be looking on the surface under which Nantgwyllt and the house belonging to Shelley's cousin lay submerged. On a long day, first climbing the stairway that started from their liberated spring, they circumambulated the reservoir, the highest, under which, night after night, they slept, and located, to their satisfaction, the place a diver would have to sink himself who wished to visit the anchorite's roofless cell. Question, said Seth. Does the well still bubble up oppressed by tons of water? They took out the deeds of their home, Craig Ddu, and climbed the little stream, to see where they began and ended, their forty or fifty acres. But this was harder than imagining a village or a dwelling fixed for ever under sheets of water. The walls had collapsed, the bracken and sedge were over all. At the head of the stream, where it split, where its three strands were plaited together into one, there was a ruined fold, one hawthorn clinging on, its roots in rock, its shape, set by the wind, offering a threadbare roof over a waterfall. Emblem: the survivor. I don't know what we own and what we don't, said Seth. Whatever, wherever, the land was given up, for humans it was long since finished and the crows, the kites, the buzzards and the kestrels were left at liberty to scour it lot by lot.

Seth's work was changing. Carrie looked over his shoulder now and then, his concentration was intense, he did not mind. She loved to watch his hand, so quick, so deft. But what came of it troubled her. At first she thought she must make a new effort of understanding, to do him justice. He had said his way must be that of groping through failure towards the truth. But in truth she had to confess to herself that she understood him perfectly well. The lines of his art were forfeiting all insistence, one figure elided into another. One that by the shock of black curls and the steady eyes most resembled Benjamin had the bodily shape of an adolescent girl; she saw herself with Seth's short hair and features haunted by all his previous alienations. Everywhere there was doubling, tripling, echoing, fragmentation and dispersal, fleeting as Welsh weather, faithless as water. Even that she might have said yes to, and praised his courage. They were change, flux, movement, or they were dead. That was their principle, was it not? What distressed her were his trials with colour, the way he exceeded and overrode his slight outlines with a willed carelessness, like a child's smudging and genial mess, the watery colours running and giving up their selves whilst the draft of some elusive shape ineffectually showed through. But this was a man with the keenest sharpest gaze she had ever known. She had watched him when he bore on a thing and truly saw it. She knew how exact and knowing he was: when he dashed off a likeness for a favour; and in the devising and execution of a particular pleasure. So why this allowing a world in which nothing belonged, nothing had shape or fixed identity or an outline marking it off from anything else? She remembered his axiom, and it chilled her: Whatever I *can* do will not do. He was reneging on his peculiar abilities. For what?

Seth took off his boots and entered on stockinged feet, quite silently, though he had no intention of stealth. Carrie and Benjamin were sitting in the window. She was buttoning her dress, he was cradling Gwen and murmuring over her. Carrie was contemplating him and her baby with a contented love. The light from outside was on the three of them. Seth stood, he saw the beautiful ordinariness of their intimacy, the daylight fact of it. He turned, quitted the room, his movement alerted them, Benjamin came out to him as he was putting his boots back on. Seth kept his face averted. Nothing, he said. I was going to show you something. Benjamin touched him on the shoulder. What then? Seth shrugged, still averted, but walked across to the stone barn, allowing Benjamin's arm along his shoulders. And step by step he felt the virtue going out of him.

In the barn, standing still, he couldn't for the life of him remember what he had wanted to show Benjamin. He was attending dumbly to the transmutation taking place in him, a sort of petrifaction, the replacement of every atom of faith with an atom of hopelessness. He stared in stupidity at the tractor. It had slumped forward on burst front tyres. He motioned vaguely at it. The weights? said Benjamin. No, no, said Seth. Nothing. The weights, a couple of cast-iron pyramids, were still slung from their rings under the tractor's front bar. Stop you going over backwards, said Benjamin. He was staring at Seth, who at last looked him in the eyes. Tell Carrie, will you, Ben. I'm very sorry. Then he covered his face. The tears forced through his fingers, the wells of his hopeless sadness burst their strong restraint.

He curled up on the bed of love, tight as an embryo, and sobbed; he choked on his own snot; he was a grub, a grown man with his knees up to his brow, smelling his own terror and despair; in overalls, with dirty working boots, a competent man, weeping over his exile from all fellowship with love; shoved into space, into the cold and the dark of the interstellar spaces, turning for ever like a finished capsule. For an eternity, for an hour or so. After that, uncurled and lying quietly in his wife's embrace, behind the curtain of her hair, he said in a level voice he was not fit to live, he had a coward soul, he cringed in shame that he had ever associated himself – in a far-off laughable mimicry – with any of his saints and heroes, the artists and the poets. He begged in the flat, the leaden voice that she would burn every scribble of his or daub she ever found. He begged her to promise there would be nothing left, not a scrap or jot to show the world his folly and ridiculousness. And he said again that he wasn't fit to live, that on her house and home and child and love he was unfit to have the smallest claim. Then shame over these his speeches. Dumbness then, the mute inability. And a vague terror, hard to pinpoint, hard to lay a finger on its whereabouts. Inside or out? The air he breathed, the wreath of atmosphere around his neck and shoulders. Or in the blood, coursing around him for as long as he was he. The nights had terrible gaps in, rents and pits, and every morning waking he felt sheeted under lead.

Ten days of this, a bad passage. He came out lachrymose and vastly sentimental. He sat with Gwen in the bedroom window like a grandfather, her hand clasped tight on his little finger as though she anchored him and nurtured him. With a large benevolence he watched Benjamin, like his own younger self, labouring at the finish of their steep track to the bridge and the beginnings of the outside world. The thistly grass was gay and innocent with rabbits, like a tapestry. Carrie, her hair coming loose from under a red headscarf, pushed manfully at the wheelbarrow. She waved, said something to Benjamin, he looked up and waved. They swam in tears as far as Seth could see.

Then his return began, unhoped for, miraculous, never biddable but somewhere in the depths of him insistent as a germination or water forcing up. He wandered about in the house and out of doors with Gwen on his hip, she was easiest to be with, he could babble at her or murmur like a breeze and what delighted her in the early summer delighted him, thistledown, dandelion clocks, forget-me-nots around their neatly stone-flagged spring whose water was a clear continuous beginning again. He viewed himself with more indulgence now, with a wry friendliness. Held up the child against the soft blue sky and intoned while she kicked and chortled: My own heart let me more have pity on; let/ Me live to my sad self hereafter kind… Brought her close, kissed her nose, went down on his heels and toddled her towards him. Her cool hands warmed in his; he marvelled with her over the unpractised action of her legs. Scooped her up to admire the woodpile, Benjamin's special pride, and the new plots set as well as possible for the growing season's sun. The stone barn, the very sight of it, tilted his spirits towards a steep collapse, so he walked away, down the slope past Benjamin and Carrie smoothing the last few yards, to the water where the wagtail liked to visit and sat there till they called him, willing his fears into submission in the happy consciousness of the child. Returning, admiring, he suddenly saw where a new plot might be dug, on the slope itself, with some terracing, almost Mediterranean; he would begin it next day.

That evening he read in the Shelley Benjamin had given him. He read Mary Shelley's notes on the poems year by year, until the last. They were brave, these people, he said. It's brave just being in a place like that, so far from anywhere, facing the open sea. And Mary collecting everything afterwards and writing her notes, that's brave. What happened to Harriet? Benjamin asked. Seth made no answer so Carrie said: She went in the Serpentine. He had left her for Mary. They married and went to Italy. Seth was thinking of her heavy clothes, sodden, the mud, the weed. And her heavy belly, she was very pregnant. They didn't look after one another, Carrie said. One to another they were a catastrophe. I suppose everybody is responsible, Seth said. I mean for what he does. They left one another their own responsibility. He was feeling bolder. He was thinking about his terracing – whether to tell them or not, or make a start first thing, for a surprise.

Next morning Seth appeared at the foot of the bed. He whispered a strange sentence: the boat has come. It was early, he had parted the curtains slightly and the sun shone on the black paint and the golden brass. Carrie woke. Benjamin was asleep on her left arm. He looked, to Seth at least, much as he had lately in his drawings and paintings, only more beautiful, the black curls, the lashes. Carrie smiled, gently disengaged herself, sat up. Seth said again: the boat has come; but with his eyes on Benjamin shook his head in wonder and added the words: sweet thief. Carrie joined him outside in the sunlight. You've been working already? Yes, he said. Come and see. He took her to the edge and pointed down to where he had begun hacking out a terrace. We shall grow what we like, he said. Carrie put his arms around her. Was I dreaming, she asked, or did you say something about a boat? I did, said Seth. That's the strange thing. But not strange at all really. Not for this place. I was working and I looked up at the dam and thought how lovely the water must be with the sun on it already. I thought I might go and swim and when I got up there I saw the boat, a little rowing boat with the oars in. It was bumping against the land where I might have gone in swimming. It's nobody's, we can use it.

Everything from the far end drifts before the wind and arrives sooner or later up against the dam or lodges in a near angle. They claimed the boat and the shipped oars until they should hear of someone who had a better claim. They made a mooring in a tiny inlet, out of sight of the rampart should anybody walk there, which was almost never, and whenever they liked, which was often, the four of them were out on the water. There was nearly always a breeze but rarely too strong to make headway against. And besides, by keeping close and following on water the path they had followed or made to the far end of the lake, they could creep along, like a yacht skilfully tacking. They packed a picnic, landed where they pleased: by two or three hawthorns, by the broken line of a drystone wall where it descended and entered the water. Poignant, these traces, these indications of a connection and a use gone out of sight. Keeping an eye on the weather – they were never foolhardy – they crossed with steady strokes the width near the far end, to experience, said Seth, the imaginable tremor of the hermit's holy well still bubbling out of the ground invisibly below. And best were their returns, scarcely rowing at all, idling down the centre, confident of safety within reach on either bank, wafted by the breeze and what felt like the bent or inclination of the water always to be coming from the west and heading, however quietly, towards the ruled line and the little tower that made the limit and the brink. It was sweet to drift like that, as though to a sheer falls but knowing they could halt when they chose, safe in a secret harbour, and disembark and descend their secret stairway into their house and home. Often they had a soft music on these returns. Carrie sat in the stern, holding Gwen and singing; Seth rowed, his eyes on them, and behind him in the bows Benjamin, become accomplished, played and murmured an accompaniment. Seth was between them, between their music. Their last such return was at full moon. They had not thought of it. They were idling down the length of the water, the music dying behind them like a wake, there was the merest breeze, and the blue of the sky was becoming pale so very gradually they were beginning to drift into nightfall before they would notice. Then Seth saw in Gwenny's face what she had seen. Her eyes were all amazement, she thrust out her pointing finger, as though she were the inventor of that gesture of an astonishment demanding to be shared, then Carrie saw too and suffered likewise a childish shock and pause or gap in her adult comprehension. Moon! The moon! White as a bone, frail as a seed, big as a whole new earth, the moon was rising over the rim of the dam, dead centre, clearing it, first with the ugly stump of tower intruding, then free, sovereign, beyond measure beautiful and indifferent. Seth turned sideways on, so all could see, and like that they drifted nearer and nearer, in silence but for the water lapping.

Carrie woke. The curtains were slightly parted, which made her think he must have stood there and looked at her. She went to find him on his terraces. There was fresh earth dug but the mattock had been flung down. She turned and called for him, the echo came back, a single note, distended. Benjamin came down. He'll be swimming, he said. Or in the boat. Look for him, will you, Carrie said. Benjamin began the climb, Carrie went indoors, dressed, saw that Gwen was still asleep. Then downstairs again, uneasy, and met with a shock, an absence: the table was cleared of his sketches, drawings, paintings; the portfolio, that had stood by it, also absent. She ran out, Benjamin was coming down from the dam, too fast. She waited by the spring, he hurried by her, not a word, averting his face. His breath was coming in sobs. He ran to the stone barn, she followed, the door was open, he took a step in, bent forward, turned to face her, ashen, smitten white. The weights, he said. He's filed them off. They're gone. He began to whimper, a queer unstoppable distress, bolted like an animal for the cliff again. Carrie fetched the child and laboured with her oblivious up the stairway to the ugly level rampart of the dam. She saw Benjamin already distant, small, making haste along the bank, visiting every inlet, in all his bearing, his sudden leaps and halts, hurting her even as he diminished with his manifest dread. How large the water, vast the hills and without bounds the sky.

Now she must wait on the dam in a steady breeze. Everything drifts that can sooner or later down the length of the water and bumps against the terminus, the ugly wall. The little boat will come, with its oars shipped, empty. Everything that can float will drift this way, the work, the distorted likenesses, they will be for a while like spawn, like a flotilla of vaguely coloured rafts, till the colours run and all weighs heavier and they sink. The boat will come. But what cannot kick free, anchored at the feet, what cannot rise on the body's insistent buoyancy, pulling towards the daylight on the will to live, that must stay where it is and in her lifetime will never rise, only toll like a bell, like a sunken, silent and useless bell. On the dam, the baby on her hip, Carrie reflects that she has said she will never forgive him.